A Second Chance

The Chances
Book 2

Emily E K Murdoch

© Copyright 2024 by Emily E K Murdoch
Text by Emily E K Murdoch
Cover by Dar Albert

Dragonblade Publishing, Inc. is an imprint of Kathryn Le Veque Novels, Inc.
P.O. Box 23
Moreno Valley, CA 92556
ceo@dragonbladepublishing.com

Produced in the United States of America

First Edition September 2024
Print Edition

Reproduction of any kind except where it pertains to short quotes in relation to advertising or promotion is strictly prohibited.

All Rights Reserved.

The characters and events portrayed in this book are fictitious. Any similarity to real persons, living or dead, is purely coincidental and not intended by the author.

ARE YOU SIGNED UP FOR DRAGONBLADE'S BLOG?

You'll get the latest news and information on exclusive giveaways, exclusive excerpts, coming releases, sales, free books, cover reveals and more.

Check out our complete list of authors, too!

No spam, no junk. That's a promise!

Sign Up Here

www.dragonbladepublishing.com

Dearest Reader;

Thank you for your support of a small press. At Dragonblade Publishing, we strive to bring you the highest quality Historical Romance from some of the best authors in the business. Without your support, there is no 'us', so we sincerely hope you adore these stories and find some new favorite authors along the way.

Happy Reading!

CEO, Dragonblade Publishing

Additional Dragonblade books by
Author Emily E K Murdoch

The Chances Series
A Fighting Chance (Book 1)
A Second Chance (Book 2)

Dukes in Danger Series
Don't Judge a Duke by His Cover (Book 1)
Strike While the Duke is Hot (Book 2)
The Duke is Mightier than the Sword (Book 3)
A Duke in Time Saves Nine (Book 4)
Every Duke Has His Price (Book 5)
Put Your Best Duke Forward (Book 6)
Where There's a Duke, There's a Way (Book 7)
Curiosity Killed the Duke (Book 8)
Play With Dukes, Get Burned (Book 9)
The Best Things in Life are Dukes (Book 10)
A Duke a Day Keeps the Doctor Away (Book 11)
All Good Dukes Come to an End (Book 12)

Twelve Days of Christmas
Twelve Drummers Drumming
Eleven Pipers Piping
Ten Lords a Leaping
Nine Ladies Dancing
Eight Maids a Milking
Seven Swans a Swimming
Six Geese a Laying
Five Gold Rings
Four Calling Birds
Three French Hens

Two Turtle Doves
A Partridge in a Pear Tree

The De Petras Saga
The Misplaced Husband (Book 1)
The Impoverished Dowry (Book 2)
The Contrary Debutante (Book 3)
The Determined Mistress (Book 4)
The Convenient Engagement (Book 5)

The Governess Bureau Series
A Governess of Great Talents (Book 1)
A Governess of Discretion (Book 2)
A Governess of Many Languages (Book 3)
A Governess of Prodigious Skill (Book 4)
A Governess of Unusual Experience (Book 5)
A Governess of Wise Years (Book 6)
A Governess of No Fear (Novella)

Never The Bride Series
Always the Bridesmaid (Book 1)
Always the Chaperone (Book 2)
Always the Courtesan (Book 3)
Always the Best Friend (Book 4)
Always the Wallflower (Book 5)
Always the Bluestocking (Book 6)
Always the Rival (Book 7)
Always the Matchmaker (Book 8)
Always the Widow (Book 9)
Always the Rebel (Book 10)
Always the Mistress (Book 11)
Always the Second Choice (Book 12)
Always the Mistletoe (Novella)
Always the Reverend (Novella)

The Lyon's Den Series
Always the Lyon Tamer

Pirates of Britannia Series
Always the High Seas

De Wolfe Pack: The Series
Whirlwind with a Wolfe

Noble titles throughout English history have, at times, been more fluid than one/you might think. Women have inherited, men have been gifted titles by family or gained them on through marriage, and royals frequently lavished titles or withdrew them as reward and punishment.

The Chance brothers in this series agreed to split the four titles in their family line, rather than the eldest holding all four. It is a decision that defines their brotherhood, and their very different personalities.

Get ready to meet a family that is more than happy to scandalize Society...

Chapter One

July 5, 1812

IF IT WERE possible to literally fade into the wallpaper, Miss Florence Bailey would have managed to do it about three years ago.

As it was, however . . .

Florence smiled weakly as Mrs. Pullman laughed riotously at a joke of her own making. "Yes. Yes, I see. Very amus—"

"And of course, Prinny darling nearly wept with tears—wept!" cried Mrs. Pullman over the polite mutterings of the younger woman. "The man could barely see, he was enjoying himself so much!"

If she knew anything about Prinny, Florence thought, it was that his lapse in vision was probably due to the sheer amount of brandy he had likely consumed, or the snuff he had borrowed with no intention of repaying the favor from his friends.

She did not say these words, of course. Florence may not have learned how to disappear in public, but she had certainly taught herself to hold her tongue when her sharp mind presented it with a less than flattering remark.

Most of the time.

"—howls of laughter, I really thought I had broken him!"

"How amazing!" said a wide-eyed woman about Florence's age, whose name she had already forgotten. "To merely be in the presence of a prince is one thing, but to actually make him laugh . . ."

The conversation continued. At least, Florence was almost certain it did. She couldn't be entirely sure, because she had already taken advantage of Mrs. Pullman's momentary distraction in the way she had hoped to do for over eight minutes.

Florence had stepped back, slowly, out of the small gaggle of women, and was now creeping slowly toward the drawing room door.

That was it. She was almost there.

Almost free. Almost out of this cacophony of sound, the constant stares, the well-meaning smiles, the people consistently asking her—

"Ah, Miss Bailey!" boomed Mr. Knight with a wide grin. "Or are y'married by now?"

Florence's weak smile almost faded under the barrage of the goodhearted man. It certainly faltered.

Well, it was the question everyone asked a woman of a certain age, did they not? Even if that certain age was naught but four and twenty . . .

"Still M-Miss Bailey, Mr. Knight," she said quietly, her voice barely strong enough to be heard over the violent laughter that surrounded Mrs. Pullman.

"Well, can't be long, I'll be bound," said Mr. Knight jovially. "My wife has said how awfully pleasant it is to have you about the place. We couldn't have had the house party without you!"

It was on the tip of Florence's tongue to point out that having her at a house party made little to no difference, that she was a wallflower, desperate to hide, desperate not to be noticed, hoping from one moment to the next that she would not be called upon to speak. Or sing. Or breathe loudly. And his dear wife had not spoken a word to her since she had arrived at the Knights' nearly four whole days ago. She doubted the woman could pick her out of a—

"How k-kind," Florence murmured.

There was no point in attempting to speak those things. Not when her cheeks flushed a heavy burning pink at the mere thought of them.

Mr. Knight puffed out his chest. "It was quite a coup to get this group of people together, y'know! I don't mind telling you, getting some of these toffs to leave their houses is quite impossible. And we have more guests arriving this afternoon!"

Florence's hopes sank.

More people? More names to remember, more faces to gawp at her—more people?

Were the ten who were here already insufficient?

Mr. Knight misunderstood her expression. "I knew you'd be pleased!"

Florence swallowed. She tried to remind herself it would all be over in a few days, that the constant commiserations that she was entering her fourth Season—fourth!—unmarried were not a slight on her family. It was just a comment on her, and it would all soon be over and done with. She would cease to be asked who was courting her, cease to have to explain that no, she had no younger sister who was prevented from coming out, and cease to be forced to acknowledge that no, she herself had not yet managed to find a husband.

In short, soon she would be able to escape the marriage mart completely.

In just a few days.

Until then . . .

"You look a little tired, if I may be so bold as to say so, my dear."

Florence blinked, and the face of Mr. Knight swam back into view. As did her excuse.

"T-Tired—yes, I am greatly f-fatigued," she said hastily, almost doing the unthinkable and reaching out to touch the man's arm. *Dear Lord, what was coming over her!* "I think I sh-shall go upstairs to m-my room and—"

"Can't have you abandoning afternoon tea, can we?" said Mr. Knight happily, as though it would be the end of British civilization as they knew it. "Here, let me deposit you on a sofa, far away from the chatter."

Just for a moment, Florence considered arguing with the man. She didn't want to stay in the stuffy drawing room, a fire lit even in July, filled with people she didn't know. Even those she knew, she didn't like.

There was lace everywhere, cushions and wall hangings and crochet, the place was fit to bursting. And Mrs. Pullman was laughing so loudly the sound pounded on her ear drums, and there were people everywhere, people who would stare and ask awkward questions and—

"Let me find a nice sofa for you," said Mr. Knight in what he evidently thought was a kindly voice.

Before Florence could attest to the fact that she merely wished to go upstairs and be alone, completely alone, he had taken her arm. Mr. Knight shepherded her through the crowded drawing room, acting as a sort of barrier between the guests and herself. And by the time she had been carefully lowered onto a sofa, at least ten feet from a single other person, Florence had to admit it was a decent second choice.

Just not her first choice.

"There," Mr. Knight said proudly, as though he had achieved something remarkable. "Now, I'd better be off—new guests arriving, and all that!"

Florence managed a watery smile. "B-But... I w-would much rather retire up—"

He was gone before he could even hear the end of her sentence.

Inhaling deeply and arranging her hands just so, as her mother had always taught her, Florence tried to force her face into a genteel, vague expression.

It was not difficult. It was the sort of thing she had been doing since she had first entered Society, at the late age of almost twenty.

It was her mother's fault.

And not just the inane expression or the house party, however true it might be that Florence had been most insistent that she did not wish to spend what was turning out to be one of the hottest weeks of the year with strangers. But Mama had insisted, too, and when Mama insisted, Mama got what she wanted.

No, more than that, it was her mother's fault that she hadn't entered Society until so late. That she had been kept away from the world.

Though Florence hadn't complained. She disliked the world, with all its noise and chatter and rules. Rules that didn't seem to make any sense. Rules she had to abide by, even if they made her flush, and her stomach churn, and her heart cease beating.

Well. Perhaps not entirely cease.

Regardless, it had been her mother's firm suggestion that she accept the house party invitation from the Knights, and Florence hadn't had the energy to continue arguing with her once it was clear her mind was made up.

And there were only a few days left, she reminded herself as she sat alone on the red cotton sofa. Just a few days to avoid people, and try not to get caught up in conversations, and—

"—must have heard, it's all over Town!" said a woman Florence was almost certain was a Mrs. Lymington. "I read about it. The announcement was a few weeks ago."

"But I was not even aware the Duke of Cothrom was courting!" said another woman, a Mrs. Moncrieff, in tones of mild offense, as though she should have been informed.

The two of them had meandered close to Florence, much to her chagrin. Mr. Knight may have placed her far away from the current gaggles of conversation, but the sofa on which she sat was close to the afternoon tea table.

Mightily close.

"I heard it was rather a rushed affair," continued Mrs. Lymington as she helped herself to another slice of cake. "And that never bodes well, if you ask me."

"Well, titled folks have a different way of doing things, I suppose," said Mrs. Moncrieff with a shrug, pouring herself a cup of tea. "They seldom marry for love, do they? I suppose it is not much of a consideration for them, so they need not wait to see how they suit. What do you think?"

Florence started. She had hoped to remain inconspicuous here on the sofa. Her light red muslin gown, after all, was not too dissimilar a color to that of the sofa.

Dissimilar enough, it appeared.

"I-I . . . I do not know the man," she managed to say, a little proud of herself for actually replying.

Mrs. Moncrieff was not similarly impressed. She snorted. "I did not ask if you knew him, Miss Bailey. I asked what you thought!"

Heat burned Florence's cheeks.

It should be illegal, she thought furiously as her tongue attempted to work, *to ask people such things.*

What did she know? Had she ever met the duke in question? She'd never met *any* duke before, and as for the only marquess she had ever encountered . . .

Well. The less said about him, the better.

Anyway, who was she to go around passing judgment on other people's lives? It certainly wasn't something she would wish for others to do to her. And why were they so excited about the whole thing? It was only a duke's marriage. Surely that sort of thing happened . . . well, all the time!

Perhaps not all the time. How many dukes were there in England, anyway? There seemed to be more and more of them with every passing year . . .

"I said, Miss Bailey, that I asked—"

"I-I am af-fraid I do not have an . . . an opinion," Florence said stiffly.

The hope had been, naturally, that that would be the end of it. That she would not have to concern herself with any further nonsense, and the two women would take their tea and cake and return to whatever inane conversation they had departed.

And they did. In a manner of speaking.

"Well!" Mrs. Lymington said, with a gasp that suggested Miss Bailey had mortally wounded her. "I never heard the like!"

"Too well-bred for the likes of us, I see," sneered Mrs. Moncrieff, peering at Florence with a most bad-tempered eye. "At least we've been put in our place, and I thank you for it, Miss Bailey!"

The two ladies flounced off to the other side of the room.

It was all Florence could do not to drop her head into her hands.

Why was it that Society was so eager to force gossip upon and from its members? Why could she not just read? Or leave the room in search of solitude? Or even better, disappear from this house party altogether?

It was most infuriating that she had no carriage to whisk her away. It was most irritating that merely leaving this room would cause comment, even suggest offense to her hosts. And it was infuriating that no matter what she did, Florence thought with still-reddening cheeks, she was still the person no one wished to talk to.

And from there, the afternoon wore on in much the same manner that she expected it would, but for two incidents.

The first was the sort of thing Florence had grown accustomed to over the years, though it did not make it any easier to endure. About an hour after her last conversation—the unfortunate one with Mrs. Lymington and her companion—Florence had, ironically as it turned out, been congratulating herself at fading into the background.

Rarely, she did manage it. The red gown on the red sofa helped, but so had the arrival of Miss Quintrell, who was apparently a great wit, and it was an impressive feat for the Knights to have her at their house party. Florence's only thought on her was delight that she had taken the attention of the room, but most unfortunately, that delight did not last. Not when the woman strode over confidently to help herself to tea, waving away a maid who seemed desperate to do it for her—and spotted Florence.

"Goodness, I hardly saw you there," said the young woman with a grin. "Miss Quintrell. And you are?"

Florence had to swallow twice to make it possible for her mouth to work. It was most embarrassing, but not nearly as embarrassing as the vague gurgling noise that exited her mouth.

"I . . . beg your pardon?" said the woman, pouring herself tea and frowning.

Florence cleared her throat.

As though that would help. It was the shyness that was the paralyzer, not anything to do with her throat. It was an affliction, that was what her mother had called it, and Florence had never been able to argue with her. Partly because of the problem itself, unquestionably. But partly because she agreed with her.

It *was* an affliction, this shyness that reduced her to an incomprehensible mutterer whenever she felt out of her depth. Chits of seventeen coming up into their first Season had far more bravery in company.

Florence could only be grateful that at least there had been no mention of dancing at the Knights' house party. That was a small mercy.

"I'm sorry, I didn't catch that," said the newly arrived Miss Quintrell politely. And then she did something so awful, so terrible, Florence could hardly contain herself.

She sat beside Florence.

"I hated the idea of turning up late to a house party, but I simply couldn't get away from Lady Romeril's final garden party in London," said Miss Quintrell, as though they had been friends for years and were finally catching up after a busy Season. "You know how it is."

Florence swallowed, her throat closing up more with every attempt to loosen it.

She did know how it was. Lady Romeril was one of her greatest fears. Not because there was anything wrong with the woman. She was not malicious, which in London was saying something. Nor was she cruel, or small hearted, or small minded.

But she was so . . . so . . .

"I honestly thought she would bodily prevent any of us from leaving, she was having such a great time," Miss Quintrell said in a confidential low tone, giggling at her scandalously impolite remark.

She waited for Florence to laugh with her. Florence knew that, knew what should be said and done.

And she couldn't do it. Iron had coated her veins, or steel—something that kept her precisely immobile, unable to smile, unable to nod, unable to speak.

It was mortifying. With every passing second, she could see Miss Quintrell becoming more curious, waiting for Florence to join in, to say something, and she couldn't.

Florence couldn't do it.

And she hated herself, and railed against Society that demanded so much of her, and wished to goodness the woman hadn't sat down, hadn't spotted her, hadn't wanted tea.

Oh, why hadn't she let the maid get it for her?

"Are . . . are you quite well?"

Florence coughed violently and was somehow able to shift herself. *Quick, speak!* "I-I-I am q-quite well. Th-Thank you."

Perhaps that would be all the woman would require. Surely, Florence thought desperately, she would return to the main party now that she had been polite. It wasn't as though there would be much riveting conversation on the sofa.

"You . . . you are very shy, aren't you?" said Miss Quintrell quietly.

It was all Florence could do to nod. She could feel the tension in her bones, the creak of her muscles as she made the smallest movement.

Her lungs were tight, constricting along with her throat. And her cheeks—they burned. She would not have been surprised to find blisters if she'd had the wherewithal to move her hands and lift them to her cheeks.

But that would require much more movement than a tiny nod. And such movement was still impossible.

"I . . . I see," Miss Quintrell said.

They sat there, the two of them, in almost perfect silence for several minutes.

It was not complete silence, of course. Florence's breathing was ragged, her panic continuing to rise, and she knew the woman beside her could hear her laboring lungs, and that embarrassment only made the whole thing worse! Until eventually—

"Well, good afternoon," Miss Quintrell said with a small nod.

She rose. Then she was gone.

Her absence signaled release to Florence's whole body. Her lungs suddenly took in air, and it was only then that she realized just how lightheaded she had become without its regular intake. Gasping huge lungfuls of the precious stuff, Florence wished to goodness the whole incident had never happened.

Oh, it was polite of her, undeniably. Miss Quintrell, if she had recalled her name correctly, was clearly a very well-meaning individual. They always were. But then Florence would stutter, and her shyness would make it impossible for her to do anything, say anything, contribute anything . . .

And they would get bored, as Miss Quintrell obviously had. And they would disappear.

And the worst of it all, Florence thought silently, *was that she couldn't blame them.*

They were at a house party. It was supposed to be all delight and entertainment, good conversation and games and sport, and here she was, stuck in the middle of it, unable to be delighted, unable to entertain. There had been a walk yesterday—that Florence had attended in silence. And someone had suggested bowls for tomorrow—something Florence had no wish to partake in, but she would have no choice but to succumb to the expectations of the group.

And more people were arriving...

Florence blinked back tears. It was bad enough to be so shy that one's lips simply could not work properly, but it was worse to be forced out into company to demonstrate just how ill-equipped she was to entertain.

This had to be it, she told herself. *The last house party.*

She wasn't going to permit her mother to make a fool of her any longer. No more house parties, no more balls, no more demanding that she perform in public when the absolute last thing she wanted was to even be seen by someone she wasn't related to. Suffering through it all? That had to come to an end.

In a way, Florence thought vaguely as she watched the other guests exchange gossip, laugh, and chatter away as though their mouths always obeyed them, it would be a relief. After all, she was certain her presence was a dampener on anything she attended. Had not Miss Quintrell proven that?

So that was the first incident. The first thing that occurred that afternoon that Florence had not expected.

The second was far worse.

Another hour passed and Florence's hopes had just been starting to rise again after her encounter with Miss Quintrell. It would not be long now before guests would retire upstairs to dress for dinner. *Heaven.*

Not that forcing herself from one gown into another was her idea of heaven, oh no. It was the blessed hour, or sometimes a tad more than an hour, which Florence would have to herself upstairs in her little guest bedchamber.

Sixty whole minutes of uninterrupted silence. No expectations, no conversation, no disappointing anyone because she could not reply to a quip swiftly and with a smile.

Florence sighed with happiness. Yes, in just a few minutes, she would be able to escape this drawing room, and—

The door opened. Her mind instantly assumed that a servant was arriving to tidy away the tea things—and a good thing too, that cake was in danger of spilling over onto the carpet.

But it was not a servant.

It was a man. A tall man, with dark hair, deep blue eyes, fashionable clothes which had been tailored around the man's impressive breadth, and a smile that showed the world that he was quite aware of how handsome he was.

Very handsome, as it happened.

Florence's gasp hitched in her throat the instant her eyes fell upon him.

"Well then," said the man with a broad smirk and a gaze that swept across the room. "Which of you ladies will I be seducing?"

Chapter Two

JOHN CHANCE, MARQUESS of Aylesbury, grinned. He had it. The perfect line.

It had come to him on the ride over, and the more he thought about it, the more perfect it seemed.

"Afternoon," he said with a grin to the butler who opened the door. "I'm—"

"I know who you are, my lord," said the man with a slightly disapproving look.

The impoliteness and lack of welcome only grated on John for a moment.

Well, it wasn't as though he had the best reputation, did he? He was certainly surprised to have received an invitation from the Knights to their house party, and had been genuinely disappointed he'd had to stay in Town for a few days and miss the beginning of it.

More disappointed, in fairness, that he'd been forced to because of some stupid debt. A debt he had only incurred because the blackguard had been cheating. He had to have been! There was no other way—

The point was, John interrupted his own thought as he placed his gloves in his top hat, and placed both in the butler's hands, *he had come as soon as he could.* And as almost everyone here was probably waiting for his arrival with bated breath, it was high time to give them what they wanted—the arrival of a scandalous Chance brother.

"My master and his guests are in the drawing room, my lord," intoned the butler with a sour expression. "May I—"

"Over here, is it?" asked John cheerfully, stepping forward.

It wasn't too hard to guess. The place was well-proportioned, as houses went, and was laid out in the typical style with the drawing room to the west. It had to be. He could hear chatter slowly seeping from underneath the door.

"Yes, my lord. Shall I announce—"

"I'll do it, don't you fret," said John, a smile creeping over his face. "I know my own name."

The butler was probably still glaring disapprovingly, but he could no longer tell. He'd entirely forgotten the old man and was instead striding toward the drawing room door.

Now, what was that line he had come up with on the ride over? Ah, yes.

John's fingers curled around the door handle, and he stepped into the blazingly hot room. He beamed at the myriad guests. "Well then. Which of you ladies will I be seducing?"

Just as he had thought, there were shocked gasps from around the room, scandalized noises from ladies, and guffaws from the gentlemen.

A chuckle escaped John's lips. Oh, it was almost too easy. Polite Society was all very well, but it was far more fun to shock people, to surprise them. To make ladies clutch their pearls and gentlemen mutter things like, "I say!" under their breath.

What else was going out into Society for?

And that was what they expected, wasn't it? John knew, as he stepped inside and closed the door behind him, that his reputation preceded him. It always did. John Chance, Marquess of Aylesbury: scoundrel, gambler, drinker, womanizer. He was all of those things and more.

His elder brother William, Duke of Cothrom, may despair of him, but that did not mean that John did not entertain the masses with his exuberance.

"Aylesbury!"

John turned and had his hand immediately clasped by his host. "Knight!"

"Aylesbury, so good of you to come," said Mr. Knight, wringing his hand and clearly pleased to see him. "Quite a coup for Mrs. Knight, you know—a marquess, in our home!"

"We're not really that impressive, I assure you," said John with a shrug. "Just second down the pecking order in the nobility from a duke, that's all."

He was gratified to see the man's smile broaden. "Oh, my Lord Aylesbury, you honor us!"

John laughed, allowing the habit of bravado to take over.

The *habit* of bravado.

Because this time was different now, wasn't it? Even if it was better to seem as if it weren't. This wasn't just a house party, a gathering of like-minded friends and family, a chance for people to get out of London during the heat and enjoy the countryside. Was it?

John swallowed as the little part of his mind he had once called his conscience, but rarely listened to since, tried to shout something at him.

This was his second chance.

At least, that was what Cothrom had called it.

"I'm serious, Aylesbury," his older brother had said only the day before, frowning as he wrote out a check. Another one. "I am sick and tired of bailing you out of—"

"This truly wasn't my fault this time, Cothrom," John had attempted to argue, relief settling into his shoulders that his brother was once again going to pay his debts. "The man definitely had marked the cards, there was no other way that he could possibly—"

"When I say that I am sick and tired of bailing you out, Aylesbury, I mean it." Cothrom blew gently on the ink, then blotted it with a mahogany blotter. "This is it. The last time."

And for a moment, John had blinked, not quite sure of what had just happened.

Oh, the words made sense. Individually. But William, his brother, the Duke of Cothrom—he could not be serious. Could he?

"Come again, old man?" John had said, hoping he had injected enough of a jesting tone into his words. "You can't mean—"

"I can, and I do," said Cothrom forebodingly, handing over the check. "The Cothrom coffers are nearing empty this financial year and it's all because of you and Lindow. Again."

The third Chance brother. More similar to John than he would care to admit. Than either of them would care to admit. Equally roguish, equally rakish . . . and equally poor at cards, at the moment. Terribly poor.

Poor being the operative word.

"You can't be serious," John had said, jaw dropping. "What, no more help?"

"You have taken almost six thousand pounds—six *thousand pounds*, man—from the Cothrom estate," his older brother had snapped. "You think I'm made of money? I've got a family now, a wife and child! What about the Aylesbury estate? Can it not pay off your innumerable and seemingly ever-increasing debts?"

And John had swallowed, and not said . . .

Well, he'd not said a great many things.

Like how the Aylesbury coffers were, by definition, far emptier than the Cothrom ones. It was harder to be emptier than completely bare.

Like how he had taken out a few loans, just a few here and there, and they would, apparently, need repaying. Sooner rather than later.

Like how he had mortgaged—him! A Chance, with a mortgage!— a few acres of Aylesbury land. Fine, more than a few. A few hundred.

He could have said all of those things. And he had said none of them.

"This is your second chance," Cothrom had said with a firm look over his study desk. "Second and only. I am for the countryside tomorrow, back to Alice and Maude—and I do not want to hear anything about you running up more debts, or getting into trouble, or seducing—"

"You really aren't going to help me again, are you?" John had said quietly.

His older brother had been the sort of man John had always looked up to. Partly because he was older, true, but mostly because even before he had inherited the title and become the Duke of Cothrom, had always been so very . . . very good.

Prim. Priggish, to those who did not know him. Precise.

Just the sort of man you could always depend on to act your second in a duel. Or pay off a debt that truly wasn't his fault. Not at all. Not really.

Cothrom's focus had not wavered. "Your gambling has got out of hand—no, honestly, it has. You have a problem, and I can't—I won't—watch you ruin your life. You're cut off from the family coffers, and you have to promise me you won't gamble again. Promise me. This is your second chance, man. Do not waste it."

"—said, more guests coming this afternoon, but I did not dare hope—"

"I beg your pardon?" said John, blinking in the suddenly dazzling light of the Knight drawing room.

Goodness. That was a first, getting so lost in a memory that he had momentarily forgotten where he was.

He needed a drink.

"I was saying how perfectly marvelous it is to have you, the Marquess of Aylesbury, at my little house pa—"

"Yes, yes, I am sure it is," said John, as cheerfully as he could manage.

He had to pretend that all was well, that nothing had changed. He may be on his second chance, but he also *was* a Chance. And that was quite different. The three Chance brothers—four, if you included Pernrith—did not simply give up when things grew difficult.

Not so far they hadn't, anyway.

Just don't blow it, John thought warningly. *Like you blew that check before paying the man who was owed those funds.*

He really shouldn't have done that.

"Let me get you a cup of tea," Mr. Knight was saying, glancing around vaguely. "Except—ah, I think the tea things may have been tidied away. I can ring for a footman, he can bring you—"

"A glass of your best red wine," said John firmly. Well, it was past five o'clock, wasn't it? Almost past. A quarter to. Almost a quarter to. "And I will mingle with your guests."

The man beamed. John tried not to smirk.

Yes, he had guessed correctly. He was the most impressively titled person here, by a long shot, and evidently he was the guest of honor. Mr. Knight had plainly been bursting at the seams to have a marquess at his table.

Which was all to the good. He would have to hope that it meant Knight had forgotten that one-hundred-pound flutter John had wagered him on that horserace but a few months ago. It would be pleasant not to need to pay off *every* debt.

As his host bustled away to find the best red wine his cellar had to offer, John cast a lazy eye over the guests.

Most were known to him, even if he did not particularly relish their company. Mrs. Pullman and Mrs. Lymington were here, of course. They could not deny themselves an excuse to be out in company. Their thirst for gossip was almost as great as that of Lady Romeril, which was saying something.

Their husbands, along with a Mr. Lister and what appeared to a young lady he did not know were talking in a corner. The conversation looked animated, but just as John approached in desperate need of some entertainment, a few phrases caught his ear.

"—quite an impossibility at the next election—"

"And the policies, madness when one considers—"

"—if the Americans would just accept it, then a whole host of—"

John swiftly veered away from that particular gathering, hoping he was not being too obvious.

Dear God, politics! The very last thing he wanted. Had he not just left London?

That left a pair of gentlemen along with Mrs. Knight, just to his left, who was plainly looking for a fourth.

John's stomach lurched. That could only mean one thing. *Cards.*

His fingers itched, his pulse skipped a beat, but he stopped walking in their direction, hesitating, certain he should not go forward but uncertain where to place himself in the room instead.

Cothrom would be pleased, John thought wryly. His first test, and somehow John was able to hold back from the seemingly inevitable. At least for now.

Not that he couldn't gamble. He was actually a rather good gambler. A splendid gambler. Most of the time.

It was the times when he wasn't that were tricky.

John swallowed. A second chance, that was what Cothrom had said. And it wasn't as though he had any coin on him to play. Or any coin at the bank. The manager there had been quite clear on that.

No. No, it would be a terrible decision to go over there and offer to act as their fourth.

Strange, how difficult it was not to. John swallowed, his mouth inexplicably dry. Had he ever noticed just how much delight he took from gambling? It was most odd. And yet now, standing here and forcing himself not to partake, his body rebelled at the instructions his mind was giving it.

Most peculiar.

In an attempt to prevent himself from succumbing to the obvious temptation, John turned to the final side of the room he had not inspected.

And saw her.

Florence Bailey.

John's pulse skipped a beat again—painfully—his hand instinctively moving to his chest.

Then he forced it to his side. He was being ridiculous. Showing emotion, in public? That was hardly good form for a gentleman, let alone a marquess. And he was being foolish. The last thing he wanted was awkward questions about his awkward behavior. Or any questions about anything, now it came to that.

Florence Bailey.

John blinked a few times, just to check he wasn't dreaming. It might be possible. His eyes could be playing tricks on him—the red of her gown and the red of the sofa were almost precisely the same shade.

Perhaps he had just wanted to—but by God, it had been almost two years since he had seen her. Why on earth would his mind be meandering toward Miss Florence Bailey?

It was certainly her. The instant their gazes met, her cheeks flushed deeply, a crimson red that matched both gown and sofa. Her eyes looked down, examining her hands in her lap as though they were the most interesting things which had ever existed.

Yes, that was Florence. John had never met another woman more certain to turn pink whenever a single person looked at her.

And when it was he who was doing the looking . . .

Before he could consciously think, before John could consider whether there was a better option in the drawing room than engaging in conversation with Miss Bailey, he found to his surprise that his feet were moving him forward.

Toward Florence. Miss Bailey.

Her color was deepening further with every step he took and he still wasn't sure why he was continuing forward. But John did not seem to be able to stop until he was standing before her.

And then he wasn't standing before her.

John exhaled a momentary sigh of relief, which quickly ended when he realized why he was no longer standing before her.

He was seated beside her.

How in God's name had that happened?

John's breathing was embarrassingly ragged, and he placed his hands each side of his hips on the sofa as he attempted to get his bearings.

Which was a mistake.

Because Florence—*Miss Bailey*—had unmistakably decided at the same time to leave the sofa, and so had placed her hands either side of her own hips before she rose.

Which meant that John's right hand was now covering her left.

John's stomach lurched again. Her fingers—they were just as he remembered. The softness. The closeness. The intimacy they had—

He pulled his hand back as though burned. Florence did the same thing.

"I did not think—"

"I-I never exp-pected—"

They spoke at the same time. John cleared his throat, as though that would help anything, and was just about to leave the sofa when a voice piped up at his side.

"Your wine, my lord!" said Mr. Knight cheerfully. "Ah, and I see you have made the acquaintance of our delightful Miss Bailey!"

John blinked up at the man who was proffering a glass of red wine, smiling widely at the clear pleasure the man received from seeing the two of them seated on a sofa.

As though he—

John took the wine and drank a large gulp.

"That's my best red wine, as promised," Mr. Knight babbled as John savored the burn of the liquid. "I'll leave you two to it. Two to it! What a delightful phrase, I must tell my wife."

He meandered off in the direction of the trio still looking for a fourth to play cards.

Perhaps he should have joined them after all, John thought darkly. *Then he wouldn't be . . . here.*

With her.

And yet something prevented John even now from rising and walking away.

It was the wine, he told himself sternly. He was appreciating the wine, and why not? Was it any business of his who was also sitting on the sofa beside him?

"You look well," he said politely.

It was only politeness which made him do it. That was all. A man—a gentleman ought to be polite. And she was a lady.

Very definitely a lady. Try as he might, John could not ignore the curves that reached the corners of his eye even as he stared forward. The swell of her breast, the slightness of her waist, the way her hips—

"You have been at the house party long?" John said hurriedly, forcing his mind onto better things.

Well. Not better things. There were few things better than—

"You know the Knights, of course," he said desperately.

He could not understand what was more infuriating. The fact that he was having to say things to distract his mind from the fact he was mere inches from Miss Florence Bailey, or the fact she was not contributing anything to the conversation whatsoever.

In fact, other than the slight change in her breathing which John noticed with great satisfaction, it was like he wasn't even here. And John was not accustomed to being ignored. Certainly not by pretty ladies.

Not that Florence was pretty. *Miss Bailey. Damn.*

"Are you going to say anything?" he said cheerfully, as though this were a perfectly natural conversation. "Are you going to reply to my conversation?"

Still Miss Bailey said nothing.

Eventually, John could not help himself. Fortifying himself with another large gulp of wine—Knight was right, it truly was excellent—he glared at Florence.

"You know," he muttered, "you used to like my conversation."

Now that got a response.

Florence's cheeks managed to grow, if that were possible, redder still. The coloring tinged her lips, making them a scarlet stain across her face.

"Y-Yes," she said, so quietly it was almost a whisper. "I used to."

John's irritation flared at those words. *How dare she—and to him, of all people!* He was a Chance, one of the most noble and most respected families in the *ton*. He was the Marquess of Aylesbury! He—

Though now he came to think about it, none of that had impressed her last time, had it?

John cleared his throat. Again. "I . . . you . . ."

Damned words, they wouldn't come. And all the while his body was responding to hers, even if they weren't touching anymore. Perhaps *because* they weren't touching anymore.

Because that was all he could truly think about, wasn't it? Ignoring everyone else in the room and leaning over, touching Florence, taking her hand in his own, lifting it to his lips, and tasting the warmth of her—

"Now, my lord, I simply must pull you away—I am sorry Miss Bailey—for there is someone you must meet!"

John started. Mr. Knight had come seemingly from nowhere, and had pulled the marquess to his feet before John could say anything.

Or stop him.

Mr. Knight's grip on his elbow was tight and he continued to chatter away as he pulled John across the drawing room. "I thought you two should know each other, and it would be a perfect excuse to—how do you know Miss Florence Bailey?"

John blinked. It was a most sudden change of pace, both literally and figuratively.

Mr. Knight had halted, though he still held tight to John's elbow. He was glaring, as though accusing him silently of wrongdoing.

Which was ridiculous. If he knew of John's wrongdoing, he would not have asked how he knew Miss Florence Bailey.

"I did not know that you knew her," Mr. Knight said in an undertone so no one else in the raucous drawing room could hear him. "But the moment I saw the look she just gave you—"

"What look?" said John, swiftly turning to look back at the young woman. "Ouch—dear God, man, that hurt!"

It had indeed been a mighty tug on his elbow to prevent him from looking back around at Florence.

Which was a shame. Because she was a far more delightful sight than the puce cheeks of his host.

"She is here alone, unchaperoned, and her mother entrusted her to me," said Mr. Knight stiffly, and John saw with interest that the man clearly felt uncomfortable speaking so boldly to a marquess but felt it was his duty. A good man, then. "Now I am gentle by nature, but when it comes to unprotected ladies, my sisters can tell you that I am the first man to defend their honor. And so I ask you again, my lord. How do you know Miss Florence Bailey?"

It was typically John's instinct to lie when asked about young ladies, whatever the question. It was usually safer that way. And when it came to Florence Bailey, he would rather lie. The truth was far more embarrassing than any lie he could concoct.

But looking into the stern and absolutely resolute expression of his host, John was reminded of his brother's parting words from the night before.

"Your gambling has got out of hand—no, honestly, it has. You have a problem, and I can't—I won't—watch you ruin your life. You're cut off from the family coffers, and you have to promise me you won't gamble again. Promise me. This is your second chance, man. Do not waste it."

Despite that, John tried to shrug. *Well.* A man couldn't be blamed for his bravado. "Oh, Florence? We were almost engaged, once. Almost."

Mr. Knight dropped John's arm. "I—I beg your pardon?"

"Yes, a funny old thing," John said, ignoring the twisting of his heart. Mere memory, that was all. He certainly didn't feel anything any longer. "One day I'll tell you the story."

"But—goodness, I had not realized Miss Bailey was once near engagement," said Mr. Knight, eyes wide. "I thought her mother kept her on a tighter leash than that! The stupendous dowry, after all. Any woman with a dowry like that should—"

John did everything he could to keep his voice level, charm oozing into every syllable he spoke. He had to stay calm. "I beg your pardon. Did you say, stupendous dowry?"

Chapter Three

July 6, 1812

It was all Florence could do to survive the next four and twenty hours, but somehow, she did.

Precisely how, she was not sure. If her mother were to ask—and she was certain her mother would ask, as there was no hope that the news of the Marquess of Aylesbury's attendance at the house party could be kept quiet—then Florence would tell her she did nothing but act in a most ladylike manner.

Which was true.

What she did was very ladylike.

"So sorry to hear that your headache persists," said Mrs. Knight *sotto voce* from the doorway. "I will of course leave you to rest. And if the pain has not subsided by this evening and you are unable to descend for dinner, I will send for the doctor."

Florence forced herself to sit upright. "Oh, n-no, I would not w-wish you to be p-put to any trouble—"

"No trouble at all, no trouble at all—the least I could do for one of our guests," whispered Mrs. Knight, perhaps thinking she was playing the part of the perfect hostess. "Now, rest, Miss Bailey."

The bedchamber door closed with a gentle snap.

Florence had fallen back on the bed with a heavy sigh. If this continued on much longer, she would end up with a real headache.

The trouble was, she couldn't plead a headache to escape John

Chance, Marquess of Aylesbury, forever. Not without incurring talk. And if there was one thing her mother loathed even more than her daughter's reticence for company, it was talk.

There was no possibility this could be kept quiet if Mrs. Knight had to call for a doctor. Florence's mother would be informed, and Mrs. Bailey would have a great deal to say about it when Florence returned home.

Which meant she was faced with no other option.

As the dinner gong sounded, Florence sighed and rose from the bed. It took her but ten minutes to elegantly pin her red hair up, and she wove a ribbon among the strands to make it look like she was making a bit of an effort. Her gown was perfectly fine for dinner—it was perhaps one of the more splendid she had brought. After slipping on her earbobs, her gloves, and a ruby bracelet that matched the glittering gems in her ears, Florence glared at her reflection with a stoical expression.

"It's just dinner," she told herself calmly. As ever, her voice was steady when she was alone. "Dinner. There will be plenty of people there, a great number of conversations occurring around you. The chances of you needing to speak to . . . to him, are slight. You won't even have to look at him."

And telling herself she was heartened by the thoughts, rather than actually being heartened, Florence stepped out onto the landing.

There was no one else milling about.

This was all to the good, Florence thought as she stepped down the elegant staircase and toward the drawing room where drinks would be served before the second dinner gong was rung. Better to have every other house guest in there, creating a great deal of noise and distraction, so she could slip in, speak to no one—particularly not handsome and charming rogues from one's past—and then eat in similar solitude. Or at least in silence. Solitude was not something she would be blessed with for a good while.

It was therefore quite to Florence's astonishment that she entered the drawing room, with its lace and chintz and once again roaring fire, to find . . .

No one.

No one except John Chance, the Marquess of Aylesbury.

Florence almost tripped over her gown, she was so momentarily astounded. How was this possible? Where was everyone? And why, of all the people at this house party, was it him she found here alone?

The Marquess of Aylesbury turned, and his wolfish smile was just as Florence remembered it. Just as hungry. Just as possessive. Just as—

But she could not think that way! It was mortification she felt at seeing John standing there by the drinks cabinet, and nothing more.

Nothing, Florence thought, *more*.

"Ah, Miss Bailey," said the Marquess of Aylesbury calmly, as though they had met casually while walking in Hyde Park.

But they hadn't. They were alone. Unchaperoned.

It was all going to happen again.

No, it wasn't, Florence thought firmly. *Definitely not. She was older, wiser, and much more wary.*

Even if parts of her warmed at just the mere sight of the man. Stupid, traitorous body. Idiotic, foolish heart.

"Wh-Wh-Where is everyone?" she managed to say. Eventually. Oh, it was excruciating, her tongue never obeying her when she was in public. Why on earth couldn't she just speak?

John shrugged.

There was something about the way a man shrugged, Florence thought as she stood there, unsure whether to retreat upstairs or remain here. When men shrugged, it said so much more than mere words could. It said how little they cared, and how it really wasn't their concern, and that even if someone attempted to make it their concern, they simply wouldn't bother.

A gentleman's shrug could say all that, but a nobleman's shrug said even more.

It said, such cares are beneath me. They are the cares of others, cares for those who do not have such breeding as I, the breeding to escape almost all cares in the world.

Florence found her brow was furrowing with irritation.

Well, she shouldn't be surprised. It wasn't as though John—as though the Marquess of Aylesbury had ever cared about much. Except himself.

"I was sorry to hear you have been suffering a headache, and for so long," came the irritating man's genteel voice. "Most unfortunate. You did not consider giving up and going home?"

There was something in the way that he spoke that made Florence's cheeks flush.

Not that it was an impressive feat to manage. It took almost no effort on the part of anyone around her to make her flush.

But John—the Marquess of Aylesbury was different. They had . . . well, not quite a sordid past. But a shared past, most certainly. A past Florence hoped to goodness no one else at the Knights' house party would discover.

"W-Well, I'll just s-sit here and wait for them. People. G-Guests," Florence said, walking past John as swiftly as she could manage so that she could reach the sofa again.

And she hesitated.

A sofa wasn't safe, was it? This red sofa may be comfortable, but it had permitted her a most awkward encounter just the day before when he had been so bold as to seat himself beside her without requesting her permission.

A sofa allowed intimacy. Closeness.

The man had touched her hand!

No, a sofa simply wasn't safe.

Swerving so rapidly Florence almost lost her balance for the second time since entering the drawing room that evening, she quickly located an armchair and sat there instead. A small armchair. So small that it was barely wide enough for her own hips.

But that was of no matter, was it? The point was, he could not sit beside her.

The Marquess of Aylesbury was smiling when Florence looked up—smiling as though he knew precisely what had gone through her mind.

The cheek of the man, to smile at her like that!

"You aren't going to leave? Retreat?" he said, stepping over to her and leaning against the fireplace which was a mere five feet from her.

Florence swallowed.

Retreat. Yes, that was her nature; to run and hide from anything placing her in the center of attention. She would rather disappear into the ground than perform at a recital, or scrub a kitchen floor than play charades at a gathering such as this.

But to admit defeat to such a man, within only four and twenty hours of his coming . . .

For some reason, and Florence was not sure why it mattered, she would not relent. If anyone was going to leave this house party in disgrace, it would be him.

"I-I don't have a carriage," Florence heard herself say.

Then groaned internally at the foolishness of her comments.

Truly, was that all she was going to say? Not that she had no need to leave the Knights, or that she had no intention of retreating, or that he should be the one to go?

No. No, her foolish mouth could say nothing save that she had no carriage.

She could not blame the Marquess of Aylesbury for grinning wildly at her words. "But you do wish to leave, don't you, Florence?"

"Miss Bailey," Florence corrected, heat blossoming up her décolletage.

How dare he speak to her with such—such intimacy!

Perhaps it would have been warranted, once upon a time, but that time was over, Florence told herself resolutely. The . . . the connection they had, whatever it truly was, was over. Never to be repeated. A mistake. A mistake she had made almost to such detriment to herself.

She had thought she had left that all behind. All the longing, the need for—

Florence swallowed. "There are only f-five days left of the house p-party," she said, forcing her mind onto practical matters. *Yes, that was it. Five days. That was all.* "I can m-manage five days."

John's eyes gazed into hers with a force that she could barely match.

She glanced down.

"I am sure you can," came his quiet voice. There was a teasing air to it, but certainly not as much as she had expected. When Florence looked up, John had not taken his attention from her face. "I am sure there are many things about you, Florence, that you are capable of. And many things I do not know."

"Miss Bailey," she said, her throat dry.

Why did hearing her name spoken by that man, with those lips, make her mouth so dry? Make her breathing quicken, just for a moment, before she got it under control?

You know why, a tiny voice from the back of her mind murmured. That moment, two years ago. You thought he was going to propose marriage, you were sure of it. Weeks of conversations, leading up to that moment. And instead, he—

"May I be so bold as to offer you a glass of Mr. Knight's finest wine, Miss Bailey?" said the Marquess of Aylesbury formally.

Florence blinked. His manner was such a departure from what had gone before, it was rather like emotional tennis. Her fingers tightened around the arms of the chair, but what response could she give? It would be most strange to refuse a glass of wine before dinner. And besides, she could do with something to fortify.

But where was everyone? Where were Mr. and Mrs. Knight, Mr.

Lister, Mrs. Pullman? Surely she and the Marquess of Aylesbury could not be the only people in the house?

"Miss Bailey?"

"Y-Yes?" Florence stammered.

Evidently he thought her response was to the earlier question, for the Marquess of Aylesbury stepped away from the fireplace and toward the drinks cabinet.

Her assent was worth it for this brief moment of release. Florence took in a deep yet hurried breath, hoping she would contain herself for however long it would be until she was rescued. Until someone else entered the drawing room.

They could not all be dressing for dinner. How long did it take Miss Quintrell to choose a gown? Or Mrs. Howarth, surely she—

"A Bordeaux," said Marquess of Aylesbury, suddenly far closer than Florence would have imagined possible. "Your favorite, if I remember correctly."

Florence swallowed as she accepted the glass of wine from Marquess of Aylesbury's hands. It was warm. Warmed by his palms.

Goodness. Now that was not the sort of thought young ladies were supposed to—

"You're trembling," said the Marquess of Aylesbury discreetly.

Florence stared at her wine as she considered what to say—how to reply. The trouble was, she was so conscious of the man's movements, it was impossible not to track him from the corner of her eyes as the glass of red liquid swirled in her shaking hands.

He was seated now. John. The Marquess of Aylesbury. Seated in a chair which was opposite her but a safe distance of several feet away. The scraping noise of the chair's feet against the rug grated against Florence's soul.

And now he was closer. So much closer.

"You are still trembling."

"No, I am not," Florence said softly as she lifted her eyes to him.

Which was a mistake. Heat flooded through her as she saw John's expression. It was one she recognized, one which had been fixed upon her before. Several times.

Whenever he thought no one else was looking.

And no one was looking, Florence thought frantically. They were alone here, in the drawing room—something rebellious. Certainly not something her mother would have approved of. Though having said that, she was alone with a *marquess*. Perhaps her mother would make an exception for that.

"Anyone would think," the Marquess of Aylesbury said lightly, "I make you nervous."

Florence gathered all her wits about her and did the most logical thing she could.

She took a sip of wine.

A small moan of delight escaped her lips. It truly was a wonderful Bordeaux.

"I knew it was the right wine for you," came the Marquess of Aylesbury's voice, amusement tinging every word. "I know you better than you think, Florence. Miss Bailey, I mean."

Florence swallowed a second mouthful of wine, then forced herself to look at the man who was taking such liberties with decorum. Who did he think he was?

Well. He was the Marquess of Aylesbury.

The Marquess of Aylesbury. The second Chance brother. A member of a family which entertained and scandalized the *ton* in equal measure. A man who was always in the newspapers, always in the gossip columns. Always drinking here or gambling there.

Florence's stomach lurched. Not that she had kept up with his antics.

"You are still trembling."

She knew she was, but she wasn't about to give him the honor of thinking he was having any effect on her. "I . . . you . . . that is nnothing special. E-Everyone makes m-me . . . makes me nervous."

For a moment, just a moment, Florence could have sworn she saw something strange flicker across John's face, across his eyes. If she'd been pressed to put a word to it, she would have said . . . sadness. Sadness that he was nothing special. That he was just like everyone else she encountered.

But then he rallied. The charming smile Florence knew so well fell across his expression once more, and the Marquess of Aylesbury leaned back with an elegant air of uncaring refinement.

"Yes, I suppose that is true," he said finally. "At least, it was true when I last knew you. Two years ago."

Florence nodded, relieved she was not called upon to reply to that in words. She took another sip of wine, the heady liquid providing a pleasant distraction from the heady gentleman seated opposite her.

Really, should she ring the bell? Perhaps she had mistaken the time, misheard a sound and assumed it was the dinner gong. She could still retreat—return upstairs, and—

"Two years is a long time, and you have hardly changed a bit," said the Marquess of Aylesbury, his voice velvet.

Florence said nothing, but met his look for just one shimmering moment.

It was a moment of lost control and she regretted it immediately. But in that moment, just before she could regain control of herself, Florence gave the man such a withering look of disdain, she was surprised he did not combust into flames and ruin that perfectly good Chippendale chair.

His sudden inhale told Florence her glare had not gone unnoticed.

Damn.

"We lost touch," he said. "Over the years."

Florence hesitated, but it was ridiculous to await the man to continue on with the conversation single handed. She had been born and raised to be a lady. And ladies conversed.

Wasn't that all they did?

"I am sure the loss has not been great," she said airily. "I am certain you have had plenty of lovely ladies to entertain you."

The Marquess of Aylesbury inclined his head. "I have indeed—dear God."

Florence jumped. His exclamation was so startling, it was a miracle she did not spill wine upon herself. Then she realized she hadn't only because she had drunk so much of the wine now that it was impossible for it to reach the top of the glass.

Ah. She should probably slow down a tad.

"You spoke," said the Marquess of Aylesbury in wonder.

Florence stared at the man. Was he quite well? His eyes were wide, a look of incredulity on his face. "I-I have spoken b-before."

"Not without—I mean, you spoke clearly, without hesitation, without stammer," said the Marquess of Aylesbury, agog. "How did you do that?"

Swallowing hard, Florence looked at her wine.

She did not know.

Well, she did know in truth, but she was hardly about to admit the truth to a man such as him. He would get quite the wrong idea about it, and she had no inclination to listen to the foolish man's guesses.

"These l-ladies," Florence said stubbornly, knowing this line of questioning was going to harm her far more than it would harm him. "You enjoyed them, I s-suppose?"

Her cheeks burned. She had intended to say he had enjoyed their company, but she always became tongue tied when the room's attention was all on her. And the attention of John Chance, Marquess of Aylesbury, was somehow far brighter than a whole host of people.

His roguish grin did not help. "Oh, I enjoyed them very much."

Pain as Florence had never known seared through her.

Well, what had she expected? That John—that the Marquess of Aylesbury would depart from her company and never speak to another lady again? That she would be the last woman he would ever court?

Yet the sad, aching pain that filled her was most unaccountable. Florence knew it was ridiculous, but she could not stop the pain coming.

Oh, she wanted to stop the pain—

"And yet," the Marquess of Aylesbury continued in a low voice, "none of them . . . none of them were quite like you."

Florence glanced up, meeting his gaze and for the first time since he had arrived at the Knights', holding it.

What was she to say to such a pronouncement? That he had broken her heart two years ago? That it had been far beyond confusing to have been kissed by him only to then to see him go? That it had been agony to watch him leave? That her heart had never truly been mended since?

That, in short, a part of her thought it never would be whole until he—

Florence rose hastily, placing her almost empty wine glass on a console table to her left. "I have to g-go."

"Go?" John said blankly, mirroring her and rising to his feet. "Where are you going?"

Anywhere but here, she wanted to say. Somewhere you can't reach me. Where I won't have to worry about seeing you again, because seeing you brings back memories that I cannot—that I will not live through again.

Because there is nothing, nothing worse than seeing the man who broke your heart step into a room and announce he was going to seduce all the ladies present. Or whatever it was he had said.

"I-I have a headache," Florence said hastily, no better excuses coming to mind. "And I—"

"There you are! Miss Bailey, you are positively glowing!"

Florence whirled around and saw her host, Mr. Knight, standing in the doorway. "I am n-not—"

"It appears I have inadvertently interrupted a tête-à-tête," said the man with a meaningful look at the marquess. "Oh dear."

It was all she could do not to burst into tears. What would everyone think? There would be talk, and that talk would lead to gossip, and that gossip would lead to—

"When you two are finished, we're about to finish our pre-dinner drinks on the terrace," said Mr. Knight more happily. "As agreed earlier. But don't rush on my account!"

He stepped out of the room, closing the door behind him.

Florence turned slowly to John, who had the good grace to look a little sheepish.

"Look, I—"

"You knew everyone else was on the terrace—you knew I was the only one who did not know!" she said. "H-How dare—"

"I did like our tête-à-tête," said John, stepping toward her.

Florence attempted to take a step back, almost fell into the armchair, sprang up and stepped around it. "W-Well like the m-memory, for you'll n-never have one of th-th-those again!"

He was almost right before her now, his hand almost on her wrist, and for a wild moment Florence lost herself in the memory of that kiss. The kiss she thought had been heralding the beginning of the rest of her life. The kiss that had taught her what love was, what desire was, what need was. The kiss which had meant so much to her, and so little to him.

Then she stumbled back and the memory faded and there was only John Chance, Marquess of Aylesbury, and rake extraordinaire, standing before her.

"Stay away from me," Florence said sinisterly before storming out of the room.

Chapter Four

July 9, 1812

AND STAY AWAY from her, he did.
Well. Not really.

It wasn't as though he could *completely* leave her alone. John wasn't going to simply give up and abandon the house party, and that was the only way he could entirely avoid Miss Florence Bailey.

And there was that small matter of not actually wanting to leave her alone, in any capacity.

So for the next few days, John watched her. He never got too close, always ensuring he was seated a few guests away. He never engaged her in conversation and always forced himself to stay put when he watched her slip away, seemingly unnoticed by the other guests.

Which was a puzzle in and of itself.

Here she was, one of the most beautiful women he had ever seen—and he had seen some women in his time—and the rest of the Knights' guests seemed totally unaware of her presence.

One luncheon John watched, open mouthed, as Florence managed to extricate herself from a conversation with Mr. Lister.

It wasn't particularly impressive, on the face of it. Mr. Lister was an odious man, and John was surprised Mr. Knight had thought it appropriate to invite him, in truth.

Mr. Lister had unfortunately managed to corner her. Literally, she had been standing in a corner and Mr. Lister had approached and started whittering on about some sort of horse he owned.

But what made Florence—what made *Miss Bailey's* actions most remarkable was that somehow—John wasn't sure how, even though he had been watching most carefully over Mrs. Pullman's shoulder—Florence had . . .

Walked away.

And Mr. Lister had hardly noticed. He'd kept talking about that wretched racehorse of his, but most surprisingly, to the empty corner.

John had looked at Florence in a different way ever since. Here was a woman, if it could be believed, who disliked conversation so much she had actually discovered a way to slip out of one without the other person knowing.

It was unfathomable.

Who could look at Florence and not notice her?

"Your mouth is open, my lord," said a calm voice with a hint of a smile in it.

John blinked. Miss Quintrell, to whom he had until moments ago been conversing, did not look offended by his complete inattention. "It is?"

"You're drooling, I think," said Miss Quintrell without any hint of censure. "Considering Cook's next resplendent meal, are you?"

John swiftly closed his mouth, cleared his throat, and confirmed that his constructed bravado was clear in his expression. "Of course! If that man concocts another menu like last night, I shall have to instruct my valet to start letting out my clothes!"

His quip had been quick, but perhaps not quick enough. Miss Quintrell glanced over her shoulder, saw the direction his gormless gaze had been pointed, and had a small smile on her lips when she turned back.

Much against his will, John's cheeks reddened.

Florence Bailey was seated behind Miss Quintrell. She was reading a book, assiduously avoiding everyone's attempts to converse with her.

"I see," said Miss Quintrell kindly.

Thank goodness she was the only one.

John knew he was being ridiculous—he had always been the impulsive one of the family. Well, so was Lindow, but he was also a scoundrel.

And gawping at Miss Florence Bailey was bound to attract some questions eventually. Questions he did not wish to be accosted with, questions he could not answer.

What precisely is your history with Miss Bailey?

Why isn't she speaking to you, if you were once so close?

And what precisely is your intention toward her now?

All excellent questions, ones he had wrestled with last night over a bottle of brandy. At least, John was fairly sure he had wrestled with them. He had most definitely drunk the brandy.

That evening, at dinner—and he had been quite right, his valet was going to have a job fitting him into that waistcoat which had returned from the laundry much tighter than it used to be—John watched her again.

It was easy, this time. He had heard that Florence had been seated at the right hand of Mrs. Knight, a favor he suspected had been begged of the hostess so she could be far from Mr. Lister.

But John could be equally persuasive.

"Just *begged* to be seated at my left," Mrs. Knight trilled, clearly delighted a marquess was even at her table, let alone desirous of her company. "And who am I to deny the Marquess of Aylesbury?"

"Who indeed?" said her husband cheerfully from the other end of the table.

John grinned, leaning back in his chair with as unstudied an air as possible, and studied Florence.

She had flushed the moment she'd sat down at the dinner table and realized just how close he was. So close, John realized, that if he extended his legs—

He immediately withdrew them.

No, his brother Cothrom had been most clear. A second chance. And it wasn't just about his gambling. It also meant staying out of trouble with mamas and papas, which meant no flirting openly with young ladies when he had no intention of doing anything but flirting.

And that was all this was, wasn't it?

It wasn't a nice thought, and though John rarely entertained such thoughts, sometimes you just couldn't ignore that frightfully irritating voice at the back of your own mind. Cothrom called it a "conscience," and John would be blowed if he listened to something with a name like that.

Trouble was, it had grown rather louder in the passing days. And it pointed out that it was he who had called off . . .

Well. They had not actually been engaged, had they? Not officially. Not in so many words.

In so many kisses, however . . .

"—tell me all about that book you are reading," Mrs. Knight said good naturedly to Florence.

John glanced up as he swallowed a delicious mouthful of roasted hare, potatoes, and asparagus.

Florence was, as he had known she would be, blushing. There were few situations in which Florence—he really must try to remember to call her Miss Bailey—did not flush.

Fortunately for her, the effect was most pleasing. The red of her hair was elegantly matched by the pink of her cheeks, and her lips glistened with—

John cleared his throat, looked at his plate, and tried not to think of the way Florence Bailey's lips glistened. It was nothing to do with him. She was nothing to do with him.

But it was challenging. As the hare disappeared and a new course was brought out, he listened to Florence's stuttering conversation, the way she attempted to avoid all follow-up questions, the gentle nervousness of her voice.

She was just the same. Unchanged, unspoiled in the intervening years. Very shy, very nervous, but oh so clever.

"—breeding of course is top notch," Mr. Lister was spouting loudly four seats down from them. So loudly, in fact, that he quite ruined all other conversations at the table. When he saw everyone else had fallen silent, he grinned, as though it were a compliment paid to him. "I knew the moment I saw that filly, Heart of Fire, I knew she would—"

"The Arabian b-bloodline of Heart of Fire, and her m-mother, have been disp-proven by the 1807 investigation into f-false documentation in Rome," came a stuttering voice. "You have p-paid a g-great sum for nothing, Mr. Lister."

Someone dropped a piece of cutlery onto their plate. Mrs. Pullman's mouth was most inelegantly open, and someone muttered, "By Jove!"

Florence looked liable to melt with shame and embarrassment in her chair. She was staring at her plate, as though she had not just spoken such cleverness that Mr. Lister looked just as liable to melt away in disgrace.

And John grinned.

Yes, that was his Florence. Not his Florence. Obviously. Someone's Florence.

The thought hit him with the force of an upper cut.

Dear God. Was it possible—no, he had heard nothing of an engagement. Not that he was a frequent peruser of those particular pages in the newspapers. Should he have been?

Mr. Knight cleared his throat. "Well. My goodness. We shall be sure to come to you, Miss Bailey, when we next decide to buy a horse!"

Gentle laughter murmured around the table, a footman stepped forward to replenish the wine, and a chatter arose. And still, no one was looking at Florence.

Except him.

John tried to concentrate on his meal, but he'd lost all appetite for food. Florence—she was such a puzzle. Even when you thought she wasn't listening, slipping into a world of her own, Florence was able to swiftly contribute something insightful and clever.

Her nerves always showed. The stutter had been something she had loathed, from memory—though now John considered it, she'd said something once about that, hadn't she?

"It's n-not a stutter."

And he had grinned and said, "What do you call it, then?"

And just for once, Florence had glared and replied, "A s-stutter is a difference in speech, but m-my . . . my nerves affect it. W-When I'm not n-nervous, I d-don't stutter."

Excepting that one brief moment the other evening, he had never heard her speak without it. Which, John realized as he sipped his wine and tried to follow the conversation which had now moved onto styles of bonnet, meant Florence had always been nervous in his presence.

Was that a good thing or a bad thing?

By the time the dessert course was brought out, John had drunk three glasses of wine and was finding it difficult to bring his spoon to his mouth.

Not because of the wine. He'd imbibed far more than that in an evening and still managed to win a game of billiards. Badly, to be sure. And his opponent had ended up sleeping the night away under the table.

But still. He'd won.

No, it was the captivating picture of beauty seated opposite him that was the trouble. Whenever he lifted a spoonful of the rhubarb crumble and disgustingly thick custard to his mouth, John would look up, see Florence, see her flush at his attention, and . . .

After the third attempt led him to use his napkin to clean away the custard from his cheek, John put down his spoon.

Agog. That was the only word he could think of to describe his utter fascination with the woman.

He was truly agog. The refined motions of her hands, the slender slope of her waist that rose to swell over breasts that ached for his touch—

No, wait. That was him doing the aching. Damn.

The point was, John told himself firmly as the last of the desserts were taken away and the ladies departed, *he was getting distracted*. And by Florence Bailey! A woman of good family, it was true. And beauty. And cleverness.

And a stupendous dowry, muttered the traitorous voice in the back of his head.

And that, John agreed with himself as port was brought round and cigars offered by their eager host. It would be churlish of him to deny that a dowry, any dowry, would be convenient right now.

Any money was preferable to no money.

A stupendous dowry, on the other hand . . . what counted as stupendous?

He had been unable to winkle the exact amount from Mr. Knight, and there were no other gentlemen here John trusted well enough to inquire without the news getting out that he had done so.

That left him guessing.

Ten thousand? Surely not stupendous. Twenty thousand? It would be unusual, true, but hardly worthy of the description.

Thirty thousand?

John found his mouth had gone dry. And it was attached, this stupendous dowry, to the person of Miss Florence Bailey. A person he would quite like to be attached to himself.

At least for a night.

"This is your second chance, man. Do not waste it."

John sighed as he puffed on his cigar and attempted to put the beautiful, shy creature from his mind. Second chances. Well, he supposed that was more than fair. Cothrom could have made a significant argument for how this was actually John's three hundred forty-second chance, so ignoring the first... the first few hundred or so misdemeanors was good of him.

And that meant staying away from Miss Florence Bailey.

But that was proving to be easier said than done.

The dinner had run so late, when the gentlemen rejoined the ladies after the cigars had been smoked, many of their number had already gone to bed.

"Ah, Knight," said his wife with a heavy yawn. "Now you are here to entertain our guests, I admit my fatigue has gotten the better of me. I will retire."

"And I will join you," said Mr. Lister. His face immediately colored. "I-I mean—not join you, obviously, I meant—"

"We know what you meant, Mr. Lister," said Miss Quintrell with a wry look. "Off you go. Sleep well."

There was something immensely chastising about her tone, something John noted with delight. Anything to help keep Mr. Lister away from the ladies. Why, the stories he had heard—he'd even attempted to kiss the now Duchess of Axwick against her wishes! Before she became the duchess, obviously. John could hardly see old Axwick permitting something like that.

Within an hour, there was only himself, Florence, and Mr. Knight still remaining in the drawing room. Then—

"I really don't think I can keep my eyes open any longer," yawned old Knight, stretching out his arms and smacking his lips as the yawn subsided. "You don't mind me taking my leave, do you, Miss Bailey?"

John's head snapped up from the letter which had been in his lap, unread, for nigh on thirty minutes.

Florence decidedly did not look at him as she replied, "I-I have my b-book. I will be quite w-well."

A flicker of excitement, of anticipation, raced through John.

She must wish to speak to me.

It was the only explanation, he thought as Knight bowed to them both and departed from the drawing room. That had been the perfect excuse for Florence to retire to her own guest bedchamber—or be left alone with him.

She had chosen to stay.

The idea heartened his resolve to speak to her and yet unfortunately did not supply anything in particular to say. As the minutes ticked by, John found himself once again staring at her—agog—his brother's letter remaining mostly unread in his hands.

Try to keep away from the gambling tables, you idiot, came his older brother's encouraging words. And . . .

And what else, John could not tell. His gaze had drifted over once again to the woman who was reading a book that looked most serious, bound in a blue leather. They were not that far apart, seated in two armchairs. His eyes meandered along her fingers, holding the book carefully; to her collarbone, just begging to be kissed; to the way her lips—

"You are s-staring at me."

"No, I'm not," John said instinctively.

It was a lie. It was also not a very clever lie, and it did not take long for Florence to refute him.

"You are l-lying."

A smile crept across John's face. *She could tell. She could always tell.* "I suppose I am."

And then the most wonderful thing happened. Florence's eyes flickered away from the page before her, just for a moment, and a brief smile curled her lips.

Oh, she was beautiful. John had never seen a more captivating woman. She was a creature designed as though by God to distract him, to make it impossible to think of anything but the space in which she inhabited.

And when he had kissed her, when he had tasted the sweetness and the worry, the desperate need for him he had never imagined could be found in those trembling lips—

John cleared his throat, his smile disappearing as he shifted uncomfortably in his seat.

Damn. Could she see, perhaps, just what a . . . ah, physical effect she was having on him?

He would have to talk to his valet about the tightness of these breeches. Except he wouldn't, because it was the stiffening between his legs that was proving to be the problem, rather than Cook's fine offerings.

Florence had returned to her book. The smile had gone, the genial atmosphere between them disappeared. It was like she had not said anything to him at all.

John looked at his letter again, but his eyes could not take in a single word.

So, he liked her. There was no crime in that. It was hardly new, either—he had liked her when they had met two years ago. Liked her a great deal. Far too much, in fact, to leave her alone, which had been the trouble.

Because when he realized Florence expected—her whole family expected—a proposal of marriage . . . a proposal to restrict him forever, tie him to one person, one family, one experience, for the rest of his life . . .

John had ended the courtship. Badly, probably, in hindsight. But still. It was better than continuing on with nefarious intentions, wasn't it?

Wasn't it?

Two years later, John was starting to wonder whether he'd made a mistake.

And his manhood seemed to be wondering along with him.

"H-How is the book?" John asked, astonished at the stutter that had crept into his voice.

"W-When I'm not n-nervous, I d-don't stutter."

Hell, could she be right?

Florence glanced over at him, just for a moment, as though ascertaining whether he was teasing her or not. When it became clear it was just a question about the book, and nothing more, she nodded briefly.

John's shoulders slumped. Dear God, he couldn't even get a word out of her? His charm was failing him.

"I never had you down for a bluestocking," he said cheerfully.

That got her attention. Florence carefully placed a bookmark on the page, then closed the book on her lap. When she met his eye, it was steady, though her cheeks were already pinking.

"I would n-not call m-myself a b-bluestocking," she said in a hushed tone. "M-More a wallf-flower."

John leaned forward, eagerness overcoming his resolve to remain aloof. Or at least, to try to pretend to be aloof.

Florence Bailey, a wallflower! No, she was just shy. There was a difference. Florence wanted to be part of the conversation, had plenty of things to say, thoughts that astonished and astounded whenever she shared them.

She was just shy, that was all. That could be overcome.

Reducing Florence Bailey to the description of "wallflower" was like reducing the throne of England to "a chair."

"You said that to me once before," he said aloud. "You told me, the first day we met, that you were a wallflower."

It had been a cold spring morning. She'd worn blue.

Now how the devil did he remember that?

"And y-you said," Florence murmured with a smile. "You s-said that you'd n-never seen such a p-pretty flower."

John's stomach lurched. *She remembered? After all this time?* "I meant it."

"I'm s-sure you mean all th-the p-pretty things you say to the l-ladies," Florence said, her voice at least managing to be tranquil.

Ah. Well. He did. He had, at any rate. "I'm not sure about—"

"You s-said yourself, there h-have been other ladies since m-me, and you n-never truly had m-me," said Florence lightly. "Though n-not for the lack of trying. You whispered p-pretty things to me th-then, all th-those years ago. If you hadn't m-meant them, why s-say them at all if . . . if you were n-never g-going to do anything about it?"

It was perhaps the longest she had spoken in John's presence since . . . well, since two years ago.

And it was a well-asked question. *A well-deserved question*, John thought bitterly.

"Except," Florence said, her voice so low now that he could barely catch it. "E-Except . . ."

Her voice trailed away as her gaze moved to his mouth.

That simple gesture said so much more than mere words could.

John swallowed. That kiss. Oh, God, that kiss—he had never known anything like it, before or since. It had been the only kiss they had shared, but it had . . .

God's teeth, it had frightened him.

He'd never almost lost control like that. Never almost wept to have a woman in his arms give herself to him in that unfettered and passionate way. Never realized how much he stood to lose if Florence decided to walk away. Never known a single kiss could tear him apart, revealing all his fears, his needs, his craving.

His craving for her.

John couldn't help it. As Florence continued to stare at his mouth, he bit his lip.

The sudden gasp was a hiss between Florence's lips—lips his own attention had been fixed on. A burning need to kiss her again, to tell Florence, to show her just how much he wished to repeat that scandalous kiss, shot through John.

It was urgent and nearly overpowering. But not quite.

John had rocked forward as the instinct rushed through him, but he pulled himself together and leaned back in the armchair.

Dear God, that had been close.

He'd come here with the words of his brother ringing in his ears—that he was dancing on thin ice, and this was his second—and by the sound of it, last—chance. He wasn't about to cause a scandal by being discovered kissing Miss Florence Bailey in the drawing room.

Even if it that sounded most agreeable.

He wasn't going to prove his brother right.

Florence's look was wistful. "Y-You never int-tended to marry me, did you?"

John swallowed. They were on dangerous ground here, and he wasn't sure what to say next. Time to escape.

He shot up. "My goodness look at the time is that the time it is so late I must be abed goodnight Miss Bailey."

The words poured from his mouth and before John knew what he was doing, he had marched across the room and then slammed the door behind him.

He stood, panting heavily in the empty hallway, having just retreated—*retreated!*—from a woman.

Well. There was a first time for everything.

Chapter Five

July 10, 1812

WHEN FLORENCE OPENED her eyes, it was to breathe in a sigh of relief.

This was it. She had done it. The last day of the house party.

In just a few short hours she would be departing the home of the Knights and returning home. Her mother would have sent the carriage, as was proper, and the moment she stepped inside it, Florence could finally do what she had been unable to do since the moment she had arrived: *relax*.

No one to talk to, no one to impress, no one to be embarrassed before. There would only be herself and her lady's maid, Abigail, who had been with her long enough to know that Florence would have no interest in conversation during the roughly three hours the journey home would require.

Florence sat up in bed. She had survived. And that would mean saying goodbye to . . .

She swallowed hard, forcing down all foolish thoughts about a certain gentleman who had made her time here even more difficult.

John Chance, Marquess of Aylesbury.

The Marquess of Aylesbury had gone out of his way to—to look at her, and smile at her, and do all manner of vexing things. The man had been purposely irritating, and he knew it. And she knew it. And he knew she knew it.

Florence considered the tangle of that particular thought as Abigail dressed her for the final part of the house party—breakfast—but she knew what she meant.

She should be glad she would be rid of him. She was glad. She was most certainly not upset that she would shortly no longer be able to look over at him and remember what had been. Consider what could have been.

It was therefore most infuriating that the Marquess of Aylesbury was not downstairs for breakfast, robbing Florence of her last chance to show him and the world how infrequently she looked at him.

The toast was dry and the marmalade sour. Or perhaps that was just her dour mood.

When Florence returned upstairs to the guest bedchamber which had been her home the last week or so, it was to discover Abigail had already finished most of the packing.

"There y'are, miss," said her maid cheerfully. "I left you out your favorite scent. I thought you may wish to freshen up before the journey."

Florence blinked. "J-Journey?"

It would be several hours, surely, until the house party broke up. Many of the guests were vocally disappointed to be departing, and she had hoped—

She pushed aside the ridiculous thought.

No, she had not hoped to see the Marquess of Aylesbury again, Florence told herself sternly. She had most definitely not wished to have another conversation with him. Another private conversation. A conversation that might lead to . . .

"Miss?"

"I-I think there is a l-little time before d-departing," Florence said hastily, though she stepped over to the little toilette table where the scent had been left. "It is only n-nine, I d-do not think—"

"Ah, but you see, I knew how's as you would like to be away early, like," said her maid with a conspiratorial air. "So's I said to young Roberts, when he left us here, I said come nice and early and we can be away straight after breakfast. And he asked if that was your wish, and I said it were, and so the carriage arrived ten minutes ago. We'll be gone in a dash!"

She beamed at her mistress and Florence forced herself to smile.

It was kindly done. In any other scenario, she would have taken a few shillings from the meager pin money her mother permitted her and given it to Abigail as a demonstration of her gratitude.

Because in any other circumstances, it was precisely what she would have wanted. The excuse to leave early because the carriage was here, a swift escape from people and conversations and expectations . . .

Abigail was not to know that for the first time in her life, Florence did not wish to go.

And that was why her idea had burned in her mind when the Marquess of Aylesbury had half walked, half run away from her last night, a new thought she'd not been entirely prepared for.

It was a foolish idea, certainly. The sort of thing one heard about, but it never actually happened. Florence hardly knew why the thought had crossed her mind in the first place, it was so ridiculous.

But it had. And Florence had spent half the night awake, thinking about it.

Her original plan had been to return home once the Knights' house party was over and demand her mother cease sending her to such ridiculous places in her attempt to find a husband. She had no desire to dance, no need to play cards, and would rather hole herself up in a dungeon than sit through another excruciating afternoon tea.

That had been what she was *going* to say.

"I knew you'd be pleased," said her maid with a grin as she heaved up her mistress's trunk. "I'll just take this and wait downstairs in the kitchens. The stableboy will run and let me know when you're ready in the carriage."

Florence nodded instead of trusting her voice. Her maid carried the trunk with great effort out of the room, then kicked the door closed behind her, just as Florence's mother had attempted to teach her not to do.

She examined herself in the looking glass.

Her idea was ridiculous. And if it didn't work, Florence was likely to melt into a puddle of shame never to be forgotten. She would never be able to go out into Society again, though in truth that was more a reward than a punishment.

Florence tucked a curl of flaming red hair behind her ear. *But if it worked . . .*

No. She couldn't. It was just a passing fancy.

After dabbing the scent—jasmine and roses, her favorite—behind her ears, she placed the little bottle into her reticule and swept a quick look around the guest bedchamber.

She had not left anything here. Not even her heart.

Preparing herself for an awkward conversation with her hosts, Florence left the room and started down the staircase. She was prevented from having to find them, however, by the sight of both Mr. and Mrs. Knight near the front door, having a conversation with—

"Ah, there she is," said John Chance, Marquess of Aylesbury, airily. "I thought it was her carriage outside, I recognized the . . . you are leaving early, then."

If Florence had been a different woman, she would have glared at the man. Perhaps if she had been completely different, she would have shot back a quip, a retort, something to make them all laugh and take the focus off her and place it squarely on the man who was being so annoying.

As it was . . .

"I-I . . . I d-d-did not know m-my mother would . . ." Florence swallowed, hating how her voice simply crumbled into nothing whenever her nerves overcame her. It was ridiculous. *Ridiculous!* "I-I h-have no wish to off-f-fend—"

"No offense is given, not at all," Mrs. Knight said swiftly, rescuing Florence from her own errant tongue. "Naturally your mother wishes you to be home quickly. She must have missed you!"

Florence considered attempting to say something cutting at her mother's expense. That the woman probably missed the opportunity to berate her daughter, complain about her complete lack of suitors, and wonder audibly if she would have to bear the burden of a spinster daughter for the rest of her life.

But she didn't.

She smiled weakly. "I-I th-thank you for . . . for your understanding."

And still the Marquess of Aylesbury hovered beside her. It was most unaccountable. Here she was, attempting to thank Mr. and Mrs. Knight for their hospitality—a sentiment expressed poorly, thanks to her anxious stuttering—and he remained there.

Looking at her.

Florence swallowed as she completed her thanks. "—v-very kind, I th-thank you."

And she meant it. Though she had dreaded this house party, Mr. and Mrs. Knight had proven themselves to be exemplary hosts. Most importantly, they had never forced her to join a card game, or dance about playing charades, or do anything to draw greater attention onto herself.

It was a rarity, and she wished them to know just how grateful she was.

If only she could wrangle her tongue.

"It was our pleasure to have you, my dear," said Mrs. Knight with a kindly look.

"Oh yes, you must come back," Mr. Knight said eagerly. "We're thinking of having a hunting party in the autumn! I don't know if you hunt, Miss Bailey—"

"Miss Bailey does not hunt, but she rides superbly," came a quiet voice.

"Oh, capital!" said Mr. Knight enthusiastically. "I should have guessed that, the way you put down—ah, I mean, explained to Mr. Lister about bloodlines. I thought at the time . . ."

Precisely what the man had thought at the time, Florence did not know. She had rather lost the thread of what he was saying as she was too busy staring at the man beside her to pay enough attention.

The Marquess of Aylesbury was smiling. No, not smiling. There was no curve on his lips, but there was a twinkle in his eye that told her precisely what he was thinking.

They had cantered together. The rest of the pack had been left behind and Florence had laughed joyfully, not a tremor in her voice, as John had attempted to keep up with her.

"Slow down!" he had cried.

Florence had barely heard him, the rush of the wind and the euphoria of riding almost overcoming her.

And yet she had slowed. Riding had always been a passion, an escape—but riding with John . . . his laughter beside her, his admiration, the way he had attempted to grow close whenever he helped her dismount . . .

As if she needed help dismounting.

Then the moment was broken.

"Well, bring your own horse when you come in the autumn," Mr. Knight said, and Florence turned from the Marquess of Aylesbury hastily to nod. "Excellent. Wonderful! And you, my lord, you must—"

"Anywhere Miss Bailey is, I will be certain to be," said the Marquess of Aylesbury. "Her ability to ride anything is second to none."

Boiling heat splashed across Florence's face. *Did he have any idea what that sounded like—how could he even think of—*

But apparently their hosts had noticed nothing. "How impressive," said Mrs. Knight cordially. "You have hidden depths, my dear! I look forward to getting to know you better."

And a wave of guilt washed over Florence. They really weren't so bad, Mr. and Mrs. Knight. They had been truly good hosts, and perhaps Mrs. Knight, who was perhaps only a few years older than herself, could have been a friend.

She would have plenty of time to regret her behavior at this house party in the carriage, Florence told herself. And even more time when she arrived home and her mother grilled her about the number of gentlemen, and how many of them Florence had flirted with.

The very idea!

"G-Goodbye," Florence muttered, curtsying low and turning to the front door, which was immediately opened by a footman.

She stepped forward. And then could not step forward farther.

There was a pressure on her arm.

Florence looked at it to see a hand placed upon it, preventing her from moving. A hand that was strong, yet gentle. A hand she recognized.

She swallowed, and looked up into the serious expression of the Marquess of Aylesbury.

"I-I can find my own w-way to my carriage," she managed, heat searing as she met his blue gaze.

"I am sure you can," he said cheerfully. "But I wouldn't dream of you being forced to find your own way there. The very idea!"

There was nothing she could do. No matter what Florence's thoughts were on the matter, it was clear the brute—*perhaps that was too strong a word*—was not going to let go of her arm until she reached her carriage.

Fine, Florence thought darkly. He could walk her to her carriage. Then she would be in the carriage and away from this very confusing man. Free to weep over the missed opportunity, once again. *Unless . . .*

She again pushed aside the plan she had concocted last night then dismissed in the cold light of day. Absolutely not. She was no harlot, acting in such a bold and outrageous manner. Certainly not!

All she was going to do was walk with the Marquess of Aylesbury. Unwillingly.

"F-Fine," she managed to say aloud.

The Marquess of Aylesbury's face split into a grin. "Excellent."

Florence had been certain the man had merely intended to accompany her, to walk beside her across the gravel drive with an appropriate amount of space between them, then come to a halt when they reached her carriage.

But apparently John Chance had a different idea.

As Florence came to the portico steps, John attempted to lift her hand and place it on his arm.

The sudden intimacy was overwhelming. That the man would assume they would walk arm in arm—like a couple betrothed, like two people who shared a connection deeper than mere words...

He was out of his mind!

Worst of all, Florence could not help but be suddenly intoxicated by his presence. The heat of the day was only just beginning to make itself felt, but her mind had been instantly overcome by the heat of John Chance.

His touch, his scent, the very masculine presence that was and only could be John. Sandalwood and cedar, the warmth of his fingers, the ease with which he reached for her own—

It was too much.

Florence stumbled down the steps, mind reeling from the sudden intrusion of the Marquess of Aylesbury's presence, and she was falling, falling, the ground whooshing forward at a terrible pace and she would be injured, the marble steps were approaching so rapidly she could not—

A strong arm swept her to the left, pulling her into the solid chest of a man who chuckled.

"See," the Marquess of Aylesbury murmured so only she could hear. "You need me."

Florence knew she should push him away. Should use the splayed hand against his linen shirt above his waistcoat as leverage, and force the man to release her.

Which was why she did so—after a few heart-stopping moments, during which she felt his pulse race, race to match the throbbing pulse aching through her own body.

"I-I don't n-need your—"

"Careful, Miss Bailey!" called Mrs. Knight from the doorway. "They can be awfully slippy, those steps!"

Florence carefully ignored the smirk on the Marquess of Aylesbury's lips and stepped onto the gravel. At least here she was unlikely to fall.

Because it had been the step's fault, obviously, that she had stumbled. Not the overpowering presence of a certain gentleman, who she most certainly was not in love with, not at all, and was not heartbroken about in the slightest. Most definitely not. Not at all.

"You need me."

Shaking her head as though that could remove the echo of those words, Florence looked up to see her carriage. There, only about twenty feet away. She would be there in a moment.

And every moment she would be accompanied by the Marquess of Aylesbury.

If only there were something there. Something mutual.

Florence had allowed herself to hope, two years ago, and she had been proven to be most foolish in doing so. She was hardly about to make the same mistake again.

Was she?

This time she was not startled, nor did she attempt to escape him when the Marquess of Aylesbury placed her hand on his arm. Perhaps it was better not to resist the warmth of his arm. Or the sense of peace that flowed through her as they walked in step together—slowly, far more slowly than Florence would have intended. Perhaps instead she should resist the painful thought that this could be the last time she was ever close to the man who—

"H-Here we are," Florence said aloud—mostly to force away the hurried thoughts swirling through her mind.

It was best to forget him. Forget what could have been. Forget what she had hoped.

Her driver, Roberts, must have gone to the kitchens to find Abigail, for there was no servant by the carriage to open the door and help her in.

And she was not, Florence told herself firmly, *going to permit the Marquess of Aylesbury to—*

"John!" she gasped, instinctively using the far more intimate first name in the shock of what he had just done.

Because what he had done was outrageous. Instead of opening the carriage door and helping her inside—which would already have been a little reckless, the two of them without gloves—John had tightened his grip on her hand and pulled her around the carriage.

Out of sight of anyone who may be looking out from the house.

Florence's pulse quickened as she tugged her hand away from the miscreant. "Wh-What do you th-think you're—John!"

She had not intended to say his name again, but for the second time, she had not been able to help it. What else was a lady supposed to do when a gentleman suddenly pushes her up against a carriage, his face somehow serious and eager at the same time?

The solid carriage behind her and the breadth of John Chance, Marquess of Aylesbury, before her, Florence's pulse skipped a beat as she looked up at him.

What on earth was the man playing at?

"I miss you, Florence," John said in a low voice.

Florence's gasp hitched in her throat. *This wasn't happening. This could not happen!* "Y-You can't m-miss me—"

"Why not?" he asked insistently, his voice remaining hushed. "You are beautiful, Florence. And kind. And far too tempting for a man like me to resist."

The aching longing Florence associated with the impetuous marquess was flooding back into her body, and just for a moment, she considered giving into all those desires, all those feelings, and giving herself to him.

Just one kiss, a part of her moaned. *Just one.*

The rest of her, the far more sensible part of her, rebelled at the mere thought. The Marquess of Aylesbury was a rogue, and a rake, and a brute, and a scoundrel!

And besides . . .

Besides, she had been down this path before. Florence sagged against the carriage, unable to bear her own weight as the Marquess of Aylesbury stared at her with a hungry expression. She knew where this path ended. Florence wasn't going to waste any more tears on this man again.

Probably.

"Florence," said the Marquess of Aylesbury with a teasing air.

Florence wetted her lips before she spoke—an instinct which had never had any dire consequences before.

The man groaned, placing his hands either side of her head as he leaned toward her. "I very much want to kiss you, Florence."

Her panting breaths were short and she knew two things most clearly, despite the whirling of her mind.

Firstly, that she absolutely was not going to let this man kiss her. *The very idea!*

And secondly, that if she did, she would not be able to regret it.

"Florence," the Marquess of Aylesbury whispered, lowering his head so his forehead touched hers. "Talk to me, Florence."

Florence swallowed hard, not sure how she was still standing, and tried to speak. It was impossible. Her breathing was shallow, her lungs straining for air, and her throat was so dry it was a wonder she could swallow at all.

This was not happening! Where was Roberts? Where was Abigail?

Was it possible she was going to have to escape the Marquess of Aylesbury herself?

"I still want to kiss you, Florence," he whispered.

His breath was warm against her cheek and Florence forced down the sudden urge to lift her lips to meet his own.

"Y-You wouldn't," she managed.

It was the wrong thing to say.

Or the right thing. Florence wasn't sure. All she knew was that as the two words were spoken, the Marquess of Aylesbury groaned and captured her lips in a fiery, desperate kiss.

It was most unlike the kiss they had shared before. That had been filled with desire, of restraint which had been borne too long. It had been a kiss stolen in the kitchen gardens, a kiss Florence had not expected and could never have prepared for.

This was different. This kiss was filled with aching need and lust, a physical ache Florence could not believe was being sated by such a man.

But sate it he did. The Marquess of Aylesbury knew precisely what he was doing, precisely, it seemed, what she liked. Florence moaned, parting her lips beneath his under the aggressive need he poured down upon her. His tongue wetted her lips, and when hers darted out to meet his, it was the Marquess of Aylesbury and not herself who groaned.

Somehow, and Florence was not sure how, she had managed to tangle her fingers in his hair and was doing something most irregular: pulling him closer.

With the bulk of the carriage behind her and the strong chest of the Marquess of Aylesbury against her, Florence could do nothing but succumb to the aching pleasure that flowed through her body as he worshipped her mouth.

And then it was over.

Florence blinked in sudden dazzle of sunlight as she opened her eyes.

The Marquess of Aylesbury was smiling at her ruefully. "I would," he growled.

She nodded hazily, exhaling slowly before she spoke the words she knew she had to say. "Well. I think we should get married."

Chapter Six

July 15, 1812

"No," said William Chance, the Duke of Cothrom, calmly. "No, I don't believe it."

John stared. "What do you mean, you don't believe it?"

"I don't believe it," repeated his older brother with a frown. "And there is absolutely nothing you can say to me that will make me believe it, either."

This was not the auspicious start John had hoped for.

When his older brother had invited him over to Cothrom House in London for tea, John had seen it for what it was: an excuse to check up on him, to ensure the second Chance brother hadn't caused any mischief.

And he hadn't. Much.

He had waited, patiently, too—*well, mostly patiently*—for an opportunity in the conversation to share his news. His new sister-in-law, Alice, had been a most gracious presence in the room while Cothrom complained about the antics of the third Chance brother, the Earl of Lindow, and John had listened, nodding in all the right places. He had earned the opportunity to share his good news. And now Cothrom was saying he wouldn't believe it?

"Well, it's true," said John, perhaps more testily than he should. "And you can go on disbelieving it as long as you wish, but that doesn't make it any less true. And—Alice, what is this tea?"

Cothrom rolled his eyes as John beamed at his wife. "You always were one to get distracted."

"Only by the best things in life, and this tea is sublime," said John, gesturing with his teacup at his hostess. "Wherever did you find such an exquisite blend?"

"I make it myself," said Alice with a teasing look at her husband. "William found it so refreshing, when I was sent to—when I went to the Dower House, I mean, he got rid of my entire stock due to missing me. I had to make a fresh batch, and I must say, I am quite delighted with it."

"There's assam in there, am I right?" asked John with a smile.

He nodded as Alice spoke about the careful blend of tea. He was only doing this to annoy Cothrom, which was perhaps bad form. But really! Here he came with the best possible news—the sort of news Cothrom had been demanding for months now—and the man did not even wish to give him the benefit of the doubt?

"—and just a tablespoon of—"

"Hang the tea!" exploded Cothrom. "My apologies, my dear," he said swiftly to Alice, flushing at his own rudeness. "But you know my idiot brother is only—"

"That was a low blow, don't you think?" protested John, leaning back in his chair and grinning.

"—only asking you about the tea so he can avoid the topic," his brother persisted.

He wasn't wrong. But John wasn't going to tell him that.

"You turn up here," said Cothrom, violently pointing a teaspoon at him, "at my home—"

"William," said Alice calmly.

"—and you try to make us believe—"

"You were the one who invited me to tea!" countered John.

He shouldn't be enjoying this. He really shouldn't. He could see the pressure building in the oldest Chance brother, knew it was irritating him beyond belief. And Cothrom had just gone through a rather stressful experience of his own already this year. Marriage to a woman who turned out to be not quite what you thought was very taxing on a man who always had to have things just so.

But that didn't mean Cothrom could berate him for this!

"—make us believe," continued Cothrom stoically, a dark gleam in his eye, "you are going to be married!"

John grinned. "Yes."

"Married."

"Yes."

"To a woman."

"Yes."

"And she has consented?"

"On purpose and everything," John said cheerfully.

He should have done this years ago. He hadn't had this much fun aggravating his brother in ages, and it was markedly entertaining. He should have made sure Lindow would be here. The man would have loved it.

"Married," Cothrom repeated in a monotone.

John threw his free hand up in the air in mock exasperation. "Married, yes. As in, a wedding. To a woman who will then be a wife. I think you are familiar with the concept?"

He chanced a glance at his new sister-in-law and saw to his delight she was stifling a giggle.

Oh, it would do the old man good to have a wife who could, and would, laugh at him. If there was one thing that Cothrom needed more than anything, it was taking the large stick out of his—

"I don't believe it," said Cothrom flatly.

"We're going around in circles," Alice said, putting a placatory hand on her husband's arm. "I understand your astonishment, William, truly. I never would have thought any woman would agree to—"

"That's a bit harsh," interrupted John with a wink. "After all, you agreed to marry this brute!"

Cothrom actually went to rise from his chair, which was not something John had anticipated, but the tightening of his wife's fingers on his arm steadied him.

John watched the two of them in barely hidden wonder.

It was astonishing. You thought you knew a man. The same parents, the same household, raised by the same nanny then governess. They had both gone to Eton—all three Chance brothers had—and had attended the same college at Cambridge, though taken very different degrees.

And then Cothrom could go and get married, and you saw an entirely different man from the one you'd known your entire life.

Well, nothing of the sort would happen to him, John thought impressively as he tried to hear the gentle words Alice murmured to her husband. He knew precisely what and who he was.

None of that was going to change.

John grinned as his older brother fixed him with a look. "Yes?"

"Married?" Cothrom said. "Ouch!" He rubbed at where his wife had jabbed him with her elbow. "Well! It's a perfectly reasonable—"

"Who is the fortunate woman?" asked Alice firmly. "I'm tired of going around in circles, it's like having a conversation with Maudy about what she wants for breakfast. Who is this woman you are marrying?"

John grinned. "How is Maudy?"

Discovering his brother had decided on a whim to marry a woman he had met once at a ball was one thing—finding out that she had a child already had been quite another.

Still. If he was going to have a niece, he'd want one like Maude. Bright, mischievous, and utterly in control of the Cothrom household.

"She is fine, and you are avoiding my question," Alice said with a smile.

Ah. And his sister-in-law was clever, too. More's the pity.

"I am getting married," John said enthusiastically, finishing his tea and placing the cup on its saucer on the console table beside him. "I am, Cothrom, really—and to a perfectly respectable woman with a good dowry." *A stupendous dowry.* "You've met her!"

"I sent you to that house party to behave yourself," Cothrom said with a sigh. "To get away from London and the gambling hells. Not to propose to random women!"

And a flicker of something unfamiliar curled around John's torso.

Possessiveness. No, that wasn't it. A need to defend. It was, in fact, an absolute fury that Cothrom had spoken so casually about the woman he—

Well. Probably best not to interrogate that thought any further.

"She is not a random woman," John said, discovering to his surprise that his response was more curt than he had meant it to be. "She is Miss Florence Bailey."

Cothrom stared. "Miss Bailey?"

"Yes," said John tightly.

For some reason, sharing the name of his betrothed felt exposing. As though he had revealed something of himself he had not intended. As though he were now . . . vulnerable.

His brother snorted. "I don't believe it."

"For God's sake, man!"

"Now, please," Alice said peacefully.

The two brothers halted immediately. John swallowed, trying to force down the anger that had just made him bellow across the little parlor. Cothrom crossed his arms like a petulant child, but managed to hold his tongue.

Good, John thought fiercely. He didn't even deserve to speak Florence's name.

Oh, and you do? The irritating little voice was back.

She asked me to marry her, John pointed out silently. *Mostly.*

"William," Alice was saying. "You have been saying ever since I met you—before that, I am sure—that you wished for your brothers to settle down. To marry, to—"

"Yes, but not like this," Cothrom said, cutting across her with an expression of exhaustion. "I hoped they'd put a little more thought into the choice!"

His wife grinned. "What, like you did with me?"

The two of them shared a moment John was not a participant in. He watched, though. Curious.

Because it was strange. Odd, to think of his brother as a spouse. It was not something he had ever truly considered. It was like a different part of Cothrom had blossomed. A part that John had known, sort of, but never seen grow. And he was happy, there was no denying it. No explaining away the look of deep affection that passed between the two of them. It was so intense, John felt awkward just being in the same room.

Cothrom turned back to him. "Miss Bailey."

John inclined his head. "The very same."

"You've known her for . . . for some time, haven't you?" came the stiff reply.

"Some time, yes." It wasn't exactly a lie, but it wasn't the truth either.

Because how could he tell the whole truth? How could John admit that two years ago he had ended up falling into a courtship he had never intended, and then, when he realized just what matrimony would mean, he had . . . escaped?

Escaped was not the right word. Fled.

Just one kiss. That was all it had taken for John to realize, in that moment, just what he would lose by walking away.

And yet he had.

"Look," John said aloud, forcing the memories of that time away. Where they belonged, right at the back of his mind. "I have not lost my head or anything. This is not a love match."

Alice raised an eyebrow at the firmness of his last few words. "It isn't?"

"It isn't," John said steadfastly.

"It isn't?" said Cothrom, mystified.

"Look, let's not construct a new circle for us to go round and round in," said his wife hastily. "You are not marrying for love—"

"Most definitely not," said John swiftly.

Far too swiftly. Why had those words tumbled out of his mouth? What was he afraid of—being presumed to be such a ridiculous man that he had actually permitted his feelings to get involved?

Ludicrous!

"Which means," said Cothrom darkly, "you're marrying for money. The poor woman, does she have any idea—"

"The marriage was her idea in the first place," John interrupted, hating that he had to reveal this but knowing it would be the only thing his brother would listen to. "Florence—Miss Bailey. It was her idea."

A marriage of convenience.

He hadn't said the words aloud, yet John was astonished to find that sadness rushed over him now even as he thought them.

A marriage of convenience.

Well, it was convenient. She wished for solitude, an escape from the unrelenting calendar of Society. He needed money—respectability, that was. It was a match made . . . well, not in heaven.

John looked up from his hands, hardly aware of when his head had dropped to them. It was difficult to tell what made him more morose: Alice's clear sadness, or Cothrom's relief.

"Oh, well, that's different," said Cothrom with a brief smile. "A marriage of convenience, between two acquaintances. Yes, that makes far more sense—ouch!"

"Are you certain that's all this is?" asked Alice, ignoring her husband after her elbow had delivered its blow.

"She is a wallflower looking for an escape, and I need money," John said, repeating—or at least, paraphrasing—the hurried discussion he and Florence had shared behind her carriage. "That's all there is to it."

"All?"

"Of course," he said dismissively. "Look—I'll prove it to you."

Striding over to the little writing desk Alice had brought to Cothrom House when she had married, John pulled out a sheet of paper, dipped a pen in the ink pot, and wrote a few hurried lines on the paper. He signed it with a flourish, waved the paper about to dry it as he returned to his seat, then grinned as he handed it over to Alice.

She looked at the paper with a hint of disapproval. "I see."

"What is it?" Cothrom asked.

Alice handed him the note.

John's brother read it aloud. "I promise that I am only marrying Florence Bailey for her money, for her stupendous dowry and nothing else. John Chance, Aylesbury."

"Really, John, is that necess—"

"I'm not sure what else I could do to persuade you," John said cheerfully to his sister-in-law. "There it is, in black and white."

It had felt odd, writing such a thing. But it was true, John reassured himself silently. Florence knew it, he knew it—it was as simple as that. Everyone was going into this with their eyes wide open.

Mostly. Florence—Miss Bailey—believed he wished for respectability, an end to the mamas of Society chasing after him. In truth, her dowry had not been mentioned between them at all.

Not that it was any of his brother's business.

Cothrom sighed heavily. "Dash it all, Aylesbury, but... well, this isn't what I meant."

"Well, you will simply have to think about what you did mean, and tell me at our next meeting," said John, hearing the chime of a clock somewhere about the place. "I am afraid I have another appointment."

"What, with your lady love?" Alice teased as the three of them rose.

John grinned. "Goodness, certainly not. I'm off to woo the mother!"

It had been Florence's suggestion. Her mother, apparently, was elated with the news that her daughter had finally—Florence's word—managed to snag a suitor. Her elation had become a thrill when she discovered that he was a nobleman.

What Mrs. Bailey had said when Florence had revealed he was a marquess, John did not know.

Apparently, the best way to guarantee everything went smoothly was for John to meet her—the mother, that was—at his earliest convenience. John suspected, though he would never suggest such a thing, that Florence was worried her mother did not believe he existed. A late-afternoon tea had been arranged, and he was not going to be late.

John grinned at the world as he left his brother and sister-in-law behind and strode down the busy London streets. It was foolish, really. This joy brimming in him, it couldn't be because he was going to be seeing Florence in a few minutes.

Miss Bailey. He must remember to call her Miss Bailey before her mother.

Or could he call her Florence now, now that they were engaged to be married?

The thought was a rather pleasant one.

A marriage of convenience. John could see easily how it benefited him—forty-five thousand pounds would be more than a convenience. A careful conversation with a solicitor friend who could find these things out, and he had discovered just how convenienced he would be by marrying Florence. But he hadn't quite understood Florence's eagerness to tie herself down to a man. To any man, let alone him.

It had something to do with her mother, apparently.

John could not understand it, but then it would surely all become clear once he arrived.

Ten minutes later, seated beside Florence on a sofa far too small for two people, and opposite a severe-looking woman who was all frowns and prickles, he could indeed see why.

"Ah," he said weakly as the interrogation which had begun six minutes ago continued. "Let's see. My father was the Duke of Cothrom before my brother, naturally—"

"And just how old is that family lineage?" interrupted Mrs. Bailey, a glare surfacing as though he were trying to avoid the question. "I asked how far back your nobility went, young man, not who your father was! That's the sort of thing a mother wishes to know. Certainly it's what my mother would have wished to know."

John stared in amazement at the woman. He had never been spoken to before with such . . . such enmity. He was here to marry her daughter—to make her the Marchioness of Aylesbury. And the woman wanted to quiz him about history?

As John consumed two cups of tea, three biscuits, and a slice of dry cake that tasted as though it had been left out for some time, he endured question after question. It was more an interview than a first meeting with one's future mother-in-law.

And throughout the torment, Florence sat beside him. Silent. Her eyes cast down, her fingers gripping the cold cup of tea she had not so much as sipped from the moment her mother had thrust it into her hands.

Two painful hours later, John could see perfectly plainly why Florence would wish to escape her mother.

The damned woman was a harpy!

"And I do not think your tailor has done your collar points justice," said Mrs. Bailey with great authority. "I would have thought you, as a nobleman, let alone a gentleman, would have spoken to your valet about such a thing. If you have a valet, of course."

The prickles of irritation which had grown larger and larger with every passing moment threatened to overcome his good manners once again. But once again, John swallowed the cutting remark he wished to make and smiled painfully at the woman.

"I will have a word with my tailor and my valet," he said in an understated tone. "Though this is the latest fashion, Mrs. Bailey."

"I am glad to hear you will be taking care of it," Mrs. Bailey struck back. "Collar points of a certain angle and fabric were good enough for my husband, and I can't think why these fashions should change so quickly, can you?"

Just for a moment, John glanced at the woman beside him. Was this truly what her mother was like all the time? Did she honestly wish to transform him into some sort of replica of her husband?

Florence remained silent. Her cheeks were red, the painful sort of blotchy that John knew meant she had reached the epitome of her embarrassment. If he were to make a guess, he would estimate that it was now physically impossible for Florence to speak.

And even if she could, what would she say? This harpy—*this woman*, John corrected himself mentally—was her mother. She had evidently been ground down by a lifetime of the constant rudeness of Mrs. Bailey.

No wonder Florence would accept any marriage, any man, to escape her.

The thought was most unpleasant. Was it possible Florence had attended the house party in order to choose a rescuer, John thought with a start, and the choices were himself, Mr. Lister, and a viscount?

Was he only a better choice than Mr. Lister?

"Tell me," said Mrs. Bailey without a hint of embarrassment, "just what happened between your brother and that woman of his?"

John turned back to face his future mother-in-law and tried to smile. "You may have to be a tad more exact, Mrs. Bailey. Lindow has many—"

"Not that rascal," interrupted Mrs. Bailey. "I meant your elder brother, Cothrom, and that woman he married."

And that was the final straw.

John was not a particularly proud man. There were many topics of his personal life that almost anyone could critique without him raising even a hair of an eyebrow. In fact, now he came to think about it, he had frequently accepted rudeness from ignorant individuals and had weathered it without a care.

But not Cothrom. Not Alice.

Not his family.

Before he knew what he was doing, before he could stop himself, the words he had been wishing to say within five minutes of entering the Bailey house poured from him without pause or self-censure.

"You should perhaps mind your words more carefully!" John snapped. "It is none of your business what happened between those who have absolutely nothing to do with you—and I would thank you to speak of the Duke and Duchess of Cothrom with a little more respect!"

Mrs. Bailey's mouth was open, and she was now giving a passable impression of her daughter. "I-I . . . n-never before have I—"

"Then it's time that someone spoke to you in the manner in which you deserve," said John, an angry heat suffusing through him. "This poor woman beside me may have chosen to endure your insolence and nosiness, but I do not have to. I am to be your son-in-law, Mrs. Bailey, and I refuse to permit you to speak to me like that, and if I hear that you have done so to Florence, then you shall be very sorry indeed!"

"John!" gasped Florence beside him.

It was the first thing she had said to him since he had arrived, and John was heartened by it. The thought that his Florence—that Florence had suffered through years of this . . .

It did not bear thinking about.

"We are leaving," he said stiffly.

"W-We are—"

He did not permit Florence to continue speaking. Grabbing her hand and ignoring the splutters of Mrs. Bailey, John pulled his betrothed out of the drawing room, through the hall, and out of the front door. Only after he had dragged her along the street and taken a left, finally pulling her into a garden in the center of the square, did John pause.

And then he let go.

And then he thought about what he'd said.

"Oh, hell," John said weakly.

His temper was already cooling, regret already starting to grow in his mind.

He looked at Florence, whose eyes were wide. "I . . . damn it. I hope you don't mind. I'm not usually so—"

"I know," said Florence quietly. "But I remember how you spoke to that man who beat his footman unnecessarily. You can't bear injustice."

John stared.

Not just because she had remembered. Dear God, he hadn't even known she'd seen that. He'd pulled the whip out of the man's hands and berated him soundly. The idea of violence had always repelled him, but to see it enacted on a young lad—

No, it was because Florence had spoken. Spoken clearly. Without a single stutter.

It appeared she had just realized the same thing. Dropping her head and twisting her hands before her, Florence said, "A-Anyway, I-I don't m-mind. The r-rudeness, I mean. I've wanted to s-say that for y-y-years."

John's pulse skipped a beat as she glanced up with a wry expression.

Dear God. If she looked at him like that again, he might just do . . . do anything.

"You have a dowry of five and forty thousand pounds," he blurted out.

Regret immediately poured through him. Damn it to hell, what on earth had he said that for?

Florence was flushing, gazing at her feet. "Y-Yes."

John swallowed. "You could have suggested this . . . this marriage of convenience to anyone and been accepted. Why me?"

Why the answer to this question mattered so much, he could not explain—but it did.

Florence did not look up as she replied. "I-I d-don't want vultures circling me for my m-money. Ignoring me, happy to m-marry anyone attached to the numbers. I d-don't want to be w-wed for my b-bank balance. You need respectability. You aren't c-cruel. I chose you."

There was a moment of silence between them.

And John could have spoken. He could have admitted that he needed that money, and that he was most definitely wedding her for her bank balance. That he was out of money, in debt, and trying desperately to keep away from the card tables.

But he couldn't.

"In that case," he said aloud, hoping to goodness she hadn't seen the look of devotion he had shot her. Just for a moment. Just when his guard was down. "Let us take a walk about the park, and you can tell me what else you have wanted to say for years."

Florence went scarlet. Then she placed her hand in John's arm. "N-Not all of it."

"Not today," John countered with a grin, his stomach lurching. "No. Not today."

Chapter Seven

July 17, 1812

THE PACE, THE thrill, the rhythm, the rush—

A broad smile was across Florence's face as she rode in the early morning chill. The scent of dawn was in the air; the pollen from the flowers gently stirring, the slow arrival of sleepy honeybees venturing out, the birdsong heralding the rising sun.

And beneath her, Midnight.

It was always her preference to ride alone. Florence had seen others ride in Hyde Park in pairs or trios, sometimes even larger groups. And they talked. They conversed, the pressure of always having the right thing to say pressing constantly against a person's tongue.

She had tried it, once. Once had been enough.

Ever since, she had ridden alone. Just before dawn, as the world was waking, where no one would see her.

And she could feel alive.

Florence breathed a laugh as her mare, Midnight, shifted from an energetic canter to an all-out gallop. Wind whipped at her hair as it did the mane of her steed, the thrill of the movement stirring through her body with the thud, thud, thud of her pulse.

There was no one else here. No one else in the world. This was the one place, Florence knew, where she could be herself.

It was more difficult in the summer months. In the winter, dawn approached slowly and later in the day, giving Florence the opportunity to stay in bed far longer. In July, however, she had to be up so early there sometimes seemed little point in going to bed.

But still. It was worth it.

Florence expertly slowed her horse to a swift trot as they approached the edge of the Serpentine, looking out curiously at the water as birds chirped and ducks paddled lazily upon the lake.

Freedom.

That was it. That was what she craved, what was missing in her life. The freedom to be herself, to do what she liked, when she liked. To not be tied up in Society's rules, not be forced to attend events she had absolutely no wish to attend, all to prevent offense being given to people she had never met.

Florence leaned back in her saddle and beamed up at the sky that was just beginning to lighten. This was where she could be herself. This was the last place anyone would think to—

There was a man.

The sudden realization, borne of a glimpse of a figure out of the corner of her eye, transformed Florence immediately.

Gone was the smile. Gone was the relaxed look up at the sky, the gentle grip of the reins, the certainty she had at least another hour before anyone would disturb her in Hyde Park.

Florence curled up in herself, making herself smaller as she knew precisely how. Her ungloved hands—*what had she been thinking?*—gripped the leather of her reins so tightly the edge dug into her wrist.

A man.

After all the freedom she had enjoyed, the solitude and the silence, it was a jolt to the spirit to feel so . . . exposed.

You shouldn't have come.

Florence pushed aside the thought. She had to take advantage of these mornings while she had them. She was about to be married to John—to the Marquess of Aylesbury. He was hardly likely to encourage dawn rides alone, unchaperoned and in public.

That thought was just as disconcerting as the previous one. It was mortifying to think that to gain other freedoms, she would be forced to give up the only one that had kept her sane the last few years. But then, it was a price she'd already decided she was willing to pay.

Except that now, there was a man. He was standing under a large sycamore tree, the green leaves dappled over him as the sun continued to slowly rise.

And he was looking at her. Florence could not see much else about him, not from this distance, but it was clear he was looking in her direction. What else was there over here?

Attempting to surreptitiously look around herself, just in case there was something else worth catching the eye, Florence was disappointed to discover that she was, perhaps, the only thing of real interest.

Save for the Serpentine. Mayhaps he was interested in . . . in water birds?

Florence discounted the thought with an irritated snort. If that were so, why would he be standing over there? Surely he would be here, examining the ducks and the geese and . . . and the other birds.

Her gaze darted about her, looking for an escape. There was only one gate open this early in the morning, and it was right by where the man was standing. The Lancaster Gate.

She could remain in Hyde Park until another was opened, of course. Florence bit her lip, a quivering making it most difficult to take a calming breath. But if she stayed that long, then others would arrive at the Park. She would no longer be alone.

She would be seen. In public. Without gloves, without bonnet, hair loose . . .

Florence swallowed as Midnight continued to trot forward—the Lancaster Gate was really her only option. The man, whoever he was, was starting to come into greater clarity.

Dark hair, a tall build, broad shoulders, and—

And it was John.

Warmth seared across Florence's face, trickling down her neck and under her gown.

Well, surely that was for the best, she tried to tell herself, heart pattering against her ribcage as she slowly approached him. If it had just been some... some man, she would have had to make polite conversation. May even have been recognized.

The last thing she needed was a scandal just before her impending marriage.

As it was, it was John. The Marquess of Aylesbury. He would understand. He wouldn't try to engage her in—

"Hallo there!" John said cheerfully, waving a hand as he leaned against the sycamore trunk. "Early morning ride?"

The answer felt so obvious, Florence did not consider answering it. What she wanted to say was, "What are you doing here?" or "It's outrageous that you and I should meet here, unchaperoned!" or even "I've missed you."

But she couldn't say anything like that. Certainly not the last one.

This was a marriage of convenience, Florence reminded herself sternly. *He doesn't care for you. And you don't care for him.*

Any more than you should.

Instead, she said, "I-I didn't realize w-we had an app-pointment."

John's grin broadened. "What, at this time? Rather scandalous appointment if we did, don't you think?"

Florence's cheeks burned at the mere suggestion of impropriety. "I-I wouldn't—"

"That's a shame, because I do love an early morning appointment," said John without permitting her leave to finish her own sentence. "You look... well."

As though it were his fingers brushing over her and not his gaze, John examined her closely.

Heat poured through Florence but there did not appear to be anything she could do about it. Besides, what could she say? Stop looking at me? It was hardly as simple as that. A man could look at his wife, she knew, and one day John would be her husband. There was no law against looking.

But somehow John didn't just look with his eyes. He looked . . . he looked with his whole body. *As though he wanted to touch her*, Florence thought, swallowing hard. As though he was picturing what it would be like to touch her. Longing to be close to her. As though at any moment, he would step close to her and—

"I'm heading home for bed," said John, gazing up at her. "It's been a long night."

Florence's jaw dropped. "B-Bed?"

His mischievous grin did nothing to soothe her embarrassment, but there was nothing she could do about that, either.

She had just said that word "bed" to the Marquess of Aylesbury! In public!

Well. In public, but with no witnesses. Thank the Lord.

"I suppose you come out here so you can be alone," said John, in a softer voice than before.

This, at least, was safe ground upon which she could stand. It was a fact, there was nothing shameful or scandalous about it, and it was an innocuous topic of conversation.

Florence knew that. She also knew she could not speak a single word.

It was most inconvenient.

"I know you, Florence," John said, his voice lower still. "Better than you would think. Better than you know yourself, I suppose."

Now, she could not permit that. "Y-You shouldn't c-call me that."

If Florence had not been seated upon Midnight, she would have been in very great danger of wanting to kiss John Chance, Marquess of Aylesbury. As it was, his fiery glance did nothing but melt her core, make her thighs ache, and recall the kiss against the carriage that led to—

"What?"

"F-Florence," she said, forcing the word out. "It is t-too—"

"Intimate?" John said, a quizzical look across his brow. "But we are to be married, Florence. You do not think we have reached that level of intimacy yet?"

Florence swallowed.

Because he was right, damn him. From the little she had ascertained from those she knew who had become engaged—and there were very few friends in that quarter—being on first name terms was a natural progression of the . . . the expected tenderness.

And yet being on such terms with the Marquess of Aylesbury . . . with John . . .

Could she even say his name, albeit in private, and not melt with shame?

And then something he had said a few moments ago returned to her mind and made Florence's eyes narrow. "Y-You've been up all n-night?"

John shrugged, the picture of the elegant yet rakish gentleman. Now she came to look a mite closer, she could see the signs. The top button of his waistcoat was unbuttoned and his cravat was ruffled. His hair was mussed, as though he had run his hands through it several times, and there was tiredness as well as sparkle in his eyes.

Up all night?

"May I offer you assistance in dismounting, Miss Bailey?" John said, stepping forward with a hand extended.

Florence hesitated.

She did not need help to get down. She was an excellent horsewoman, as perhaps she should have told Mr. Knight when he had inquired about it. For years she had been perfectly able to both mount and dismount without the aid of even a mounting block. That wasn't the true cause of her hesitation.

No, it was the very idea of dismounting in John's presence. The

Marquess of Aylesbury's presence.

Up here, on Midnight, Florence was safe. Distant. Far away. Able to depart at a moment's notice without any fear of being caught up. Giving up that safety, that distance . . .

He was asking a great deal. Did he not know?

John's hand lowered slightly but did not return to his side. "I'm not going to hurt you, Florence."

Florence's stomach lurched. *You did last time,* she wanted to say, knowing her tongue would fail her. *You hurt me. You kissed me then disappeared—no one else knew why you left Lady Romeril's house party after three long weeks when you seemed so happy. I had thought you were happy.*

"Florence?"

There was something about the way he spoke her name. It caused a shiver to rush down her spine as she stared into his blue eyes.

And despite all her decisiveness that she would most definitely remain upon the horse—right here, right where she was safe—Florence found herself offering out a hand.

Which was ridiculous. She should have just dismounted herself, preferably on the opposite side of the horse to where John was standing.

That way, he would not have suddenly pushed her against the horse the moment her feet touched the ground. Then Florence would not have been pinned between Midnight, who stood still quite happily, and the crush of John's chest.

"John!"

"Oh, you'll say my name now," said John with a wicked grin. "Aren't you going to ask me?"

Strange ideas were flooding Florence's mind, so swiftly it was difficult to grasp onto one.

What on earth did the man think he was doing? Pinning her like this, against her own mare—there should be a law against it!

And despite all that, Florence's body was betraying her. For though her mind knew it was quite ridiculous for a man, any man, let alone the Marquess of Aylesbury, to be accosting a woman like this, and in public too...

It was nice. More than nice. Pleasant, to feel the strength of his torso against hers, to know herself hemmed in by his presence. To breathe him in. To feel the welcome of his arms around her, to be close to that throat, Adam's apple bobbing as he swallowed hard.

Was... was it possible, Florence thought wildly, *that John was just as affected by their closeness as she was?*

Not that she was affected. Not at all. That would be ridiculous, she told herself tightly as her pulse hummed in her ears and she tried to think. Think of something, anything to say—

"A-Ask you?" Florence whispered, eyes fixed on his. "A-Ask you wh—"

"What I've been doing all night, of course," said John with a chuckle. "If I have been with a woman. It would be within your right to know. Ask me, Florence."

And the last three words were whispered like a prayer, like a benediction, as though he were begging her.

Her breath caught in her lungs. How could she ask him such a thing? How could anyone even think it, let alone ask the question? This was all too much—and yet John had taken a small step back, allowing her to escape him if she chose.

Florence stared, something twisting within her that she did not like.

Desire.

She could not go around desiring her own betrothed! Had one heartbreak not been enough to teach her?

With a great effort, far more than she had thought herself capable of making, Florence stepped to the side and escaped the heady presence of John Chance, Marquess of Aylesbury.

She had thought it would bring relief. Florence had been sure, once she was a good five or so feet away from him, that she would breathe more freely, that the sense of panic would dissipate.

And yet it did not. Her lungs were still tight, her pulse still frantic, and it crossed her mind in a flash that perhaps it had not been panic she had been experiencing at all.

Perhaps it had been . . . something else.

"You don't ask," said John flatly.

Was that disappointment?

Florence did not interrogate the thought. She did not have time—her mind was working at half speed, as it always did whenever she was in John's presence. Did he know? Did he have any idea, the effect he had on people? On ladies? On her?

"I-I d-don't . . ." Florence swallowed, hating anew that her voice betrayed her. She looked at her hands, the marks of the leather reins still upon them. Then she looked back up at the man she knew she loved, even though she hated that she did. "I do not like the idea of you with someone else."

The words echoed out into the early dawn.

Unaccountably, John's balance was suddenly interrupted, his feet tangling a bit as he attempted to find his balance and accidentally knocked into Midnight who nickered irritably. "I . . . yes well, I cannot help but be pleased to see again that I am the only person you speak to without stammering. You must . . . there must be something between us. Something unique."

Florence swallowed. *Now he had pointed that out* . . . she could speak clearly and plainly to herself, in solitude, to be sure. But with another? That was indeed rare.

"Not entirely unique." Pulling herself together, she did her best to hold her head up high. "I-I have spoken to y-you before—"

"But not to others," said John quietly, stepping toward her. "Am I correct?"

Florence hastily took a step back. The motion came from instinct, a certain knowledge that getting too close to John was a recipe for losing her voice all over again.

Most unaccountably he kept stepping forward, and Florence was forced into a half retreat, half run. When her back hit the trunk of the sycamore tree, she gasped—partly at the shock of the jolt, and partly at the realization that once again, she had nowhere to run.

Before she could think to step around it, John had reached her. He placed his hands on the trunk, either side of her waist, and looked deep into her eyes. "I am special to you."

Florence raised her hands—why, she was not sure. To ward him off? To push him away?

The trouble was, the moment her palms splayed against him, John's throat cleared loudly.

Florence blinked. *Was she—she couldn't be having any impact on John, could she?*

He was a rake. A scoundrel. She had once overheard a viscount whose name she had forgotten mutter to a footman that John Chance, Marquess of Aylesbury, was not to be permitted anywhere near a gambling table unless he proved he had coin on his person. He was a rascal. A brute, apparently, of the highest order.

And he was breathless . . . because of her?

"I wondered if your shyness alone was what prevented you from speaking," John was saying in a low, intimate voice. "I wondered whether over time, you may be able to . . . speak to me."

The comment was heady, and not one Florence could even consider replying to. How could she? There was nothing she could say.

This had never happened before.

"Y-You . . ." Florence swallowed, willed herself to stay calm. Calm while pinned against a tree in Hyde Park by a man who made her want to take all her clothes off. *Easy.* "You don't have to explain your whereabouts t-to . . . to me."

"Even as my wife?" John said with a twisted smile.

It would be much easier, Florence could not help but think, if they could have this conversation while they were both even more fully clothed. Gloves, hats. Perhaps even overcoats. And ten feet apart.

As it was...

As she tried to take in a deep breath, her breasts pushed against John's chest and he groaned.

He groaned?

No, she must have imagined that, Florence thought hastily. "Ours is a marriage of convenience, J-John."

Perhaps she should not have attempted to say his name—but there, again, a hitch of breath in his throat.

And a wicked idea struck Florence that she could, if she wished, disorient him just as much as he was affecting her. It was a strange thought. One she liked.

To test this wild idea she shifted, twisting her hips from side to side as though attempting to get away.

The movement had the desired effect—and more. John stiffened, his whole face suddenly flushed, and there was something else, too. Something pressing most oddly against her hip.

Florence looked down, and saw—

She looked up again, her cheeks burning, as she met his gaze.

Goodness.

"A marriage of convenience," she said aloud steadfastly, as though reminding them both that this attraction, this whatever it was—it was nothing. "I-I get aw-way from m-my m-mother, a-a-and you g-gain respectab-bility."

John's grin was dry. "Is my name truly that disgraced?"

"N-Not the n-name of Ch-Ch-Ch—"

"But the name of Aylesbury," he said.

Florence nodded, rather than attempt to speak again. It was, after all, why she had suggested the marriage of convenience to him.

Oh, it was true that she had made the mistake of entirely falling in love with him two years ago, and that was certainly part of the decision. She could not deny that, not even to herself. But Florence had kept track of John in the newspapers. Seen the scandals, one after another. Heard whispers about how the oldest Chance brother, the

Duke of Cothrom, was attempting to keep his brothers in line. Knew that having a wife would give John—give the Marquess of Aylesbury a veneer of respectability which could not be gained any other way.

That had to be it—his reason for accepting their deal. It wasn't as though there could be any other reason. The Chances were famed for their wealth, and of the two of them, he was the one with the title.

"J-John?" Florence whispered.

His focus sharpened. "Florence."

"Are . . . are . . . are . . ." Florence forced her tongue into submission. "Are you going to l-let me free?"

It could not be more obvious that John had been hoping to keep her pinned up against the tree, but with her question now out in the open . . .

John shook his head ruefully as he stepped away from the tree, releasing her. "You know, I would much rather have kept you there."

"I bet you would." The words had escaped Florence's lips before she could stop them. They were the sort of thought she had frequently, but never permitted herself to say.

Her cheeks burned as she glanced over at John. His mouth was open.

Turning away before he could ask her to repeat herself—or God forbid, laugh—Florence grabbed the reins of Midnight.

"May I walk you home?"

She turned. There was an expression she had never seen on John's face before in all the time she had known him. It was disconcerting, to tell the truth.

It was eagerness.

"Wh-What if we're seen?"

John's grin broadened. "Gosh, I don't know. I'll have to marry you, I suppose."

And Florence laughed, the tension that had built in her body melting away as his chuckles joined hers.

"It's nice to see you smile," he said, still chuckling as they started to walk toward Lancaster Gate. "I suppose you haven't had much to smile about."

Because of your mother.

The unspoken words were not necessary. Florence knew precisely what he meant, and nodded as she said, "L-Losing my f-father... it was a terrible time."

"I lost my father young, I know that pain," John said quietly, seriousness in his voice as they passed through the gate.

Florence looked over, surprised. She should have known, of course. His older brother could not be the Duke of Cothrom without the loss of their father, yet it had never occurred to her.

"You never said," she murmured as they started down the empty street. "When we first met."

"I didn't," said John. "I think... I think I did not tell you a great deal about me when we first met. I wasn't... well, I wasn't particularly interested in matrimony then."

It was an understatement, but it was true. And he had been the one to say it, which she had not anticipated.

She glanced over again, and John met her eyes steadily, with no shame.

"But I am interested now," he said earnestly. "I'm interested in you. A... a second chance, call it. To get to know you."

Heat burned Florence's cheeks. "I see."

"I hope you do," John said. "I'm just sorry that you had to be the one to suggest a marriage of convenience. But I'm glad now we have our second chance."

Chapter Eight

July 20, 1812

"This," John muttered to himself as he glared up at the townhouse, "is not where I want to be."

Not that it mattered. When one received an invitation from Lady Romeril, one did not decline it.

At least, he had never heard of anyone who had. Which proved the point—if one did refuse the invitation, one was no longer in polite Society.

Still, that didn't make her gatherings any more enjoyable. For a start, Lady Romeril did not seem to believe in serving delicious food to her guests. Nor did she provide cigars for the gentlemen, or in most situations, a single card table.

It was an outrage.

But a ball hosted by Lady Romeril was a ball. Even if it was out of Season. Even if half the *ton* were in the country, surviving the heat rather than being baked alive in their own waistcoats.

John tugged at his cravat as he waited for the carriages to pass before crossing the road and entering the house.

"Your invitation—"

"I am the Marquess of Aylesbury, I need proffer no invitation," said John smartly as he sidestepped the footman.

Which was a ruddy ridiculous thing to say, he thought as he handed the crimson-cheeked footman his top hat and gloves. It wasn't as though he were a duke, like old Cothrom. He did need an invitation, most of the time.

Apparently his arrogance got him by this one, though. It was only a minute later that John was stepping into the hallway which was almost empty. The only two people within it were—

John snorted. "Lindow."

His younger brother turned and grinned as he saw who it was. "Aylesbury!"

If John had been asked to picture precisely what his brother would be doing if found *almost* entirely alone in Lady Romeril's hallway, it was this.

The young lady who had until moments ago been receiving the kisses of John's younger brother George, the Earl of Lindow, flushed pink. "Oh my!"

"Oh, don't worry yourself, it's only Aylesbury," said Lindow easily. "Stay here."

"But—"

Lindow did not give her another glance. He strode over to Aylesbury, clapped him on the shoulder, and said, "My commiserations."

John blinked. It was not exactly the levity that he had grown to expect from the third Chance brother. "I beg your pardon?"

"For your loss," said Lindow seriously, his expression morose. "At this difficult time, I am sure you don't need me to say that you can come to me at the drop of a hat—"

"Loss?" John repeated, trying to ignore the giggles of the woman behind his brother. "What on earth are you—"

"The loss of your freedom," Lindow said with such solemnity, it was only the twinkle in his eye that proved he was being an absolute idiot. "Your engagement. Such terrible—that hurt, you know!"

"Good, I am glad it did," said John, his cheerfulness having returned now he'd smacked his brother in the chest. It always did him good to have Lindow put back in his proper place. He was the baby of the family, after all.

Well. Sort of.

"You've told Cothrom, I suppose."

John nodded. "He wasn't pleased, the old devil."

Lindow's mouth dropped. "The rascal! And he's the one who's been telling us to get married since the day we were born!"

"Slight exaggeration."

"But only slight," said his brother with a roguish grin. "Marriage! Dear God, when there is so much of the world still to enjoy!"

John was under no illusion at all what his brother truly meant by "the world," but just in case any emphasis was needed, Lindow glanced over his shoulder toward the woman who was obediently still leaning against the wall.

Lindow's smile became wolfish.

John tried to smile, too. Well, it was the sort of thing the two of them enjoyed, wasn't it? Had enjoyed for years. Gambling, drinking, laughing with friends, and bedding women. Preferably in that order.

And the woman looked pleasant enough. Pretty enough for Lindow, though that wasn't saying much—he was hardly picky when it came to women. Nice features and a willingness to spread their legs, that was all he cared about.

Perhaps even just a few weeks ago, John would have joshed his brother about the woman, wondered whether there was a sister he could have for himself. And that would have been it.

But now . . .

"I wasn't particularly interested in matrimony then."

Something twisted in his chest—not an unpleasant movement.

"You're not taking her to bed, are you?" John found himself saying.

Lindow snorted. "You sound like Cothrom."

"I'm serious, man, she looks like part of the *ton*, not one of your serving wenches," John said darkly.

His brother was right. He did sound like Cothrom. It was usually the eldest Chance brother who attempted to keep the other two—

other three in line.

John shifted uncomfortably on his feet. The fourth Chance brother was only half a Chance, their father's bastard. Legitimacy was impossible, but Cothrom had given the man a viscountcy, part of his gift as the head of the family.

It had surprised and delighted Frederick, who became Viscount Pernrith. It hadn't delighted Lindow.

With only a few months between the two youngest Chance brothers, Lindow had never accepted the sudden arrival of another son into the family. Now he came to think about it, he'd have to work that out for the wedding.

John's pulse skipped a beat. *The wedding.*

"—daughter of the Earl of—"

His attention was suddenly dragged back to the present. "You can't bed the daughter of an earl!"

"Why not?" Lindow grinned. "I'm an earl."

"But you—" John inhaled deeply and tried to remind himself that months ago, he would have seen nothing wrong with his brother's actions. In truth, he wasn't sure why he saw a problem with them now.

What had gotten into him?

"There'll be a scandal."

Lindow shrugged. "There's always a—"

"And I am about to be married," John said.

If he had hoped for his brother might be a little more understanding due to that fact, he was now sorely disappointed. In fact, he was to endure quite the opposite effect.

His brother rolled his eyes. "It's a marriage of convenience though, isn't it? I mean, you don't actually feel anything for her."

John opened his mouth to say of course not. That he didn't have any feelings for Florence save those of wanting to bed her, which were perfectly natural. Anyone in her presence would want that. She was delectable.

But somehow the words did not come.

A strangled cry croaked in his throat, but other than that, John was unable to speak.

He closed his mouth. *Well, this was damned irregular.*

Was this how Florence felt all the time, a small part of him wondered. God almighty, that would be awful.

"You can't stop me," said Lindow flatly.

John sighed. He knew full well that he could not—more, that he had encouraged his younger brother for years to do precisely what he was about to do. He could hardly reverse that course now.

"Just . . . just try to be discreet, will you?"

His brother's grin was unconcerned and indifferent. "Where's the fun in that?"

John had no choice but to laugh as he watched Lindow pull the woman out of the hallway and out of Lady Romeril's ball.

Well, he would read all about it in the gossip papers in the morning he supposed.

It was with that disconcerting thought that John stepped into Lady Romeril's ballroom.

There had been no additional decoration. Just the Romeril ballroom that he already knew: two chandeliers at each end of the wide open space, tables along one wall covered with food that was inedible and punch that was delicious, and musicians together in a corner, tuning up their instruments.

And people.

Despite the time of year, Lady Romeril had clearly rustled up a good few guests for her ball. John inclined heads with a few of the gentlemen there. Politicians, a few admirals, and friends from Cambridge who had evidently thought there was nothing better to do on a Monday night.

And Florence.

John's chest swelled as he saw her. *Florence. His woman.*

His woman? Now where on earth had thought come from?

It certainly wasn't something he had consciously considered her—until that moment, that was. But it was difficult to look at Florence and not feel a little possessive, a little territorial about her.

She was dressed in a most elegant silk gown. The light cream color would wash out most people, but thanks to her red hair and sparkling hazel eyes, along with the richness of her complexion, the gown merely enhanced what was already there.

And there was a great deal there. Curves that no amount of silk dropping to the floor in an empire line could hide, a bust that was delightfully shaped, and—

John swallowed. *Oh, their wedding day could not come soon enough.*

And he blinked, and Florence was no longer the only person in focus. There was another person. A person beside her.

A man.

A sudden jolt of rage John could never have predicted shot through his body. A man! Standing there, so close to Florence they were almost touching! A man standing beside his woman with just as much possessiveness in his stance as John felt from twenty feet away.

It was unhinged. It was inexplicable. But John wished to stride over there and rip the man limb from limb merely for having the presumption to stand so close to the woman he—

He caught himself just in time.

It was rudeness, that was what it was, John tried to tell himself. He was merely scandalized by the impropriety of the way the interloper—the man was standing. Because it was very close. Indeed, as they spoke, or rather, he spoke at Florence, John saw the man's cuff gently brush against Florence's bare arm.

Just a touch. Nothing more.

Yet it was enough to spur John to march forward, unbale to bear it any longer. As he walked, his mind attempted to flag a few things for his consideration.

Firstly, that there was no actual crime in talking to a beautiful woman. Even if it was Florence.

Secondly, that this was a marriage of convenience, and his emotions about this—*Emotions! Him?*—were quite unwarranted.

Thirdly, that he was likely to make a scene if he did, indeed, rip the offending trespasser limb from limb.

Fourthly, that he probably could not undertake such a feat, even with this molten rage pouring through every muscle of his body.

Fifthly, that it wasn't as though he were in love with Florence. He wasn't in love with anyone. Being in love with Florence might explain this behavior, but he wasn't—he couldn't be—it wasn't possible that—

Sixthly, that—

"You," barked John, pulling up before Florence and the criminal before his mind had time to finish running down its list of seemingly important facts. Not that he'd paid much attention to any of them.

"M-M-My lord," stammered Florence, looking up with . . .

John could hardly tell what her expression contained, which was itself odd. Florence had always been an open book. She was hardly able to hide her emotions, even if most of the time those emotions were fear, shame, and nerves.

But somehow, standing this close to her in that silk gown—a silk gown he would much prefer to be pooled on the floor—he could not comprehend the look she was giving him.

Was it delight to see him? Confusion as to why he had shouted a word rather than bowed and asked for an introduction to her companion?

Introduction! John scoffed in the privacy of his mind. The lucky beggar should be on bended knee thanking Florence for her company! The scoundrel! Standing there, as though he belonged there!

"A marriage of convenience, between two acquaintances."

But Cothrom's words, which had been running through his mind since he'd heard them, had swiftly departed from John's mind the moment he had seen the two of them together.

What *had* managed to make its way through his beleaguered mind was this: *I may be in more trouble here than I thought.*

The intensity of that knowledge frightened him. He was John Chance, Marquess of Aylesbury. He didn't go around catching feelings. He'd never get anything done.

"You," he repeated, this time directing his gaze straight at the offender.

Who, most infuriatingly, did not appear to look abashed at all. Instead, the brute raised an eyebrow of surprise and looked at Florence.

"Don't look at her, look at me!" snapped John, wishing to goodness he'd brought a pistol.

Wait, what? No, of course he didn't wish that. Probably. He couldn't go around challenging men to—

"John," Florence said.

And hearing his name on her lips, in such an intimate way, in public, soothed part of John's scalded heart—but it was not enough.

How dare she stand here in public so familiarly with a man who was not her betrothed!

The fact John had never particularly cared for the rules of Society in his life did not occur to him. Not in this moment. Not when it was his Florence who had been standing so calmly so close to a man who was—what? Attempting to flirt with her? Kiss her? Bed her?

Lindow's recent conquest flashed through his mind. Was that all this ball was? A hunting ground for dissolute men?

"Just what do you think you're doing?" John hissed, jabbing a finger into the man's chest.

It was reckless, yes, and it also did not elicit the usual response. Instead of apologizing profusely, stepping away, and promising he would never even deign to think of Miss Florence Bailey ever again, the man frowned.

Actually frowned!

"I don't understand," said the man, glancing at Florence once more. "I—"

"John," Florence said quietly. "L-Let me—"

"You should be ashamed of yourself," John snapped at the man, attempting to keep his voice low but conscious that people were starting to turn to look at them.

That had to be the reason for Florence's tinged cheeks. What else could it be?

Perhaps, and the thought made his hopes soar, perhaps she was grateful to him for rescuing her! Perhaps she had been hoping someone would relieve her of this vagabond's company!

Spurred on by that new certainty, John cast an irritated eye over the man. "Who do you think you are? You sir have overstepped the mark, and by God, I'll teach you what happens to—"

"John, you sh-should listen t-to—"

"What the devil are you talking about?" the man interrupted, his voice sharp. "Begging your pardon, Florence."

And it was that intimacy, that casual mention of her name in the middle of Lady Romeril's ballroom, that pushed John over the edge.

Anger and rage had been spilling over the moment he had seen them together, but now there was something more. Something darker. Something uncontrollable.

John's shoulders heaved as his breathing quickened, and he opened his mouth to call out the blackguard.

And halted.

There was a look not of shame, or of delinquency but . . . confusion in the man's eyes. Bewilderment. Genuine shock.

When John looked at Florence, it was to see to his own shock that she had placed a hand on his arm.

Not John's arm. The man's. Their connection was evident, the familiarity strong.

And in sudden pain, the like of which John had never felt before, he realized that Florence had something with this man that she did not have with him. A level of comfort that permitted her to reach out and touch him—and in public!

John took a half step back, almost staggering under the weight of the disappointment that was crushing his lungs.

Florence and . . . and this man?

Could it be that he was truly only the first man that she had chosen out of many possibilities, when she suggested that they wed? How could he go through with the marriage now, now it was so obvious there were other men she liked just as well as him, men she might prefer to him?

"Answer me," John snapped, pushing aside the thoughts that were giving him such pain. "Who do you think you—"

"John," Florence said determinedly.

He halted in his tracks, unable to continue after she said his name with such force. Their gazes met, and something inside him hardened. If she could look at him like that, with her hand on another man's arm . . .

How much did he know about Florence, really?

"M-May I introduce my b-b-brother," said Florence with something akin to a wry look. "Philip Bailey."

All the air deflated from John's lungs so all he could manage was a wheezy, "Brother?"

The man, now identified as Mr. Bailey nodded curtly. "Sir."

John stared.

Brother?

Brother. Oh, well. Well. That made . . . that made more sense. Brother. Of course.

Why the devil hadn't he thought of that?

"Brother," he repeated again, this time his voice stronger.

Florence's face was scarlet as mutterings started to encircle them. "Y-Yes."

"Ah," said John weakly. "Right."

An emotion he did not quite recognize was pouring through him. It took him a moment to decipher it, as it was something that he could not recall ever feeling before, though he had invoked it quite recently on Mr. Bailey's behalf.

It was . . . shame.

"You must the Marquess of Aylesbury," said Mr. Bailey curtly.

John tried to smile, but it was an effort. How could he have been so stupid? The very idea he would accost Florence's own brother—and in public!—just for the crime of standing close to his sister . . .

Oh dear God, this was going to be in all the newspapers. Cothrom was going to need a lie down.

"You understand, ah—"

"Yes, yes, I'm sure," said Mr. Bailey with a raised eyebrow. "We can't be too careful when it comes to my sister's honor, can we, my lord?"

John's weak smile faltered. "Right."

"Now, if you'll excuse me, I must speak with Viscount Braedon," said Mr. Bailey with a short bow of his head. "My lord. Florence."

He stepped away without another word, leaving John and Florence standing together in the growing crush of the ball.

Ye gods. John wondered whether it would be politer just to leave, rather than stand here and submit Florence to the gossip which surely must be growing around them. There were a startlingly high number of people staring at them.

Oh, hell.

Florence's hesitated. "S-So . . . you've m-met my brother."

"You could have said something," John said faintly.

It wasn't a reprimand, not exactly, but the flush of her cheeks proved it had been taken as such. "I-I t-tried. You w-wouldn't listen."

Gone were the relaxed tones, the easy speech they had shared yesterday morning. John could kick himself for putting this wallflower into harm's way—for there was no other word for it. She would be mortified by the attention now, and undoubtedly even more mortified when the scandal sheets were printed.

John opened his mouth to defend himself, and saw Florence's expression.

It was . . . warm.

Not warm with embarrassment, though that might have played a part in it. No, warm toward him. There was a smile on her face, and the connection between them—

John sighed heavily and shook his head with a rueful grin. "Remind me, the next time I do something like that, that I am a complete idiot."

Florence's small gasp was like a balm to his soul. "I can't do that!"

She hadn't stammered.

Almost as soon as John noticed that, Florence did too. She looked at her hands.

"You're going to have to," said John. "I'm not an easy person to live with, you know. I have it on good authority."

Florence looked up. "You . . . you've lived with a w-woman before?"

"No!" John was startled by his own haste at clarification. "No, I mean my brothers! They . . . well, they've had to give me a second chance more than a few times. I always hope for them from . . . from the people I care about."

She looked at him slightly askance. "Is . . . is this you r-requesting a second chance?"

"You know, I think it is," said John heavily, though he attempted to smile. "Now, shall we dance?"

"We sh-shall not," Florence said firmly.

He couldn't help but smile at that.

"But you can f-fetch me some p-punch," she continued, eyes sparkling. "And we can s-stand at the s-side and watch others. And you can t-tell me more about how d-difficult you are to l-live with."

Chapter Nine

July 23, 1812

"I can't believe it!" squealed the woman excitedly. "You're marrying a marquess!"

Florence tried to smile as she poured the tea, thankful her elevenses companion had more than enough conversation for the both of them. "Y-Yes."

It had been her mother's idea to have a friend over for elevenses.

"You never see anyone, Florence," Mrs. Bailey had complained over breakfast the previous morning. "You are dull. Dull! But that does not mean you should not entertain. Entertain, girl! That's what my mother would have said to me."

And so Florence had.

At least, she had sent out an invitation to the most pleasant woman in her acquaintance. Whether or not she was managing to entertain her guest was quite another matter.

"And that means that you'll be a marchioness," said Miss Quintrell, carefully selecting a pastry from the array on the plate before them. "A marchioness! Can you believe it?"

And Florence discovered, to her general surprise, that she could not.

With three days to recover from the stir John had caused at Lady Romeril's ball, she had started to think a little more about the future, but that had been practicalities. Wedding decisions like invitation lists and flower choices and whether or not it was feasible for her mother not to attend.

Not that Florence would ever dream of saying such a wish aloud.

The idea she would have a title, and one so grand as marchioness, had rather passed her by.

"G-Goodness," Florence said before taking a sip of tea.

Miss Quintrell squealed. "Oh, how exciting!"

Florence nodded faintly as her new friend chattered on about how wonderful the whole thing was, and how half the *ton* was envious as sin, and the other half were wondering how on earth she'd done it. Florence wondered herself.

"May I have another cake?" asked Miss Quintrell interrupting her own monologue about how wonderful it must be to fall in love with a marquess after just five days together at a house party.

Florence blinked. "Of . . . of c-course."

Miss Quintrell reached out and helped herself. "And the man is so charming! Honestly, I have rarely met a man so easy to converse with. Of course you know that . . ."

Nodding as she allowed her friend to continue, Florence attempted to push aside the memory of what her mother had said when Miss Quintrell had arrived just an hour ago.

"Her?" muttered Mrs. Bailey. "You're about to have a title, you ninny. Shouldn't you be aiming for a better class of associates now?"

"M-Miss Quintrell is m-my friend," Florence had said, shocked at the boldness of her answer, that she had answered back at all.

And her mother had frowned and said, "When you and I and that marquess of yours live together, I hope you shall respect me better!"

Which had left another painful conversation for another day.

"—tell me," said Miss Quintrell in a matter of fact way. "How does he kiss?"

Florence's teacup wobbled. "I-I beg your—"

"The Marquess of Aylesbury, how does he kiss?" repeated Miss

Quintrell, without a hint of shame about the question.

It was certainly not the sort of conversation Florence had thought they'd be having! Wasn't it rather shocking, asking such a personal detail?

Miss Quintrell's grin was broad. "Oh, come on—you wouldn't have agreed to marry him if he hadn't already kissed you. Was it any good?"

Florence swallowed her mouthful of tea and wished to goodness she had helped herself to a cake too. Then she could have pretended to choke on it.

Besides, it wasn't as though she could tell her companion the truth. If the *ton* discovered it was Miss Bailey, not the Marquess of Aylesbury, who had suggested the marriage, they would never hear the end of it.

"How was his kiss?" insisted Miss Quintrell.

Florence considered telling the truth. Just for a moment.

But she was hardly going to speak about something so personal with Miss Quintrell. Even if she was a pleasant conversational partner.

"It . . . it was f-fine," she managed, taking a sip of tea as though she could hide behind the teacup.

"Fine? Oh dear," said a new voice, tinged with mirth. "I believe more practice is needed if you can describe my efforts as merely *fine*."

Fortunately, Florence did not drop her teacup. But it was a close-run thing.

"John!" she gasped.

John Chance, Marquess of Aylesbury, stepped across the threshold into the parlor and grinned at both her and her guest. "Florence."

Florence flushed.

It was all very well for him to call her by her first name in private, when they were alone—which was fast becoming her favorite time of the day. If a day went by without it, she felt rather . . . diminished.

But saying it before someone else—someone who wasn't even family! It was outrageous!

The trouble was, it was almost impossible grow angry with a man like John. Not just because of his roguish charm, Florence thought wistfully. Nor because of his good looks, which were far superior to those of any other man she had ever met.

No, it was because she liked him.

That was the problem. Ladies should not like the men they have chosen to be their escape route from awful mothers and gossiping Society.

Miss Quintrell was giggling. "Oh, goodness, my lord!"

"Florence's lord, actually," John said with a wink. "But don't worry, I'll allow it."

"My lord!"

Florence's flush burned her cheeks. *How did they do it?* These ladies entered Society with no more experience of life than she had, and yet they could jest and quip and flirt to their heart's content without even a hint of embarrassment.

How did the words come so easily to them? How could they speak so comfortably, making it look to the world as though they did not care a fig what words came out of their mouths?

"Just fine," said John, shaking his head with a tut. "I am heartbroken."

"I-I d-d-didn't m-mean," Florence said, desperately trying to get her words in order as the shame of being overheard saying such a thing rushed through her.

Of course, the one time that she attempted to downplay her attraction to the man, he overheard her!

"I would not worry about it," John said with a look of such potent desire, Florence was surprised she hadn't melted into the sofa. "I'm willing to be taught."

Miss Quintrell's giggles became a gasp and Florence looked furiously at the man who was doing an incredibly good job at mortifying her. Did he not have any compassion for her?

"Well, I can see that the two of you have a great deal to . . . ah . . .

catch up on!" said Miss Quintrell, still giggling as she rose. "I am due home for luncheon anyway. Thank you for your tea and conversation, Miss Bailey. May I take your carriage home?"

It was an excellent suggestion. Not just Miss Quintrell taking the carriage, but leaving altogether. Florence had had her fill of people for the day.

She nodded mutely, not trusting her voice. There was no point in attempting to speak. There was nothing she could try to say that anyone in the room was going to listen to.

For a moment, as John and Miss Quintrell exchanged a friendly goodbye, Florence wished that he would leave too. Leave, leave her in peace. Leave her to cringe over the things she had said, to worry over every syllable she had managed to utter. Leave her alone. As she so often was.

As she usually craved.

But though being left in solitude would typically have been her greatest desire, Florence found herself unexpectedly pleased John would be remaining with her. Just the two of them. Alone, as it were, together.

Still. The whole experience would have been even more gratifying if she hadn't said such a foolish thing.

"How was his kiss?"

"It . . . it was f-fine."

The door snapped closed behind Miss Quintrell and Florence gave a sigh of relief.

Well. That goodness that was over and done—

"Right, Florence, shall we begin?" said John briskly.

Florence's eyes widened. *What on earth did he mean?* "I-I don't know wh-what you—"

"Our kissing practice," John said blithely, though there was a hint of mirth in his features he evidently could not quell. "I am disheartened in the extreme to discover my kissing has not delivered, and—"

"John!"

"No, I insist! It's outrageous that you have been left unsatisfied and silent," said John, moving swiftly to sit beside her. "I've never received a bad report before, and—"

"John!"

"If you keep exclaiming my name like that, I really will kiss you."

Florence's lips parted in astonishment.

John's voice had suddenly become . . . different. More intimate, more sensual. And his attention had left her face and—well, not quite left her face. Had left her eyes. Were now tracing the lines of her lips with his pupils, which flared with something that couldn't be desire.

It just couldn't be.

Florence wetted her dry lips but apparently that was the wrong thing to do, because John shifted closer in his seat, making it impossible for her to think.

And she had to think. She couldn't just sit on this sofa with the Marquess of Aylesbury advancing on her like . . . like . . .

Like you had always wished, a small voice pointed out in a smug tone.

No, she hadn't, she thought hastily, banishing the thought away swiftly.

Liar.

"Tell me," said John quietly. "Tell me what you didn't like about my kisses."

Oh, this was sweet torture. Florence wondered whether she could pretend to faint. At this rate, she may actually do so. The room had been boiling as it was, the hot summer sun pouring through the windows, and now that John was here—

Here, in the room, seated beside her, asking for her assessment of his kisses . . .

"Or if it's easier, tell me what you want from my kisses," murmured John, leaning so close his breath rippled across her skin. "I'll take instruction, I promise . . ."

Florence's eyelashes fluttered, unable to help themselves, as John lowered his head and pressed a kiss upon the curve of her neck, just below her ear.

Oh, God.

Tingles of pleasure flickered through her body and Florence found herself grasping the end of the sofa with her left hand.

This was not happening. This was impossible—handsome and charming men did not attempt to make love to Miss Florence Bailey in the middle of the day!

At least, they never had before.

"John," she whispered, hoping to goodness her voice would stay steady. "John, you mustn't—"

"Either tell me what my kisses are really like, or tell me how they can be improved," John murmured with a chuckle as he pressed a kiss after each word slowly down her neck. "I know you were lying, Florence. I know what I do to you."

Florence almost whimpered but managed to contain herself. Something was shifting inside her, heat flowing down her neck to where her breasts tingled, pressed against the stays and corset that were suddenly far too tight.

"Y-Your . . . your kisses . . . oh, John—"

"Tell me," he said mercilessly as his lips grazed her collarbone then nipped at her décolletage.

Florence closed her eyes, just for a moment, as though that would aid her concentration—but all it did was remove one sense and heighten the others.

"Tell me," John said urgently.

And no longer resisting, Florence found herself saying, "Kissing . . . oh, John, kissing you is the most incredible thing I've ever experienced. I—I never thought I could . . . you make me want to—"

And she probably would have continued, speaking nonsense, the truth spilling out from her lips because she simply couldn't hold it in any longer.

Would have.

But it was rather difficult to do with John's questing lips now pressed hard against her own.

And this time it was Florence who opened for him. She did not need his hungry tongue teasing apart her lips. She welcomed him in, her tongue darting out to meet his own in heady desire.

John moaned, twisting so his body covered hers, and Florence found herself pressed against the sofa in an agony of delight.

This was what she wanted. This was what she craved—this connection, this intimacy with the man who had charmed her two years ago then made it impossible to forget him.

His hands were on her upper arms, holding her tight, but Florence didn't know why. She was hardly going to wish to escape this cacophony of delight, this aching need to be close to him, these kisses which—

John sprang away from her just as the door to the parlor opened.

"Shall I ring for more tea, miss?" asked the Bailey housekeeper before she entered the room. "And some cakes for—oh. Oh my."

Florence tried to breathe normally.

Oh, she must look like a state. Her hair was undoubtedly mussed, she knew her cheeks were pink—she could feel them burning—and her lips had to be crushed red from all the ardor which had just moments ago been lavished upon them.

Mrs. Harris obviously had guessed what had been occurring just seconds before she had stepped into the room, for her cheeks were as pink as Florence's felt. "I-I . . . cake and . . . and tea and—"

"N-No, th-thank you, Mrs. Harris," Florence managed to say, though how, she had no idea. "W-We are . . . we do not need . . ."

It appeared that was enough. Mrs. Harris bobbed a curtsy and backed out of the room, closing the door behind her.

Florence's breathing was still ragged as she glanced over at John, who had a sheepish expression on his face.

"Damn," he said. "That's what comes of trying to stay away from you."

Whatever could he mean by such a thing? It was preposterous, that's what this was. She should never have allowed him to—

"I think I'll move seats," said John, rising to his feet.

Florence did not think, she merely acted. "Don't."

He halted and looked at his hand. So did Florence.

She was holding it.

John's fingers were soft, as soft as she recalled from when he held her against the sofa and kissed her silly. But there was something else there, too.

Was that her pulse, racing away? Or his?

John slowly lowered himself back onto the sofa. "You should be careful, you know."

Florence nodded, releasing his hand as though burned by it and dropping her eyes to her own hands, now clasped in her lap. "I-I know. Mrs. Harris c-could have—"

"I meant in your words to me. The most incredible thing you have ever experienced, you said," he murmured, repeating back her own words to her.

It was mortifying hearing them spoken like that. *What had come over her?*

"If you're not careful, I may actually end up falling in love with you."

Florence's mouth went dry as she looked up at the rake seated beside her.

Much to her surprise, John held her gaze—and even more astonishingly, there was no mirth in his expression. The jesting man she had been so enchanted by was still there, but there was something different about him now. Something . . . not serious, either, but somewhere in between.

He certainly looked as though he was speaking in earnest. Which was ridiculous. Theirs was a marriage of convenience, that was all, Florence told herself sternly. She had been most clear with him after that kiss against the carriage in the Knights' drive. They would both benefit, and they wouldn't have to worry about . . . about that.

Besides, a man like John Chance, Marquess of Aylesbury, did not go about falling in love with wallflowers who couldn't string more than ten words together!

No, she needed to keep her head. Even if it was being kissed spectacularly by a handsome man.

"Y-You didn't fall in love with m-me the first time," Florence said, in an attempt to make light of the situation.

It did not work. Instead of laughing and agreeing with her, John merely nodded his head seriously. "No. I was an idiot."

What did that mean?

Florence's head ached with the effort of always trying to understand the world, but with John, it was more like jolting unexpectedly off a horse. There were times when she understood him exactly, did not even need words to decipher his thoughts. And there were other times, like this.

He was looking at her with all the solemnity of a priest. His chiseled jaw was taut, as though . . . as though he regretted the past.

That had to be a nonsense. Didn't it?

"John," Florence said firmly. Time to reiterate their agreement. "We—wh-what are you doing?"

"Holding your hand," John said simply. "Do you mind?"

He was not just holding it, but entwining his fingers with hers. It was . . . intimate. And though the aching need for him which had never truly dampened down from the moment he had kissed her at the Knights' still burned in her core, Florence was astonished to find something else was curling around her breast.

The love she had suppressed. It was getting out!

"You know, I wasn't jesting," John said quietly. "Earlier. If . . . if you did wish to practice. More often, I meant, in the lead up to the wedding, I would be quite happy to—Florence?"

She had jerked her hand away from his and risen, managing to take five steps away before he said her name. Said it with such disappointment, such surprise.

Florence tried to slow her breathing, placing a hand on her breast and feeling the panic pump her lungs like bellows.

He was suggesting lovemaking. To her!

It was the one part of their agreement which had not been spoken—but she had not thought it needed to be. Of course they would not . . . John had no need to . . .

"I will not be pitied," Florence said with restraint before turning.

To her surprise, John looked just as confused as he did before. "Pitied?"

"I am not—I-I will not be . . ." Try as she might, it was impossible to get her lungs under control. And the panic that rose, panic she knew would overwhelm her, making it impossible to—

"Florence."

She gasped as John's hands once again clasped her upper arms, but this time it was not a clinch of passion, it was—

"Breathe, Florence," John said quietly, his worried eyes raking her face. "Breathe with me. In. Out. In—yes, that's right. And out."

Florence's fingers grasped in horror at John's chest, finding his lapels and holding onto them for dear life. For if she did not, how would she breathe? How would she be? She would fall apart into a million pieces and then there would be nothing left of her.

"Breathe, Florence," John repeated, his determinedly solid presence calming in a way Florence had never known. "Breathe with me."

And she did. Concentrating as best she could, hardly aware of the spinning room or the dazzling light or the overpowering heat, Florence clutched onto John . . . and breathed.

When she finally had a semblance of control over her lungs, she looked up from the elegantly tied cravat and forced herself to meet

John's eyes.

"I am sorry," he said.

Florence's eyes widened. "I-I was going to—"

"You do not have anything to apologize for," he said, and his voice remained low. "I should not have—teasing you was only supposed to . . . I am sorry, Florence."

She nodded hastily, unsure whether she could say any more.

How had he done that? Seen the pain in her, the panic, and known precisely what to do? How had he calmed her with nothing but his own presence, his own breath?

"I am sorry," he said again.

Florence swallowed. "I-I-I . . . I do not . . . I am not just an object to desire."

"I know that—I should have known better," John said. "Look, I'll make this easy for you."

Easy for her? What on earth did that mean?

His smile was sorrowful, and there was a catch in his voice as he said, "I can see what happened, and it's all my fault. I should have said, from the very . . . Florence. This marriage of convenience, it does not behold you to—I would never expect . . ."

Florence stared, trying desperately to understand what on earth the man was trying to say.

"When we marry, I will not expect, nor demand, *that* from you."

"That?"

"Lovemaking," he said calmly, his voice now steady. "Kisses whenever you want them, yes. You'll find me most . . . most willing. But I am taking marital union, for want of a better word, off the table. You don't have to worry. I'll never ask you for that again."

Florence's lips parted in astonishment.

It was kindly done. It was spoken well, and with respect, and more than a little reverence. It was the last part of their agreement which had not been discussed, and now it had been.

In quite the opposite direction of what she had hoped.

"There," said John brightly. "Now you can relax."

Florence slowly released the man's lapels and stepped back, before she did something foolish.

Like kiss him.

Like tell him she wanted more, so much more, just as long as he wanted her, not just a willing body.

Like tear off his jacket and—

"Well. Good," Florence said faintly with what she hoped was a smile. "That's settled then. Excellent."

Chapter Ten

July 25, 1812

"Now I'm warning you—"

"Yes, yes, you're warning—"

"No, I mean it, Aylesbury—"

"You always mean it," said John, attempting his most wolfish grin. "And I never listen."

William Chance, Duke of Cothrom, rolled his eyes. "Do you have to be so aggravating?"

"Not in the slightest," John rejoined as they stepped into the drawing room all set out for the card party that Viscount Bysshe was hosting. "I do it especially, just for you."

His brother's groan of irritation was thankfully drowned out by the delightful playing of the pianoforte in the corner of the room. Otherwise it would have been most embarrassing. Quite a few of Lord Bysshe's guests turned out to have already arrived.

John inclined his head at several of the gentlemen he already knew, and discovered to his surprise that he had no interest in sweeping his attention over the gaggle of ladies.

Well. That was new.

"This is a card party," muttered Cothrom brightly as though there were nothing amiss. "Not an opportunity to—"

"We went over this in the carriage," said John, smiling just as broadly. "In fact, I seem to recall you went over it several times, despite me saying that I had listened the first—"

"If you listened the first time to anything, then you would not be on this second chance, you blackguard," Cothrom said, with a laugh for the benefit of the room.

John's jaw tightened, but there wasn't much he could say to that.

After all, his brother was right. And he had no wish to return to the countryside like a schoolboy sent home from lessons for misbehavior. Oh, the shame!

Besides, it would be most dull. What do gentlemen do in the country all the time, anyway? He could hardly make it out. Something about nature, which was all to the good, to be sure. But there must be more than that, mustn't there?

"—heed me well," Cothrom was muttering as they stepped into the room and closer to the other members of the *ton* who had received invitations. "This is not an excuse to lose more money!"

"I know that," snapped John, unable to bear the lecturing any longer. "You just worry about what we do if Lindow turns up."

That was sufficient to derail his brother. "And I don't want to have to pay—what do you mean, if Lindow turns up?"

John grinned. "Well, you know he's starting betting on horses, don't you? And now he's gone a step forward. A large, hefty, financial step further."

Cothrom's face was a picture of panic. "You don't mean—he hasn't—"

"Oh, hello, Lord Bysshe," said John pleasantly, waving over a gentleman with a penchant for conversation who could hopefully distract his older brother. Nursemaid, more like. "How pleasant to be invited, we thank you. Now, tell Cothrom all about . . ."

With his shadow carefully distracted by another person, John stepped back quietly and scanned around the room.

Not looking at the card tables. Much as he wished to rib his brother, he knew perfectly well that sitting down and gambling was not a good idea. It wasn't that he *couldn't* stop once he had started. He just had no wish to.

He wasn't looking at the ladies, either. Not really. There were a couple here this evening he did not recognize, and perhaps the John Chance, Marquess of Aylesbury, of three months ago would have secured introductions and wondered whether it were possible to find a nice nook to . . . get to know each other better.

But as it was now, none of them intrigued him. No, his gaze was searching for one woman in particular: Miss Florence Bailey.

It was ridiculous, really. It had only been . . . what, days since he had last seen her?

John swallowed, a flicker of uncertainty within him. That was odd. Since when was he a gentleman who noticed such things?

Apparently since now. And for each of the intervening hours since he had been with Florence, he had spent an inordinate amount of time thinking about her. Worrying about her, mostly. Wondering about her. Regretting what he had said to her two days ago.

"*I am taking marital union, for want of a better word, off the table. You don't have to worry. I'll never ask you for that again.*"

It had been a damned foolish thing to say. John could hardly believe the words had sprung from his mouth. What was he doing, cutting off perhaps forever the one source of pleasure he now craved?

But the memory of Florence in her panic, her breath short and her whole frame quivering with alarm—he would have done anything, anything in that moment to calm her.

And he had.

Now he would have to pay the price. But his words, their agreement had said nothing about spending time together, about appreciating each other's conversation. Which was why he had agreed to come to this card party in the first place.

The little pencil note on his formal invitation had obviously been scrawled in haste, perhaps not even by Lord Bysshe himself but by a butler. But it could not have been clearer.

Miss Bailey invited in your honor.

So she must be here, mustn't she?

John's eyes flickered across the room once more. It was strange. Just weeks ago, he would have gone whenever a card table could be pulled together. Especially if there were some wiling victims—sorry, participants to play with. The chance to win some coin would have been too difficult to give up.

Now...

Well, damn it, he missed her.

John almost laughed, his mirth hidden by the continuous playing of the pianoforte, which was most excellent.

Missed her? Missed Florence—missed any woman! It was unheard of.

And yet there was something about her. Something more about her that no other woman possessed, he was sure of it. And until he understood it, John was discovering that he couldn't really leave her alone.

The pianoforte music stopped as Lord Bysshe stepped forward and placed his hand on the instrument.

"Thank you, Miss Bailey, for such excellent playing," he said with a nod. "And now, let us take our seats! Shilling buy-ins for each table, we have whist, we have cribbage, we may even start a..."

Whatever the third game was, John was not sure. He was certain Lord Bysshe said, but the words drifted in one ear and out the other.

His attention was wholly focused on the woman seated on the pianoforte stool.

It was Florence.

How in heaven's name could he have missed her? There she had been, right in front of him—only six feet away. Her flaming red hair was now a beacon, one which he should have seen.

And he had not.

She looked up, cheeks pink at the momentary attention she had gained by being singled out by Lord Bysshe by name, and met his gaze.

And gave him a small smile.

John had to be careful that he didn't trip. Trip over what, he wasn't sure, but his legs were weak and his balance off the moment she had smiled at him.

The Marquess of Aylesbury, felled by a smile?

Remembering to smile back, John was delighted to see Florence's cheeks flush pink, her expression brighten—which then set his stomach to swooping.

This was ridiculous. He was no young slip of a man, just entering Society! He was almost thirty, for goodness' sake. He couldn't stand here, mooning over a woman he was already engaged to, unable to step forward and talk to her because he was smiling too much!

Move, man!

John half walked, half stumbled toward the pianoforte. "Miss Bailey."

"My lord," Florence said, rising and then curtsying low.

Strange. The last time they were alone together, he had kissed her most heartily. John could almost taste the sweetness of her mouth on his lips, the recollection was so strong.

"If you're not careful, I may actually end up falling in love with you."

And now they had to stand here in polite company, as though they had done nothing more scandalous than perhaps hold hands. Without gloves.

"I-I did not . . ." John swallowed.

What was it Florence had once said?

"A s-stutter is a difference in speech, but m-my . . . my nerves affect it. W-When I'm not n-nervous, I d-don't stutter."

Was this what it was like, to have no dominion over one's faculties? To struggle to get the words out, even though you knew precisely what you wished to say? It was maddening.

"I did not see you there," he said, forcing his tongue into submission. "By the pianoforte, which is ridiculous, I should have seen you there but—"

"It is one of my h-habits," said Florence. "No one n-notices servants, you see? And so I considered to m-myself, and asked: what is the c-closest thing to a servant I can become? And I th-thought—"

"Pianoforte," John blurted out, unable to help himself.

Florence's expression twisted. "It is probably unb-becoming of a lady to consider such things. And y-yet . . . yet I cannot go out riding all the t-time. I must be in Society, I s-suppose, until . . . until we are married."

Married.

John swallowed, trying to ignore the thoughts that sprang up. About marriage. And marriage beds. And kisses like those they had already shared, scalding hot and melting a part of him he had not even realized had been there. And aching. And longing. And wanting to—

"How was his kiss?"

"It . . . it was f-fine."

His fingers unconsciously curled into fists—fists John had to force himself to relax.

Fine! Fine? He had never received any complaints before. Though of course, he rarely requested an evaluation before. In fact, as far as he could remember, John had never inquired of his conquests if his kissing was sufficient.

It was an uncomfortable thought, one he had not permitted himself to wonder in the Bailey drawing room. But if he was lacking in the kissing department, did that mean he had insufficiencies elsewhere? Was it possible—God forbid—that his lovemaking skills—

"John?" Florence reached out and brushed her ungloved fingers down his own gloved ones. "I-I mean, my lord?"

John's expression sharpened and he gave her a brief smile. "Just . . . just lost in my thoughts. Do not mind me."

And those thoughts were: I will prove it to you, and to myself, once and for all. That I can give so much more pleasure than a mere kiss.

"I am taking marital union, for want of a better word, off the table. You don't have to worry. I'll never ask you for that again."

His heart jolted.

Damn. Or, he wouldn't.

"Let us sit down," he said aloud, conscious Florence was now staring at him with a most concerned look. "Here—a table tucked away by the wall without a game set up, only a pack of cards, so my brother won't have an excuse to complain."

Leading her to the table which only had two chairs—all to the good—John tried to collect himself as he helped Florence to her seat.

"Your brother?" she said lightly, twisting her head to look about the room. "Y-You mean the duke?"

"He's forbidden me to play again, as usual," John said darkly without thinking.

Florence turned back to him. "Wh-Why?"

Ah.

Well, it wasn't as though he had actually lied. This was a marriage of convenience, after all, and Florence had not asked about the state of his financial affairs. It was the bride's family who paid for the wedding, after all, and John saw no reason to enlighten her about his . . . well, his womanizing and gambling debts.

It wasn't as though he was going to stagger down that path again. Probably.

"He just wants to make sure I'm respectable in public," John said with a shrug.

Florence's eyebrow twitched. "As respectable as you are in private?"

Delight soared through him as he noticed again the complete lack of stammering in her words. So, she was starting to relax around him, was she? He wasn't sure whether to be pleased or offended.

Another young lady stepped over to the pianoforte, eager to perform, so they were able to continue their conversation under the sound of her playing.

"I . . ." John swallowed as an impulse overtook him. Where precisely this instinct came from, to spill the truth, he did not know. But he suddenly found he could no longer hold it back. "I have a gambling problem."

And all at once, a heavy weight he had never known was lying on his chest was removed.

John gasped. Dear God, how long had that been pressing on him?

Florence was watching him carefully. "G-Gambling problem?"

Shifting uncomfortably in his chair, he spoke quietly so that no one else could hear them. "I couldn't stop. Or I could, but I didn't. It was bad for me, bad for the family, so Cothrom . . . he's given me a second chance. To prove myself. To stay away from the cards."

Her gaze flickered to the table before them. "D-Do you w-want to m-move away, or—"

"It's fine, I have enough of a distraction," John said, his mouth dry.

Florence frowned. "You do?"

"I am pleased to see you, Florence," John told her, wishing to goodness he could reach out and take her hand. But he wasn't a complete dolt. "And I hope you will consent to sitting here with me, all evening, without speaking to another soul."

There was a glitter of mirth in her eyes. "Y-You know that is what I would prefer over all things. But . . . is this n-not a tad scandalous?"

John frowned, attempting to understand what she meant. "Scandalous?"

"The two of us here, tucked in a corner with n-no one else," Florence said gently. "You . . . you c-could be saying anything to me."

His stomach lurched. *Well, fine. A bit lower down lurched.*

He certainly knew the sort of things he would like to say to Miss Florence Bailey, but some of them were frowned on in parts of Europe. He definitely couldn't vocalize them here. Not without a special license from the Archbishop of Canterbury tomorrow, permitting them to marry that afternoon.

John cleared his throat. *Concentrate, man!* "We are in plain view, and we are engaged. To be married."

"You and I know th-that's only an agreement," Florence said in a muted tone. "One we made for our convenience. It . . . it doesn't mean anything."

Something in John rebelled at the sentiment, even if he couldn't explain it.

Because it was painful, somehow, to hear Florence say that. Even if it was true. Even if it was a completely accurate description of how they had organized things, it felt callous, somehow.

Because things had changed.

John pushed the thought aside, but he couldn't remove it from his mind.

Yes, some things had changed, he told himself. He had kissed Florence and given her what could only be described as a panic attack. And that was quite enough.

"Doesn't mean anything?" he said aloud.

Florence dropped her gaze to her hands, as though the intensity of his thoughts had somehow crept out into his expression. "I-I just meant . . . I-I . . . w-when we . . ."

"Let's deal out these cards," said John, taking pity on the woman. "Then people will think we're playing, and not worry about the look of the thing."

After all, that's all most of Society was, wasn't it? The look of the thing.

Florence nodded and picked up the cards, deftly shuffling them and spreading them out into a simple game of Commerce.

John blinked. "You know," he said without thinking. "There's something about you."

When he looked up, she was flushing a deep pink. "I-I'm a wallflower."

"That's not what I—"

"It's why I know how to p-play the card game Commerce," Florence said quietly. "Wh-When I refused to go out, my b-brother would play with me."

John recalled the protective, almost defensive look on the man's face that he had accosted at the ball. Accosted quite erroneously, as it turned out. Yes, there was most definitely a look in that man of someone who had spent a great deal of time caring for his sister.

"It's more than just being a wallflower," said John, examining the cards in his hand. Excellent. A flush. "You—"

"Why is everyone s-so insistent that I not be a w-wallflower?" asked Florence, perhaps for the first time interjecting over John. "I-Is it so bad?"

She looked at him steadily over her cards.

John's stomach dropped. "No—no, that's not what I—"

"It is difficult at t-times, yes," she said, though there was weight behind every single syllable. "I-I am overlooked. Often m-made to feel unwanted. But . . . but I am just shy. Th-That is all, and if people . . . if people made an effort to know me . . ."

Her voice trailed away, her confidence evidently only able to take her so far.

John stared. He had never . . . well, never considered it like that. "Wallflower" was about as offensive a term a lady could be given in polite Society. No one wished for the moniker, and those who had it rarely escaped it.

Hark at him—escape it? Was he truly so blinded by Society's view of wallflowers that he considered being one to be such a detriment, a failing?

"But I don't think of you like that," he said.

Florence gave him a wry look. "I d-don't suppose you do. But I . . . I want to be valued for what I can bring to a conversation, even if it does often move too quickly for me to contribute. I want to be shy, and still be welcome. Be quiet, and still be respected. It is not a great ask, is it?"

"No," John said, dazed. "No, I suppose it's not."

If anyone had ever asked him whether he had set out to change Florence, to alter her in any way, John would have given them a resounding, "No!"

And yet he had, hadn't he?

Whenever he was with her he had encouraged her to open up—but on his terms. Speak more, speak louder, speak often. Laugh loudly and flirt and jest and . . .

And be like all those other ladies in the *ton*.

John swallowed, and glanced back down at the widow cards laying face up between them on the table for want of a distraction.

"I want to be loved," Florence said in a subdued way, laying down her own cards. A tricon of of aces. "Not just tolerated."

She looked up and met John's gaze, and there was such fire in it, such blazing fury, he was rather surprised the whole room did not burst into flames.

How could he have misunderstood Florence so utterly? How could he not have noticed the depths of the woman? Not just of mind, but of character. Oh, she may be a wallflower, but underneath the petals was a center of steel. A woman who had gone through Society's upbringing and decided to be her own person, no matter how painful that was.

A woman like that could rule the world.

She could certainly rule him.

"You win," John murmured.

Florence blinked. "I-I wh-wh-what—"

"The cards," he said hastily, pointing at them. "You win. I don't know how you did it, but—"

"B-By distracting you, of c-course," she said.

John noticed the stammer was back, but said nothing. The hasty agreement they had made, pressed up against her carriage outside the

Knights' home, felt foolish now. How could he have made such a deal with a woman who was fast demonstrating her superiority to him in every way?

Because, by God, he liked her.

Had liked her before. Two years ago, the captivating if shy Miss Bailey had been a welcome amusement at the house party he had been certain he would find most dull. Flirting with her, courting her much against his typical taste, had been a pleasant diversion.

And then that kiss.

John had told himself then he had retreated because matrimony was most definitely not for him. But was it something else? Could he now say, with the beauty of two years of distance and hindsight, that instead it had been . . . fear?

Fear of caring too much?

"I-I find I am tired," Florence said quietly.

John blinked. "I beg your pardon?"

"I am t-tired," she said with a shy smile. "Do you th-think Lord Bysshe will mind if I—"

"If you wish to go home, go home," said John, hating that he was encouraging her to leave. He rose, offering out his hand. "But do me the honor of allowing me to escort you to your carriage."

There was a small stir in the card party as the Marquess of Aylesbury took the arm of Miss Bailey and led her out of the room—but after all, they were engaged, and it was only polite decorum to see her to the door.

Polite decorum was the last thing on John's mind.

"You know," Florence said in a murmur as they stepped into the empty hall. "The l-last time you saw me to a c-carriage, you kissed me, and we ended up engaged to be m-married."

"Don't tempt me to kiss you again," John muttered. "I told you before, we took that . . . those sorts of things off the table. You didn't want—"

"I didn't want you t-to feel pity for me," she exhaled, eyes wide. "To only d-do it because you f-felt you—you ought to, or—"

"Ought to?" he repeated blankly. Had she ever looked at herself? Did she have any idea what she did to him? John swallowed. "Well, I don't feel like I ought to. And I want to, but I don't want you to—"

Florence pulled the ties of her pelisse together into a tight bow, then looked up with sparkling hazel eyes. "And if I ask for it?"

Desire was rising, but John knew he had to ignore it—he would not put her in that position again. "You would have to be very sure, Florence, and I don't think—"

"I'm sure," she said softly, placing her hands inexplicably on his chest and leaning into him, her breasts straining against him. "Just . . . just stop if I ask, w-won't you?"

John swore under his breath. "Of course—of course I will, but—"

He groaned. How could he do anything else, with Florence Bailey kissing him?

She was eager. He could not have predicted the way her fingers were attempting to get underneath his waistcoat, scrabbling to get close to him.

Well, what was a man supposed to do?

Florence gasped in his mouth as John pushed her back, pinning her against the wall. It only gave him better access to plumb the sweet depths of her mouth, twisting her tongue into agonies of pleasure that roared through him.

"John," she moaned as his lips trailed kisses down to her breasts, breasts that rose and fell with frantic movement. "John—"

"Do you trust me?" John asked, lifting his head only for a moment to confirm her consent. "Will you allow me to—I want to give you—"

"Yes," said Florence, her eyes wide. "Yes."

He didn't understand it, couldn't understand it. Mere days ago she had refused his touch, refused his offer of lovemaking—and now she craved it?

But with the straining need of Florence against him, there was little thinking John could do. Besides, had she not demonstrated how much she wanted him? She had kissed him, had somehow managed to undo all his waistcoat buttons and was making swift work of his shirt ones.

No, she wanted this. And she had consented.

"You can tell me to stop," John said with a ragged voice. "Anytime you—"

He moaned, unable to help himself. As he had been speaking, his hand had been lifting up the skirts that were entirely in the way. His questing fingers had found soft skin, then softer skin, then—

Oh God. Her core, her center, the very soul of her. She was dripping wet.

"You want me," John said in a whisper, hardly able to believe it.

And Florence stared with wild eyes, and her lips parted. "So much."

Groaning as he dropped his head onto her shoulder, hardly able to stand, John allowed one finger to slowly tease over her slit.

Florence bucked under him, and he crushed his lips on hers to prevent her cry alerting the card party guests that anything untoward was occurring just feet from them.

Untoward? Damning hell, there was nothing better than this.

Straining to control himself, desperate to make this the best moment of her life, John tasted the eagerness in Florence's mouth.

And slipped a finger inside her.

Slowly, slowly, he built the rhythm he knew would edge her closer and closer to absolute ecstasy. Florence whimpered, twisting her hips, bucking slightly as his finger slipped over her nub, and that only made him want her more.

But this wasn't about his pleasure. It was about hers.

Manhood straining in his breeches and hoping beyond hope he was giving her the sweet, decadent, sensual experience she so deserved, John noticed when Florence's quivering heightened.

He slipped in his thumb, circling around her nub as his finger twisted and sped up the pace.

Florence fell apart.

It was so sweet to watch, to feel, to taste, John could have wept. This was everything—all he wanted, for the rest of his life, was to give this woman bliss like this. To see her come, to feel her core squeeze around his fingers, to taste the honeysweet dew of her orgasm.

When Florence collapsed against him, John held her without saying a word.

There were no words for a moment like this.

She blinked up at him as though he were a blinding light. "Th-That . . . that was . . ."

John waited, but when it became clear she could not continue, he grinned. "Now, I believe you had a carriage waiting?"

Florence gave an unsteady laugh. "You think I can walk a-after that?"

"Fear not," said John bracingly. In one movement, he lifted her into his arms and stepped toward the door. "I have you, Florence. I have you."

Chapter Eleven

July 30, 1812

FLORENCE HESITATED, THEN lifted the heavy knocker and allowed it to fall on the imposing door before her.

She hadn't actually intended it to be a particularly loud knock, but that did not appear to matter. The heavy iron slammed down onto the brass circle, rebounding several times and making it sound like she was demanding access.

She winced. She would have to hope the butler would be understanding.

But it wasn't a butler, or even a footman, who opened the door of Aylesbury House.

"John."

She would have to get back into the habit of calling him the Marquess of Aylesbury in company, or at the very least "my lord." But the trouble was, that would mean missing out on seeing John's lips break into a delighted smile whenever she said his name.

A habit she most certainly did not wish to break.

"Florence," he said softly.

Florence beamed, trying not to melt onto a puddle on the doorstep.

It had been at the card party, she was certain. That was when something had changed between them. Florence wasn't sure whether it was the fact that she had finally opened up about being a wallflower, and how limiting it was to be treated in such a way . . . or the fact that he had brought her to ecstasy with his fingers in the hall of Lord Bysshe's home.

One or the other.

The point was, she told herself determinedly, *something had shifted.* The last few days had been some of the happiest she had ever known.

Which, thanks to her mother, was not saying much. But still.

"It looks like it's g-going to rain," Florence whispered.

She would have jerked her head behind her, or even turned to look up at the rainclouds which had been scudding over the London sky all day. After what felt like an eternity of blistering heat, the sudden dull clouds were a welcome relief.

But that would mean looking away from John.

And she couldn't. Florence didn't think she would ever encounter a gentleman so liable to make her beam as John Chance, Marquess of Aylesbury. Even when he wasn't intending to be, he was most amusing.

Not something she had ever mentioned to him.

"Rain?" said John vaguely, not looking away. "What care I about rain, when you're here?"

Heat blossomed up Florence's body, across her décolletage, and up her neck to her cheeks. And in any other situation, that would have bothered her. Blushing, as her mother so often said, was an attempt to attract attention—and there was nothing more shameful in Mrs. Bailey's eyes than attracting attention. At least, in that way.

But with John . . . oh, what did it matter? He never seemed to notice whether she was flushing or not, Florence reasoned, and so why should she care?

How could she care about anything when he was looking at her like that?

"Come on in," said John quietly, stepping back so she could enter the building. "Welcome to Aylesbury House."

Florence swallowed as she stepped inside.

It was perfectly fine, she told herself as John's fingers smoothed across her shoulder as he removed her pelisse. John had invited her and his brothers to dinner. It was an opportunity, he had said, for her to get to know the Chance family better.

The idea of having to converse with so many people—two brothers and a wife—had hardly filled Florence with joy, but still.

She would be with John.

"Aylesbury House?" she said, gazing around the large hallway in which they now stood. "I-It's not a very original name, i-is it?"

John grinned. "I suppose not—but the Chance family isn't particularly known for our creativity. My older brother's London townhouse is Cothrom House, Lindow's is Lindow House . . . you get the general idea."

Florence matched his smile, then swiftly looked away and at the splendor of the place.

It was incredible. A high ceiling, carefully painted with swirling clouds, gods and goddesses peeking out behind rose bushes and fruit trees. Cherubs flew about in the sky, glinting with gold paint. There were columns around the hallway, marble with exquisite carvings that must have taken an age to craft. It was magnificent.

"Beautiful."

"Yes," said John.

When Florence turned back to him, he was looking not looking at the spectacular chandelier, or the paintings, or the most interesting sculptures that sat either side of the doors. He was looking at her.

Florence's pulse skipped a beat, fluttering almost painfully. He had a way with him, this man. Oh, she'd known that from the minute that he'd flirted with her when they first met—had known John Chance was a charmer.

But this was different. There had been moments, these last few days when they had ridden together in Hyde Park, or wandered through an art gallery Lord Palmerston had opened, or discussed politics over a cup of tea at Twining's...

Moments when John looked at her almost as though she were the only woman in the world.

Which was a ridiculous thought, Florence told herself sternly. There were many ladies in the world—most of them prettier and more delightful in their conversation than she.

It just happened that she was the one John was looking at in that moment.

John cleared his throat, breaking the silence. "A tour, my lady?"

Florence gave a nervous laugh. "I'm n-not a—"

"But you will be," he countered with a smile, taking her hand and placing it on his arm, where it burned. "In not too long, you'll be the Marchioness of Aylesbury. You'll be mistress of all this."

All this . . .

It was a heady thought, but Florence managed to retain her equilibrium as he led her into a beautifully appointed morning room, with sky-blue drapes and a rug that picked out the same color.

"Sh-Shouldn't we wait for your brothers?"

John shrugged. "They've seen it all before anyway, they won't mind missing the tour."

"N-No, I meant—"

"Look here, this is where I thought you could place your books," he said eagerly, speaking over her in his excitement as he gestured to a bookcase which was only half full. "And through here"—he pulled her onward, into a spacious drawing room with an impressive marble fireplace—"I thought there would be room for your pianoforte. If you have one. If not, we can buy one."

Florence stared about her in wonder. "P-Pianoforte?"

"Yes," said John, beaming. "Though now I say that, I realize I'm not sure if you actually like playing, or just use it as a clever excuse to avoid people."

"I . . . I d-don't—"

"Well, let's get one, and then if needed you can use it to avoid me," John said with a wink. "I'm sure I am most irritating at least half the time, so it may come in handy."

Their mingled laughter moved through the drawing room into the dining room—resplendent in red—then into a parlor that looked out onto the garden, a study which John said sternly she was never to enter for it was packed to the rafters with boredom, and a small library with a small writing desk in the corner.

"I suppose I should stop the tour there, and not tempt you to come upstairs with me," said John with a wicked look.

Florence flushed, looking at her hand so comfortably tucked into John's arm. She'd almost forgotten, for a moment, why he was giving her the tour in the first place.

Her future home.

One of them. She still had to have the awkward conversation with her mother—Mrs. Bailey was most certainly not accompanying the new marchioness into her marital home—but it was starting to occur to Florence that there would be, in the absolute worst-case scenario, a solution.

Why, the Marquess of Aylesbury had many houses. Why not simply deposit her mother in one of those?

"Unless . . ."

Florence looked up. "Unless?"

"Unless you would *like* a tour of the upstairs of your future home," said John.

There was more than a little hint in his expression, but Florence discovered she could meet his teasing air with relative equanimity. "P-Perhaps not," she said with a smile. "If we can do . . . do *th-that* in a hallway, I'd hate to th-think what we'd get up to in a bedchamber."

The instant the words had left her mouth, Florence's cheeks burned.

Well! It was a most scandalous thing to even think, let alone say—and she had spoken those words not just to herself, which may have been permissible . . . but to her future husband!

A future husband who had already given her a glimpse of the pleasures of the flesh that lay before them . . . if they wanted them . . .

"I am taking marital union, for want of a better word, off the table. You don't have to worry. I'll never ask you for that again."

Florence hesitated. It had been a kindly gesture, she was certain of that—or perhaps he had never intended to do much of that sort of thing with his actual wife, and intended instead to take up a mistress the moment their vows were spoken.

It was a rather disconcerting thought. But not unusual. In fact, as far as she could make out, it was unusual for a gentleman *not* to take a mistress, to stay loyal to his wife.

"Dear God, you're right," said John with a sigh. "And I made you that promise—I shouldn't have even . . . come, let us sit in the drawing room and attempt to act like rational human beings."

Florence let out a laugh as he swung her around, her head reeling, and then pulled her through the house back to the drawing room.

At this time of year, it would be several hours until the sun went down. The fireplace therefore remained unlit, and John deposited her on the sofa beside the empty grate.

He sat beside her. Very close beside her.

"You'll have to let me know if you don't like any of it," he said quietly.

Florence blinked. "Don't like what?"

"Any of the house," John said, gesturing vaguely about the room. "It'll be your home, you'll be mistress of it. The Marchioness of Aylesbury. It will be for you to decide what furnishings are suitable, what color you want the walls, that sort of thing."

Her stomach lurched at the thought.

Her own home. It wasn't something she had ever given much thought to. Florence had known from a young age, almost as soon as she had realized what Society's requirements were of a person, that she did not match them. So finding a husband and imagining their life together had been something other ladies did, not her.

And now here she was, facing the prospect of not only her own home, but freedom within it. Freedom to choose how a room looked, and who would be invited into it . . .

John shifted closer. "You know, as we are alone—"

"Y-Yes, we are alone," said Florence firmly, giving him a look that told him with no uncertainty precisely what they should be doing.

That was, what they should *not* be doing.

John leaned back with a wolfish look. "You're going to keep me on my toes, aren't you, Florence?"

A shiver trickled down her back. "Perhaps."

If she were fortunate.

This proposal of a marriage of convenience had fast become something Florence could not have envisioned. It had grown, spread, twisted into something like a vine. Like a bramble, suddenly blossoming flowers.

At least, it was for her. And John must like her, Florence reasoned, or else he would not have . . . he would not keep trying to . . .

Would he?

"When are your brothers arriving?" she asked, partly to keep John distracted, partly to distract herself. "Will the two of them arrive together?"

The moment Florence saw John's expression, she knew the truth. "John Chance!"

"Well, it's so rare that you and I ever get to—"

"I've been had!"

"Dear God, don't tempt me," said John in an undertone.

Florence's cheeks flushed, but she could not help but smile. "You know what I mean."

"So I wanted to have dinner with you alone," he said, leaning back on the sofa with a shrug. "It is hardly a crime."

"But . . ." Florence floundered, attempting to explain to the man—the Marquess of Aylesbury!—just how outrageous it was, what he had done. And at the same time, trying to understand this teasing he was subjecting her to. Pretending that he wished to make love to her—after his own declaration that he wouldn't ask her to do so!

A flicker of uncertainty crept within her. Except . . . except she had asked *him* for that hedonism. And he'd made her feel so wonderful—and knowing that she could stop him at any time, end the encounter with a mere word . . .

Well. It had made her feel powerful. In control, in a way she had never done before.

"I wanted you all to myself," John was saying. "And if that's scandalous—"

"You know it is—and worse, you know the only reason my mother permitted me to come was because you said your sister-in-law would be here," Florence said sternly. "And you . . . why are you looking at me like that?"

It was an odd look. John was not teasing her with this look. His grin was wide but held little mirth. It was . . . genuine. A genuine smile, one Florence could not quite unpick.

"What?" she said, a little defensively. She moved on the sofa, twisting so she could better face him. "You're staring at me as though you have never seen me before, and you're happy, and—and what?"

For a moment, John hesitated. Then he inhaled deeply and said leisurely, "Florence. Florence, you . . . you aren't stammering."

Florence lifted her hands to her mouth as it fell open. "I . . . I'm not?"

He shook his head, his expression unchanging. "You're not. It's the highest compliment you have ever paid me."

Slowly, Florence allowed her hands to fall back into her lap as she tried to take in the simple fact that she had not been stammering.

Not stammering? She always stammered. Her words were always clear and concise in her mind, and always left her lips elegantly and with refinement when she was alone. It was before others that she was unable to twist her tongue into the right shapes.

But not with John. Not now.

She swallowed, almost nervous to attempt to speak again in case the magic had faded. "I-I . . . I hadn't noticed."

"And I don't mind if you do stammer," John said swiftly, reaching out a hand to clasp hers. "You can stammer all you want, and I'll do my damnedest—oh, sorry—I'll do my utmost not to interrupt you. I promise."

Florence squeezed his hand, hardly knowing what to do with herself. "It's a p-part of me."

"And I don't want to change it," said John, his blue eyes focused on her. "I don't want to change a single bit of you."

And she could have melted right into the sofa.

Not wanting her to change? No, that simply wasn't possible. Everyone wanted her to change. Her mother wanted her to be . . . well, completely different. Her brother wished her to be stronger in her convictions. Lady Romeril wanted her to sing, God forbid, at every recital. Miss Quintrell wanted her to be a gossip. Other friends had hated her shyness . . .

But John?

He squeezed her hand, then with seemingly great reluctance, released it. "So. I lied. Sorry."

Florence tried to take a steadying breath. How was it possible to be so tremulous while still sitting down? "Well, I . . . I h-hope that is not a habit you intend to keep. When we are married."

A dinner gong rang at that exact moment, so John rose and offered his hand rather than reply to her comment. And, in a way, he did not need to. Though Florence had intended it as a jest, she had seen the flash of pain that swept across John's face at her words. Twisting agony, momentary disappointment, then it was gone. And John was smiling again.

"Here," he said as they entered the dining room.

He had led her to a chair at the foot of the table. It had been elegantly set with silver cutlery and plates edged in gold . . . and because the table could seat at least twelve people, it meant that she was at the complete opposite end from John, whose place had been set at the head.

At least ten feet from her.

"Florence?"

She blinked. John had pulled out her chair, offering to seat her—but this was wrong. Florence knew decorum dictated they sit this way, but . . . well, they were alone, weren't they?

Other than a footman, that was.

"W-Would you b-be so good as to move th-this?" she said to the man standing in Aylesbury livery. "T-to there."

The footman stared, then his gaze darted a fraction to the left.

John shrugged. "She'll be your mistress in no time, you may as well get accustomed to obeying her now."

Florence was delighted to hear that there was a teasing air in his voice. And so when the footman had finished, John and Florence sat at one end of the table, her place just to his right. Within touching distance.

"Don't you want to be proper?" John asked as the footman placed his napkin on his lap. "Do things the right way?"

"I have been p-proper all my life," Florence countered as the footman did the same for her own napkin. "Besides, I only really f-feel alive when . . . when I'm with you."

Her cheeks burned to say such a thing in the presence of another, but it couldn't be helped. *This was going to be her life*, she could not help but think. Footmen and maids and servants all the time.

Serving their marquess and marchioness.

The footman stepped over to the dumbwaiter and removed two plates of delicious looking food, placing them before each of them and then swiftly departing.

They were alone.

John poured her a glass of wine. "Well, you were proper, and you've reaped the rewards."

"Rewards?"

"Me, of course," he grinned. "A marquess. Most ladies of the *ton* would—well, not kill for one precisely—"

"I am not so sure of that," Florence interjected, marvelous at her bravery in doing such a wild thing. "I-I am not sure most ladies of the *t-ton* would praise me if they discovered that I was the one, in fact, to propose to you."

John sipped at the wine and Florence followed suit. A delicious red. A perfect accompaniment for the roasted chicken and hearty potatoes which sat before them.

"I'm hardly a success," Florence said, with as much of a laugh as she could manage.

It was only after she had taken a few mouthfuls of the delicious food that she looked up, and saw once again a most strange expression on John's face. It wasn't sadness—not quite—but it wasn't far off. A sort of melancholy which she never would have associated with the carefree bravado of the Marquess of Aylesbury.

"Well, we can be failures together," John said.

Florence placed her fork down. "You are not a failure."

"Oh, I am—quite a successful failure, in fact, though I am aware of the irony," he said with a dry chuckle that did not quite reach his eyes. "I'm always making mistakes, always needing second, third, fourth chances from my brother."

"Your brother?"

"Cothrom," John explained with a sigh, though he took another mouthful onto his fork and chewed it thoughtfully before continuing.

"If there has ever been anyone in the world who epitomizes the word 'proper,' it's Cothrom. William, the eldest of us. He's never put a step wrong in public, never caused scenes amongst the *ton*—"

"Unlike you," Florence said softly.

She watched as the man she knew she loved winced, and she hated she had been the cause. But though this conversation was evidently painful for John, it was important, too. She could not explain why, but it was. This moment. It was crucial.

"And then there's me," John said with a sigh. "Always a failure, never getting it right. I'm always being bailed out by my brother—we both are."

"Both?"

"Lindow and me. Although I suppose," he said thoughtfully, "it's possible that . . . that Pernrith is too, and I just don't know about it."

Florence frowned. "Pernrith?"

It was a name she vaguely recognized, but it was hard to put a face to the name—or place it within the *ton*. Wasn't he second son of a—no, that was someone else.

John cut viciously at a particularly roasted bit of chicken. "The fourth Chance brother—in a way. Lindow would hate me for saying that."

It was becoming less clear, not more. "I don't unders-stand."

And her hopes soared as he paused, waited to see whether she would continue, not wishing to speak over her.

Florence smiled encouragingly, and John nodded. "Well, there are three Chance brothers . . . and a fourth. Our father's indiscretion."

Embarrassment filled her. "Oh. Oh! Oh, I see."

"Yes, it's an awkward dynamic, and I can't say I like the man," John said curtly. "Lindow hates him, but that's . . . well, that's his own business. The point is, Cothrom hopes for the best and we never give it to him. I move from one scrape to the other, never making him proud, never making anyone proud . . . I'll never be enough."

There was such anguish in his words, such pain in his tones, that Florence did not have to think. She just acted instinctively. She reached out and took his hand. "You're enough for me."

John lifted his eyes to meet hers, and Florence almost gasped at the longing, the desperate need to be loved that poured from his face. "Am I?"

She nodded. "And you don't need to change for me, John Chance."

He gave a shaky laugh. "You wouldn't say that if you knew—"

"I know you, John. B-Better than I know anyone," said Florence decidedly, knowing it to be true. "And you were the one I asked to marry me. You're the one I . . . I thought I could be happy with."

Happiest with, she wanted to say. *Gloriously, ecstatically happy. If you just let me in. If you—*

Then John pulled his hand away with an apologetic shake of his head and returned to his food. "Very kind of you, Florence. You'll make an excellent wife."

Florence bit her lip, attempting to retain the memory of that moment, that instant when she had known they were connected more deeply than anything she had experienced before.

"And you'll be an excellent husband."

Chapter Twelve

"WELL," SAID JOHN slowly with a grin he could not quite hide. "It looks like you'll be staying here."

Florence glanced up, then returned to the window. There was not a hint of concern on her face. Perhaps it was her lack of apprehension that had excitement thrumming through John.

Well, she hadn't said no . . .

The rain thundered against the glass. He supposed he should have guessed. Florence had, after all, mentioned the sense of rain in the air. All this heavy heat for so long, the weather would have to break sometime. It would be a relief, in truth, to have all this strange atmosphere blown away by the winds.

A flash of light—and an answering roll of thunder that sounded far too close for anyone to venture out tonight.

Particularly if they were a specific young lady he certainly didn't wish to be drenched.

"You should not be so silly." Florence's voice was so low, it was almost impossible to hear over the thrashing rain. "I only came for dinner."

The pair of them were standing by one of the huge sash windows in the drawing room. Despite Humphreys's advice, they had pulled back the curtains and were looking up at the storm as it raged.

The rain was so heavy, John could almost feel it pouring onto his skin. Cleansing, changing him, relieving him of the habits of the past.

He almost shook his head and laughed as the droplet of a thought trickled through his brain. *What on earth was he thinking?* A little rain couldn't alter the past, couldn't change his habits or the things he had done.

He glanced over at Florence. Her eyes were wide, clearly delighting in the drama of the storm.

And something in him twisted.

But she could do it. She could alter the past, make it seem . . . better. Well, not better in and of itself, naturally. But if the cost was that he'd had to endure it all to come to her . . .

Then it was worth it. Florence Bailey was worth it.

"I can't let you go home in this," said John softly—too softly. He strengthened his voice as he realized she had not heard him over the tattoo the rain was drumming down onto Aylesbury House. "I can't let you go home in this awful weather, Florence. I'm sorry."

"No, you're not," she said as though attempting not to laugh. "It's past ten o'clock, I have to—"

"You don't have to do anything when the weather is this awful," John said firmly. "I mean, look at it!"

He watched Florence's gaze as it flickered across the garden. There was not a great deal of it at the front of Aylesbury House—that was the price one paid for living so close to the center of London. Yet even the little lawn and flowerbeds that the house afforded were being battered by the storm. Flowers had lost their last summer buds, there was a branch from the silver birch lying across a rose bush, and John didn't think the magnolia would ever be the same again.

A shiver flickered through him. What, let Florence go out in that? It would practically be murder—he would be responsible for anything that happened to her. The fact it was mightily convenient had nothing to do with anything.

"You are not stepping a foot out of this house while that storm rages," John said, speaking over the thoughts pouring through his mind which were not very gentlemanly. "You think I could permit you to risk—"

"It's not so big a risk," Florence began to say. "It's just—dear Lord!"

He nearly swore at the sight before them. Just beyond the hedge of Aylesbury House, toward the road, was a man riding along the street on horseback. Or at least, he was trying to. The wind was so overwhelming that the poor beast was essentially moving backward. Each time the man's steed raised a leg, it was shunted back over the cobbles, its shod hooves unable to find a purchase.

John and Florence watched, equally transfixed, as the man and his horse disappeared from sight . . . going the opposite direction from the way they faced.

"Absolutely not," said John with what he hoped was an air of decision. "I would never forgive myself if . . ."

He swallowed.

If something happened to you.

That was what he was going to say. It was the sort of thing one said, after all, to . . . to the people one loved.

Oh hell's bells.

Florence slipped a hand in his, and John fought against the surprising instinct to bring her fingers to his lips. "You're up to something, aren't you?"

He tried to laugh. "You think I can make it rain?"

"I think you would do anything to get your own way," she said, squeezing his hand. "So yes, I suspect you of performing a magic ritual for rain before I arrived. Do you deny it?"

Their mingled laughter was drowned out, just for a flash, by the lightning and accompanying thunder which appeared to be getting even closer.

It was all working out perfectly.

That was what John would not admit. Certainly not aloud, and hardly even to himself in the privacy of his own mind.

This dinner had been intended to be a chance for him to spend even more time with the woman he was starting to care about too much. Far, far too much. This whole marriage of convenience was supposed to get him a pleasant wife he knew he could stomach, some respectability now Cothrom was constantly at him, and access to her funds to boot.

"I sent you to that house party to behave yourself. To get away from London and the gambling hells. Not to propose to random women!"

And that was it.

That was supposed to be it. But for the last few days now, John could hardly deny that he enjoyed Florence's company. The more time they spent together, the more natural it felt, the more obvious. It felt almost as though he had been fighting against the tide his whole life, yet when he stepped to her side . . .

He no longer had to fight.

John swallowed and tried to focus on the storm. She was beautiful and shy, clever and reticent, stammering at times, and yet at others, clearer and more precise than half the people in London.

She was an enigma. She made no sense.

And now his life was starting to make no sense without her.

"Goodness, that w-was a serious thought."

John started, and realized he was still holding hands with her. The sensation had become so natural, he'd hardly noticed it. "What was?"

"Whatever passed through your mind just then," said Florence, a pink to her cheeks, as though she were being impertinent. "What were you thinking?"

The chances of John actually admitting what he had been thinking were absolutely zero. Or at least, so close to zero that there was no point even attempting to calculate those odds or to try to put his thoughts into proper words.

Thinking about how special you are.

Thinking about how fortunate I am.

Thinking about how, with every passing day, this marriage becomes less and less convenient . . .

John swallowed. "Just . . . just the storm."

"Liar."

He had to laugh at that, even with Florence's shy smile making his whole body quiver. "You used to be a lot more reticent to give your true opinion of me."

"That is probably true," she said amiably, looking up at the window as though to avoid looking at him.

John continued to gaze at her face, the elegant curve of her nose, the achingly tempting lips. Somehow, he found he simply couldn't look away. "I prefer you this way."

Florence turned back to him, cheeks flushed. "You mean you didn't like me when—"

"No!" *Hell, would he ever be able to get his words right with this woman?* "No, I meant—Florence, you are pretty damn perfect as far as I can tell, and you could spend the rest of your life as you were when we first met. But this way, I know you better. And that's . . . that's an honor. An honor I don't think many people have."

John was surprised to hear an earnestness in his voice that had never been there before. And it was genuine. He truly meant what he said.

Florence looked as though she was not quite sure. "I . . . I-I don't know."

How could he explain it? "I like . . . I like that you're shy. I like that you prefer to only speak when you wish to. I like that you have all these wild and interesting thoughts that you don't share with all and sundry. And I like . . ."

For a moment, his voice faltered. How could it continue, when Florence was looking at him like that? Her fingers still entwined with his own, John had presumed that was the height of the intimacy they would share.

And yet perhaps it wasn't. This look they were sharing, a shimmering, unspoken knowledge between them, a sense of openness and vulnerability and affection, was something much deeper. He could no longer deny it, either to himself or to Florence, even if it were only communicated through this heated look.

Affection. He felt a deep affection for this woman, deeper than he had known himself capable. He could feel it demanding more of him than had ever been expected before.

It was frightening. But he would not step back.

"I like you," John said simply.

It might have been a few heartbeats they stood there. It might have been a year or two. However long it was, John wanted to stay in that moment, inhabit it, remain there forever. Just the two of them.

Another roll of thunder echoed around the drawing room and Florence jumped. They both chuckled, the tension dissipating from the room.

John glanced out of the window, and his resolve stiffened. So did other parts of him, but it was the resolve that mattered, he told himself.

"Look," he said, "I could not permit you to leave Aylesbury House in a storm of this magnitude. It simply wouldn't be—"

"I could take a carriage," Florence said, interrupting him with a swift grin. "How bad can it be, really?"

Just at that moment, a bolt of lightning jagged to the spire of a church about three streets away. London lit up, glowing brighter than the midday sun, and when the thunder rolled, it sounded like the heavens were cracking open.

"Quite bad," John said with a shrug, releasing Florence's hand. If he kept holding it much longer, he'd find himself using other methods to persuade her—and that would certainly be most unacceptable. Probably. "Besides, I've lent my brother to my carriage. Carriage to my brother."

There was a sparkle of delight in Florence's eyes. "I beg your par—"

"You know what I meant," said John with a dry laugh. *Since when did he get his words all tangled up—and with a woman?* "And there's hardly going to be a hackney coach about the place."

Florence did not reply. She stepped toward the window, placing a hand on the glass and peering up at the sky as best she could.

John watched her. There was something intoxicating about seeing her like that. Illuminated in moments by the flashes of lighting, but otherwise a mostly dark silhouette. A figure he knew well—or at least, as well as one can just by looking at it. Continuously.

There was no one about. He could just step forward, push her up against the glass and—

"My mother will be worried," said Florence delicately.

John swallowed the aching need that had suddenly arisen, and tried to think. *Hang the mother*, his innermost being wanted to cry. *She was certainly an unpleasant person. Perhaps some fear would do her good.*

He regretted the thought immediately. What was he, cruel?

No, he may have been thoughtless, irresponsible, and childish—fine, he had most definitely been all those things, and more to boot—but he was not cruel.

John stepped forward and placed what he hoped was a comforting, and most importantly, chaste hand on Florence's shoulder. "She will understand. She would much rather you stayed inside, where it was safe, than risk—"

"But it seems so ridiculous, d-doesn't it?" said Florence wistfully. "My home is just six streets away. Seemingly no distance at all, and yet a little weather..."

The glass pane shook in its frame as the gale whipped around the house. "I wouldn't call that a little weather," said John dryly.

Florence gave him a brief nod before returning to the window. "I suppose not."

They stood there for a moment in silence.

And that was what John should have continued to do. Just remain there, standing in silence, watching the storm in the safety of Aylesbury House with Florence standing before him, his hand on her shoulder.

And perhaps, in another world, in another life, that is precisely what he would have done.

But John could not help himself. He was John Chance, Marquess of Aylesbury, and he had never turned down an opportunity like this. He certainly wasn't going to when it came to Florence Bailey.

John swallowed, his breath hitching in his throat as his hand slowly . . . moved.

Gently at first. His fingers traced a tender line down Florence's shoulder, down the back of her arm. Inch by inch, his touch so light it could almost be a breath, John allowed himself to focus on the sensation of his fingers trailing to her wrist.

And Florence did not push him away. She did not even turn around, or give any sign that she was unhappy with what he was doing.

Much to the contrary. John's pulse thrummed with the strength of the rain as Florence's shoulders dropped, a small smile just visible on the curve of her mouth.

And that was what increased his boldness beyond the level of propriety. John lifted his hand from her wrist and this time returned it to her shoulder—but as he trailed his fingers this time, it was not down Florence's arm.

No, it was down her back.

A guttural moan shuddered through him as he did so. The softness of Florence's skin had been replaced by the gentle coarseness of the muslin, but that did not matter. He could feel so much more. The pull of her corset, the delicate dip of her waist, and then—

"John," Florence said, stepping one foot away. Away from his questing fingers.

There was no censure in her tone, for which John supposed he should be grateful. But it was painful, having the distance between them suddenly increase.

"Florence," he said, astonished to find that his voice quavered, just slightly. "I—you'll have to stay. You must see that, just for the night."

Just for the night.

How long was it until their wedding—days? Weeks?

Hours would be too long. John knew that now—knew just how desperately he craved her, how simply being close to Florence was no longer enough.

He didn't just want close. He needed more.

Florence turned slowly on her heels, her hazel eyes examining him closely as she tucked a curl of wayward red hair behind her ear.

And when she spoke, it was quiet, but with all the certainty of a woman who had examined the situation and moved beyond mere guessing. "You want to bed me, don't you?"

A searing flush erupted across John's face. It was most unaccountable, and certainly not something he could recall ever enduring before. Honestly! The very idea!

John Chance, Marquess of Aylesbury, did not get embarrassed!

Except he did now. "I-I don't know what you mean?"

Florence's look was steady, amused, and not willing to back down. But the strength in her only increased John's desire. Not that he was lacking in it before.

"I think you do," she said, taking a step closer to him. "You . . . y-you don't have to deny it. I can read you like a book, John Chance."

And she could. John wasn't sure whether to be gratified and delighted, or horrified at how swiftly Florence had learned how to identify his teasing from his lies. It was most disconcerting. He had gone through the majority of his adult life always being the one able to tell what was going to happen next. The next card, the next fist, the next flirtation.

And here he was, faced with one of the shyest wallflowers in the *ton*, and he had no idea what to do next. No idea what she would do next.

Oh, he knew what he wanted...

John swallowed. When he spoke, his voice was hoarse. "I'm not the sort of book young ladies should be reading."

Any other woman would have been offended, or shocked, perhaps even mortified at such a suggestive comment.

But not Florence. Her smile was accompanied by a blush, but when she spoke, there was almost no quaver in her words. "I-I did wonder, when I suggested a marriage of convenience, if you would wish to bed me before you went through with it. The marriage itself, I mean."

John swallowed. At least, he tried to swallow. There was no moisture in his throat, nor did he seem to have any ability to control his own body.

How were they having this conversation? How was he, more importantly, having this conversation with Miss Florence Bailey?

When they had first met, he had largely discounted her. A pretty face, a terrible conversationalist, and someone who had been entertaining for a few weeks and that was all.

That was all? How could he have been so blind?

Clearing his throat as best he could, and knowing this conversation could go wrong very, very swiftly if he were not careful, John said, "I may have had hopes—expectations, certainly not."

Florence did not look away. "But you did have hopes."

Dear God, it was uncomfortable to admit this. And yet John could not think of anyone else he would prefer to have this conversation with. If he had to have it with someone, it should be her.

"Y-Yes."

"You sound like me."

John smiled weakly. Yes, the tables had in some way turned, though he still wasn't sure how. There was a new confidence in Florence, one which only emerged when they were together. Or at least, he had seen no sign of it at any other time.

"And I suppose you know what you are doing," she said softly. "In the bedchamber, I mean."

I hardly know what I'm doing now, John wanted to say. He appeared to be stumbling down a path without any map, signs, or hope. Though there must be a route to getting under Florence's skirts, he was certain of that—why else would she have raised the topic?

But where once he would have been satisfied with just being... well, satisfied, John knew now that he wanted more. A true connection. A sharing, instead of a taking. An intimacy, not an interaction.

Dear God, what was wrong with him?

"John?" Florence took another step forward. They were close now, very close. The idea of "too close" was impossible to comprehend, but her proximity was certainly making comprehension difficult. "John, you do know what you're doing, don't you? When it comes to ... to pleasing a lady?"

God help him. "Yes."

"Even ... even one who is, perhaps, inexperienced?"

John's gaze roved over the untouched skin, the innocent eyes—

Then saw something new in them, as another roll of thunder echoed through the drawing room and a flash of lightning lit up the beautiful woman before him: a gleam of lust. Florence wanted him.

Perhaps not so innocent after all.

"Inexperienced, yes," he managed to say aloud. "Though to tell the truth, I have never bedded a virgin before."

"But *you* are experienced. You know what ... wh-what a woman likes. What a woman does not like. You showed me that, in Lord Bysshe's hallway."

John's mouth was so dry now, he was amazed he could actually speak. "Every ... every woman is different."

Florence nodded sagely, as though they were discussing nothing more than the terrible weather outside. "But you can learn, can't you? The way a woman wants to be t-touched?"

And it was that faltering moment which pushed John over the edge. "We ... damn. Florence, we cannot be having this conversation!"

He had moved away, taken at least three steps, before Florence's voice halted him in his tracks, making it impossible to move, impossible to speak—almost impossible to think.

"But I want to. Not have this conversation, I mean—but be touched by you. Make . . . make love to me, John."

Chapter Thirteen

"We... damn. Florence, we cannot be having this conversation!"

Florence heard the pain in John's voice, but also the longing. The desire, a desire which she had seen bubbling away in him, just under the surface. Never to be permitted out.

Until now.

Florence knew there was a chance she would regret this conversation in the morning. When the light of day returned. When the storm had gone, and all the passion it evoked in her had died.

But there was also a chance she wouldn't.

Her gaze flickered over the man before her. Handsome, yes. Charming, yes. But also vulnerable. Open, with her. Kind and thoughtful and caring.

A man she wanted.

Florence hesitated, but only for a moment. "But I want to. Not have this conversation, I mean—but be touched by you. Make... make love to me, John."

She hadn't precisely intended those words. They were far more scandalous, far more exposing than she had planned. A part of Florence could hardly believe she had said them.

But this was right, she knew it was. After what had happened—or rather, not happened—two years ago, when she had been so certain John would propose matrimony, this was their second chance. She wasn't going to lose it just because of propriety.

"John?" Florence murmured into the silence.

He was still looking. Staring at her, as though he had never seen her before. As though he had never seen a woman before. As though language had ceased to function, his tongue mute, his mind utterly lost in the shock of what she had said.

Heat fluttered up Florence's neck, but for the first time in her life, she ignored it.

Shame would come, perhaps. But not now. Not while she looked at this man.

John Chance may be a marquess, but he was also a man—and he brought something out of her that Florence had never known before. A hunger, a desire, a passion. A need to be close to someone, to discover what delights could be shared between two people who . . .

Florence swallowed.

Words of love would come soon, she was certain. Words of affection, of admiration, words she could not quite bring herself to say. Not quite.

And they were going to be married, weren't they? In just a few short weeks, she would be Florence Chance, Marchioness of Aylesbury. That thought alone was sufficient to send a thrill of anticipation rushing up her spine.

Well, what did the difference of a few weeks make, really? Why not discover the delights of the marriage bed now, while they had this opportunity? While the rain fell and the wind blew, the lightning flashed, and the thunder roared . . .

And John looked at her like that.

Finally, he broke the silence of the drawing room. "I would never ask you to do something you would regret."

It was not a no. That was something Florence had to hold onto. *It was not a no.*

Strange. A smile crept over her face at the thought. If someone had told her, even a month ago, that she would be attempting to persuade

John Chance to bed her, she'd have thought them mad.

"I care about you," Florence said quietly. "And I wouldn't regret it."

"I care about you, too," John said, with such ferocity that Florence's eyes widened. "But—"

"John Chance," she interrupted, remembering something he had said only days ago, "you are being an idiot."

"Remind me, the next time I do something like that, that I am a complete idiot."

In the gloom of the room, lit now by only a few nearly guttering candles, she saw John's face, a picture of astonishment.

Then his features relaxed and he grinned. "I thought you'd never do that."

"I-I am surprised I d-did it myself," Florence admitted, her shyness threatening to return. "But it's true. I . . . John, I . . ."

Her voice trailed away, her courage not quite managing to stick.

Because once it was said, it was said. There was no taking that sort of statement back. She would not be able to convince John to forget it, pretend it was a spontaneous remark that meant nothing.

No, once these words left her lips, there would be nothing else she could hide behind. Florence would have no recourse, no retreat, no opportunity to step away from this man who made her feel . . . who looked at her like . . .

Florence swallowed. She had hesitated before, but this was the moment. She had to be brave—not because she was not shy, but because shyness would not rule her. Not when it came to moments like this.

"John, I . . . I love you."

The words echoed around the room. Or perhaps that was just her mind, echoing with the syllables that had been dancing on the tip of her tongue for weeks now.

She loved him.

Who could not love him? That was the trouble with John Chance, he was entirely too loveable. Florence would not be surprised if there had been others before her who had said such things. Meant such things. Wished John could reciprocate, could return the affection that so easily poured in his direction. And she wondered whether her admission had been too dull, too insipid to inspire anything—

He was kissing her.

Florence was so astonished at the sudden change that she hardly knew how it had happened. She had no memory of John moving toward her, nor of her own feet taking her closer to him. There did not seem to have been any process toward the kiss—merely that they had not been kissing, and now they were.

And all rational thought ceased.

How could it continue, with John kissing her like this? As though he had never kissed anyone else in his life. As though he were starving for affection, hungry for her in a way Florence could never have dreamed.

His lips roughly parted hers, eagerly taking possession of her. Florence welcomed him in, her tongue reaching out for his, and she did not know whether it was herself or John who moaned in that moment of connection.

His hands were not idle. Florence gasped in his mouth as John's fingers tightened around her buttocks, drawing them tight into his hips where something—

Where something she was almost certain was his manhood was straining against his breeches.

Florence gave herself to the kiss. Her hands tangled in his hair, pulling him nearer, her whole body aching to get closer to him. Time could have ceased and she would not have cared.

She was being soundly kissed by John Chance.

John's lips left her own but she could hardly complain. He remained busy as the rain poured down the windows, trapping them in this room where no other person existed in London. There was nothing else in the whole world.

"John," Florence murmured.

It was not a remonstrance. It was encouragement, encouragement in the only way she knew how—to utter his name. John's left hand remained cupping her buttocks but his right had moved to the ties of her gown, feverishly attempting to pull them apart.

And Florence laughed, her body aflame with his touch and the moment seemingly so ridiculous.

What, they were going to be thwarted by a mere ribbon?

"Here," Florence breathed, her hand moving to join his own.

Somehow in the tangle of fingers and kisses, they managed it. The tie unwound, her gown immediately loosening, and—

"John!" she gasped in wonder.

For it was wonderful. Wondrous. Beyond wonder.

As John's lips pressed against her neck, lowering to her collarbone, his fingers had moved confidently and assuredly under her gown's bodice to her corset. A corset he had swiftly forced down by a few inches.

A few inches was all it needed. Her breasts, no longer trapped beneath the whalebone and fabric, were free—but not for long.

Florence arched her back and whimpered. "J-John."

At least, that was what she had attempted to whimper, but there was hardly any air left in her lungs as John's finger scraped across her nipple. The unexpected contact did unexpected things.

Things like shooting sensuality through Florence's body as though a bolt of lightning from the storm outside had struck inside the room.

Things like make her legs weak.

Things like her mouth opening and uttering, "D-Do that again."

The swift look she had of John's face told her that he liked her being so forward. It was a strange thought—one Florence promised herself she would dedicate more time to.

After . . . after this.

John's thumb circled around her nipple, achingly close, before rubbing over it again as he plunged his head to—

Florence moaned, unable to help herself. How could anyone remain silent when John's mouth was upon their breast, his tongue licking around the peaking areola, sweeping over her nipple—

Suckling.

Sparks of decadent pleasure were cascading through Florence, making it difficult to stand. Not that it seemed to matter. John's strong arm around her, his hand cupping her buttocks, ensured she did not fall. Fall over, at any rate.

If she had not been in love with him before, she certainly was now.

How could anyone defend themselves from such an onslaught of hedonistic pleasure?

"J-John," Florence managed after a few heart-stopping minutes of him worshipping her breasts, a tugging ache pulling down from her nipples to her core.

He instantly raised his head, concern on his face. "Florence? I-I can stop, I—at least, I think I can stop. Dear God, you are so beautiful—"

Florence raised a hand and placed it on his lips, panting heavily at the wet sensation. He was so handsome, so charming . . . and he knew precisely what to do to please her.

A giddy combination.

"I need you to take me upstairs," she said.

And for some reason disappointment clouded John's eyes. "Of . . . of course. You wish to sleep, I have exhausted you beyond—you are my guest, and I will—"

Florence almost laughed, it was too amusing. The poor man had completely misunderstood her, and it would be cruel to let him to continue under that misunderstanding.

Wouldn't it?

"Here, let me—ah, I seem to have made rather a mess of your gown," John said awkwardly, trying to pull it and her corset up over her shoulders once more.

Trying to ignore the fluttering sensation as his fingers brushed against her skin, Florence said, "John, I actually meant—"

"Come on, upstairs with you, you must be exhausted," he said briskly, as though attempting to dampen all enthusiasm for what they had just so recently been enjoying together. "Come on."

Helpless against the propelling force that was John Chance, Florence clutched her gown about her and hoped to goodness they wouldn't run into anyone as they stepped into—

"Ah, my lord, Miss Bailey," said the butler as they entered the hallway. "I wondered if you—ah. Oh dear."

"Miss . . . Miss Bailey has suffered an accident," said John helplessly as he glanced at Florence with a red face. "An accident with her gown. Ahem."

"Ah," repeated the butler just as helplessly.

Mortification swept through Florence, as she had known it would, as she stood before the two men with her gown clutched to her.

And yet . . .

Yet it did not feel the same as the mortification that she had previously known. Oh, it was just as hot, scalding through her veins as though determined to burn them up. It was just as all encompassing, her whole body lost to the sensation.

But this was . . . pleasant.

Pleasant was not the right word. As the servant and John hastily muttered quickly about getting a guest bedchamber prepared, and the terrible storm, and how awful it would be for them to let Miss Bailey out into it, Florence tried to slow her breathing and understand what precisely it was that she was feeling.

When she discovered a word for it, the warmth in her cheeks only increased.

Because she was . . . *titillated.*

Titillated. By the idea that the butler knew precisely what she and

John had been doing. What they had been sharing. What John had been doing to her. And there was nothing the world could do to take that from her.

Florence could hardly believe it of herself. She was aroused merely by the knowledge that she and John had been caught.

What was wrong with her?

"—already prepared," the butler was saying, gaze averted. "Good evening, Miss Bailey."

"Th-Thank you," Florence managed to say, her mind whirling. "I app-preciate—"

But the butler had already gone, evidently so embarrassed by the discovery of his master and his future mistress that he had departed through the servants' corridor to the kitchens.

Florence and John walked up the staircase in silence. Somehow she had become disentangled from him, and she hated the distance that had crept up between them. A whole three inches.

How was such a thing to be borne?

John walked her along the upstairs passage, finally halting at a door right at the end of the corridor. "Here it is."

Florence glanced at the door. "Wh-What is?"

"The guest bedchamber," he murmured.

Leaning forward, he turned the handle, pushed open the door, and revealed . . .

Florence swallowed. *An unimaginably large bed.*

"You are very flushed." John sounded apologetic. "I hope—I know it was not ideal, running into Humphreys like that, but—"

"I liked it."

Florence clasped her hands over her mouth in shock at what she had revealed. What on earth had she been thinking? Or rather, had she even being thinking at all? What would John think of her—a harlot, no doubt, who found pleasure in the most perverse of ways!

His brow had furrowed. "I beg your pardon?"

"It's nothing," Florence said hastily, wishing to goodness he would be a gentleman and forget what she had said. "What a p-pleasant bedchamber it is—"

"Florence."

She met his gaze and knew she could keep nothing back from him. She had been about to offer him her very self, her body to worship and bring to climax, something she knew the whole of Society would consider completely indecent. Was she truly going to attempt to keep her innermost thoughts from the man she loved?

Swallowing hard, and wishing to goodness she weren't the first person in the world to feel this way, Florence pushed her hair behind her ears.

And only then realized that most of it was mussed and out of its pins.

Dear Lord, she must have looked a sight!

"I said, I liked it," Florence said in a small voice, hardly able to meet John's eyes. "I . . . oh, it was most strange, but someone knowing we had . . . that you had kissed me, and most likely disrobed me . . . it was exciting."

John's jaw tightened. "Exciting?"

She had never felt more wretched. Was it possible she was about to lose everything, just as she had been about to discover the exquisite hedonism two people could share? But she owed him this. She owed him honesty. She nodded.

John let out a ragged breath, as though attempting to get a hold of himself. Then—

"You are the most perfect woman who ever lived," he said, tilting his head as he examined her with a roguish grin. "I've never wanted to bed anyone more in my life."

Florence's lips parted in astonishment.

John groaned. "Particularly when you do that."

Her tongue darted out, wetting her bottom lip as she thought what to say, and—

This time he reached for her. "Are you attempting to seduce me?"

Florence's eyes widened. "No! No, I—"

"Because you are doing an excellent job of making it impossible for me to leave you here alone," John growled, pulling her tight into his embrace but apparently not wishing to kiss her. Not yet. "This is it, Florence."

She blinked, her pulse throbbing in her ears, between her legs. "It . . . it is?"

John nodded, his expression possessive as it swept over her. "Your last chance to retain your virtue. If you wish to leave this house in the morning still an innocent, then you need to—"

Florence did not care what she would need to do for such a thing. Leaning up on her toes, she kissed John as passionately as she was able. Did he not understand—could he not feel how much she desired him? Her lips parted his, her head turning to deepen the kiss, and her hand moved to—

John pulled away with a sudden gasp. "Florence!"

"I want you," she whispered, her heartbeat thundering along with the storm outside as she nervously stroked along the thick, heavy rod within his breeches. "Wh-What . . . what do I have to do to convince you, John?"

He moaned, his head falling onto her shoulder as though he could barely lift it. "You . . . Christ, you're doing an excellent job of it now."

Florence was surprised. All she was doing was stroking along his length, her fingers light and unsure of themselves. *This was good for him? Was it truly that easy?*

Her thumb twisted, brushing accidently on the tip of the hardness, and John shuddered. His hand scrabbled against the doorframe, holding onto it as though for dear life.

"You—I want—"

Florence smiled with delight as she increased the pressure ever so slightly of her fingers, and saw with gratified pleasure John shudder again.

Oh, to give pleasure like this—it was exquisite! She could do this every day, would like to.

She would also like to have John kiss her breasts again, now she came to think about it.

"Enough," John rasped, pulling back, but not away. He had stepped into the guest bedchamber and now pulled her through, closing the door behind them with a snap, making it quite clear what was about to happen.

Florence shivered. What she hoped would happen.

John was looking at her with a mixture of astonishment and delight. "I . . . I want you to take charge, Florence. Tell me what you want."

Her, in charge? "But I don't know—"

"Yes, you do," said John with a dry expression. "Far more than I could ever have predicted, I'll tell you that. I once said to you that I'd taken this off the table. And now it's back on, as it were, but I can't be the one to rush you. You need to ask."

Ask?

Florence glanced about the bedchamber as she attempted to collect her thoughts. It was not a large room, the majority of the space being taken up by the bed.

The bed.

Though there was naught but a candle in there, it was unlit. But that did not matter. Her eyes had already adjusted to the darkness, and she could see John clearly.

More clearly than she had ever seen him before.

"I-I want . . ." Florence swallowed, steadied herself. "I want to take off our clothes."

John's eyes gleamed. "Excellent."

It did not take long. They did not rush, but their evident hunger for each other enabled swift fingers to make light work of the layers keeping them apart from each other.

When Florence permitted her final undershift to fall, she quivered. Not from cold. The room was remarkably warm—that, or she was remarkably warm. Though her shyness surfaced, it did not overwhelm her. It was right to feel some apprehension when standing before one's lover entirely nude, wasn't it?

She looked up and saw—

Her breath caught in her throat. "Oh, John."

He was beautiful. Beautiful was not a word typically used for men, Florence knew, but it felt right. John had the sort of Greek profile that would have made Michelangelo weep. Strength and muscles, taut with the effort of not touching her, Florence thought with a thrill.

It was only a guess. But she had a feeling she was correct.

John was looking at her with much the same hunger that she felt herself.

"We should have done this before," Florence said as she stepped forward, her curious fingers reaching out to brush over his chest.

John chuckled, and she felt it as well as heard it. "What, months ago?"

"Many months ago," she quipped. "The first time we met."

His laughter returned. "I wasn't ready for you then. I wasn't worthy."

His fingers were mirroring her own. Florence arched her back as his thumb brushed over a nipple, then sighed with delight as his hands moved down her chest, curving over hips, not quite reaching—

"What makes you think you're worthy now?" Florence teased.

Every time she was worried that she had gone too far, John grinned and proved it was not far enough. "I suppose I deserved that."

"No," Florence said, her heart thumping but knowing she wanted this. "This is what you deserve."

There was a confused look on John's face as she said those words, and his confusion only increased as Florence slowly, slowly, lowered until she was kneeling before him. Before her eyes were the level of—

John gasped. "Florence!"

She would have replied if she had not parted her lips and taken in just an inch of his manhood into her mouth. As it was, her tongue was too busy tasting, shyly exploring him.

He hissed as his hand rested on her head. "You don't have to—oh, God, please don't stop . . ."

Florence placed her hands on his hips to steady herself, slowly taking in more and more of his throbbing flesh into her mouth. It was delightful, to taste him, the salty need of him, to feel the aching flex as he shuddered.

To give him pleasure . . . to share in this with him. That was all she wanted.

"Oh, God, yes," John groaned as Florence's lips finally met the base of his shaft. "Florence . . ."

Hearing her name moaned like that only caused the tugging ache in Florence to increase—and the determination to keep going.

So, what was she supposed to do now?

Drawing back, but not releasing his very tip, Florence starting to suckle, moving her head to pull more of him in, then less. More, then less. The rhythm felt natural, obvious, then—

She gasped as John pulled away, out of her reach. She blinked in the sudden shock of his absence. "J-John?"

"Damn," he breathed. "I've got to—I need—will you let me—"

"Yes," Florence whispered, still kneeling before him on the floor, looking up at him with devotion. "Yes."

There was a rumble in John's throat that she did not understand, but she did not need to. Reaching down to her and pulling her up, John tugged her toward the bed and encouraged her to lie back.

"I just need to make sure you are ready," he said. "I—Florence!"

Florence looked in alarm as John carefully drew a finger across her softness between her legs. "What is wrong?"

Nothing felt wrong. Everything felt right. The moment his finger had slid over her damp crease, an explosion of bliss had threatened to make her fall back.

She met John's gaze, which was filled with something she did not recognize.

"You . . . you're wet. So quickly."

Florence squirmed against the bed. "Is . . . is that wrong?"

John cursed under his breath. "Wrong? It's . . . it's the highest compliment you could ever give me."

She blinked. "It is?"

But she did not have the chance to ask any further questions. Before she could speak, before she could hope to understand what was happening, John had slowly parted her folds and slid his manhood within her.

Florence fell back on the bed, her lungs constricting, her whole body shaking. How could it not, when she was being so invaded, so—

And then pressure, the tightness, disappeared. It was replaced with . . .

Florence whimpered. "Oh, yes."

John cursed again, leaning on an elbow over her, teeth gritted as he slowly continued pushing into her. "You feel—"

"Yes," she moaned, unable to help herself, her hips tilting to take him deeper.

Because that was all she wanted. John, deep inside her, making her complete. As though an emptiness she'd always known was there, though she'd never been able to name it, was now somehow gone.

When John was sheathed to the hilt, he brushed away her hair from her eyes. "Are you—"

"More," Florence panted, hating that the sensations were fading as he remained still. "There . . . there must be more, isn't there?"

A look of devilish delight passed across John's face. "Oh, there's more."

All she could do was cling to him. Allow the pleasure to build as his rhythm built, as John started to move into her gently, then harder, harder, until he was pounding into her, every moment sending a new wave of sweet delight through Florence's body.

Every inch of her craved more, and as John leaned down his head to suckle at her breast, his free hand moved to touch the tip of her wetness just above his manhood.

And she exploded.

Florence could think of no other words—at least, afterward, when she could think. The frantic aching was excruciating, and she wanted more of it. It pulsed through her body, sharp like lightning, rolling like thunder, making it impossible to breathe as she came apart.

And John thrust heavily, crying out her name as he poured himself into her.

They clung to each other, tingling in the aftermath of their lovemaking. As John swept Florence up into his arms, holding her close, she knew that she would never feel this safe, this loved, this adored again.

Until, she thought with a teasing smile, her legs tangled in his. *Until next time.*

Chapter Fourteen

August 6, 1812

"You really are too kind," murmured Florence as John's stomach jolted.

Fine. Fine! Not just his stomach. Perhaps lower.

But they had relished each other again furtively in his guest bedchamber only yesterday, after a hasty lunch in which they had attempted to devour the food and not each other.

And also days before, when he had called upon Mrs. Bailey at their residence as a courtesy, only to discover—to their mutual delight—that it was only Miss Bailey who was in, not her mother, and that they were otherwise alone.

John tried to force away his wolfish smile now as he opened the opera box door for Florence and watched her pass through.

Slowly. Brushing up against him. Allowing him to breathe her in.

She was doing it on purpose. He had been foolish enough to admit to Florence only that day in the carriage ride to the opera house that he greatly enjoyed it when she purposely walked past him far too closely, brushing up against him.

Was she now going to do it each and every time she passed him?

John bit down a moan of anticipation and followed her into the box he had purchased for that evening. *God, he hoped so.*

"This is w-wonderful," said Florence with shining eyes as she looked about her. "Truly, I have n-never known anything like it!"

John's hopes fluttered as he heard the truth in her voice. He had never before known the pleasure of giving someone something they had not yet experienced.

Not *that*. Though, of course, also that.

But just experiences. The Chances had been brought to the opera since they'd been small boys. At least, when they were old enough to behave themselves.

Their mother had always adored the opera. There had been nothing like it, she had always said, for invigorating the spirit and charming the soul.

John's smile faltered, just a bit, as he continued to watch Florence stare about the place in wonder and delight. Goodness. When had he last thought about his mother? A good long while. Years. Almost decades.

"Thank you so much for the treat," said Florence as she settled herself in the plush red velvet chair. "It m-must have cost a fortune."

John's stomach lurched.

It had. Or at least, it had cost someone a fortune. He would have to hope Cothrom would not bother to look at his accounts until after the wedding, when he would be in a position to pay him back.

Forty-five thousand pounds.

Strange, it had also been a great deal of time since he had last thought about the dowry. Florence's dowry. It was a part of her, he supposed, and a part many gentlemen would have concentrated on.

He certainly had, when he had first heard.

So when had the dowry ceased to be of any interest, and the woman herself become all that he could think of?

"Come, sit," Florence said, glancing over her shoulder. "You can't stand there f-forever."

John nodded, and stepped around the chairs to seat himself beside her.

The stammer was back. It was something he was learning to understand better and better with each passing day. When it was just the two of them, in private, with no one else around them and nothing to interrupt their conversation, it almost completely disappeared. When they were in public, it was nearly impossible for Florence to string three words together without stammering.

And when they were like this, in an almost private space yet within the realm of Society, there was a halting lilt to her words. Like a bird learning its song.

"John?"

John blinked. Florence was gazing with concern. He must have been sitting there for a full minute without speaking.

He forced a smile, one which became natural as he took in the delicate red sheen of her hair, the diamond earbobs, the shell-pink lips pursed with concern. "I was just thinking."

"About what?" Florence asked quietly.

It was not like him to hesitate, but he had been thinking about this a great deal. Too much, if truth be told.

When to tell Florence he was in love with her.

Because he was. John could no longer deny it, and most importantly, he no longer wished to. Keeping that sort of truth from Florence no longer felt important, it felt ridiculous. Why should she not know just how deeply he felt about her?

Because, muttered the little voice in the back of his mind that always emerged in tricky situations such as these, *because you don't know, do you?*

Love? What did you know about it? How could you even tell?

Because he had never felt like this before, John reasoned with himself as Florence waited patiently for him to reply. Because everything in his being was centered not on himself, but on Florence.

Because her happiness was not just everything, it was the only thing.

Because being with her made his torso twist and his lungs constrict and everything in him shudder at the thought of not being with her.

What was that, if not love?

Sounds like lust to me, muttered the irritating voice. *And you've been in lust before, haven't you? And then what happened?*

"John?"

John swallowed. "Just . . . just admiring the view."

Florence, completely ignorant of the war in his mind, turned to look out over the balcony of their box. "Yes, I suppose it is spectacular."

He did not follow her gaze. He did not need to. He had seen it before, knew the Royal Opera House well. The hundreds of seats, the high ceiling designed for perfect sound, the wide stage with the red velvet curtain currently pulled across. There were the lights to ensure the stage could be seen by all. There was the orchestra pit, musicians currently tuning their violins, cellos, trumpets, oboes, all in readiment for the delightful performance. There was the conductor, arguing rapidly it seemed with someone in the Royal Opera House livery.

It was spectacle and glamor and splendor.

None of it was new. None of it was exciting. None of it was Florence.

After a moment, she turned back to him and flushed. "You're not looking at it."

"I'm looking at the view I was admiring," said John, allowing just a hint of a tease in his voice. "That's all."

And she flushed, yet continued to meet his eye with a boldness that accompanied her shyness without replacing it. "You do talk nonsense."

"Only most of the time," John quipped, his heart in his mouth.

Was that how she would take his admission of affection? As nonsense? Was it possible he had spoken so much nonsense in the past that Florence Bailey would not believe him when he professed his love?

He should have told her last week. That would have been the

intelligent thing to do, but then, John had not had much blood in his brain during the moment of lovemaking. Most of it had been . . . well. South of his brain.

Very far south.

And the trouble was, he was behind.

"John, I . . . I love you."

How Florence had found the courage to admit to such a thing, he did not know. It put him to shame, made it impossible to meet her eye at times.

John's chest swelled as he remembered the exact tone of Florence's voice as she had told him she loved him. She was so brave. So utterly beyond anything he deserved, he could well admit that.

And in just a few short days, they would be husband and wife.

He had to tell her. Now was as good a time as ever.

"Florence," John began.

"No."

He blinked. "Wh-What? What do you mean, no—"

"No, we are not going to make love in this opera box," Florence said smoothly, keeping her expression intact as her eyes glittered. "No . . . n-no matter how much we might want to."

John's stomach stirred. *Now that was an idea.* "I wasn't going to . . . though I like the idea that you were thinking of it, I must say."

It was Florence's turn to flush. "I-I thought . . . that you . . . John!"

"Don't you John me, you were the one thinking of it," he chuckled, delight soaring through him. Oh, that he had found a woman with such an appetite as this! "You, not me."

"You're making me flush," said Florence, raising a gloved hand to her cheek.

"Good. I'm trying to tell you how . . . how happy I am."

She stared for a moment, then lowered her hand to take his. "I am h-happy too."

Good, good, everything was good so far. But he wasn't just happy, was he? John had gone beyond happiness, beyond what he'd thought possible for two people to share. And not just in the bedchamber.

John sturdied himself, shuffling in his seat as he prepared himself to say the words. "It's just—after all this time, I had never thought. Damn. What I'm trying to say is . . ."

His voice trailed away as he stared into Florence's open expression.

Open, accepting, and far more caring than he had ever been. He did not deserve her.

"I-I d-don't want vultures circling me for my m-money. Ignoring me, happy to m-marry anyone attached to the numbers. I d-don't want to be w-wed for my b-bank balance. You need respectability. You aren't c-cruel. I chose you."

He most certainly would not deserve her if he could not bring herself to say the one thing that was left remaining between them to be said. That he loved her. That he loved no other, had never loved before—he was sure of that now. Now he knew what love was.

"We have a second chance," John said, his voice breaking, but he forced himself to keep going. "A second chance, one I never thought to—"

"Hush!" Florence said, squeezing his hand then releasing it.

John stared. *Hush?* Was that all she could say to him, just as he was about to pour his heart out and—

A moment later, he understood. The conductor had tapped on his music stand, the musicians were ready, and the curtain pulled back across the stage. The opera was about to begin.

John leaned back in his chair, disappointed.

Well, it was not as though he didn't like opera, he thought as the lamps were extinguished and the audience's attention was fixed upon the stage. The music started, crescendoed, filling all the air in the place.

But he had only just got up the courage to tell her. Tell Florence what she meant to him. He had to tell her.

John moved closer, leaning over the arm of his chair and suddenly breathing in the heady scent of flowers that was Florence. The scent dazzled him, interrupting for a moment his ability to think or even see. When he blinked, Florence had tilted her head.

"Watch the opera," she murmured. "You've paid for the seats, you should enjoy it!"

John tried to push aside the thoughts of cost from his mind. Future John could worry about that.

"I just wanted to say," he murmured in a low voice, just loud enough for her to hear over the soaring soprano who had taken to the stage. "Tell you, Florence, that—"

"Hush, I'm listening," she whispered, not turning to look at him this time, attention fixed on the stage.

John swallowed, then leaned back.

Well, he had tried. Not very hard, admittedly, and perhaps not in the best place. It had been foolish of him to attempt to tell Florence just how his heart ached for her in the middle of an opera.

Particularly this one. He'd forgotten how *Silvana* ended, until this moment.

Damn.

John managed to pay attention to the music for . . . what, about five minutes? It had to be at least that, though the aria the tenor was singing was still going on. The trouble was, the need to tell Florence he loved her had built up to such a fever pitch inside him, it had to come out now.

One way, or the other.

He leaned closer to her again. "Florence, I need to tell you—"

"I s-said hush," Florence said with a smile.

John took her hand in his. "But I—"

"John Chance, be quiet," she said with a teasing grin that made his stomach jolt. *Damn, he loved it when she ordered him around.* "Or . . ."

And he saw something new flicker in Florence's eyes. Something different, something he had never seen before.

A determination—no, that wasn't it. It was more like she had made a decision that she knew in some way was wrong, that was what it looked like. Yet even as he was able to identify it, the look did not disappear. If anything, it just grew stronger.

Florence turned to look at him fully, and John's manhood twitched at the calm possession of her expression. "I told you to be quiet. But that d-doesn't mean . . . doesn't mean you cannot show me what you wanted to say."

John blinked. "Show you?"

What on earth did the woman mean? They were at the opera, there was surely sufficient entertainment before them. She did not wish for . . . oh, an interpretative dance, did she? He was hardly suited to—

"W-With your fingers," Florence breathed, curling her own around his before placing his hand on her thigh. "Show me."

John stared at his hand on her thigh, then back to Florence's eyes.

She didn't . . . she couldn't mean what he . . . could she?

Florence gave him a shy look. "I'd like that."

Oh, hell.

John swallowed. Well, there was only one way to find out whether he had guessed correctly, and that was to make the attempt.

Dear God, if he was right, he most certainly did not deserve her.

Their box had been chosen carefully. John had known Florence would not wish to be gawped at by the *ton* at large, so had selected a box that was at all angles almost impossible for anyone in the main audience to look in at them. As far as they were concerned, it was an empty box.

That meant that as long as they were careful . . .

John shifted in his chair, selecting a good angle, then leaned to place a kiss on Florence's left shoulder. "You're sure?"

She quivered at his touch, the sensation of his breath caressing her skin. Then nodded.

Try as he might, John could not prevent a sigh escaping his lips. He had known, one day, he would marry. He had hoped to find a woman he could stomach for more than twenty minutes together. That was, it appeared, a success in the eyes of Society. It was certainly more than most gentlemen managed.

To find a woman like this—shy yes, but passionate—was more than he could have hoped. And now . . .

John's fingers curled around Florence's thigh, almost moaning aloud at the responsiveness of her body. Though her stays, he could see her nipples peaking. She wanted him. She wanted—

She probably did not even know what she wanted. That was fine. He knew what he could give her.

Slowly, inch by inch, John's fingers curled together and crept the fabric of Florence's skirt up. Up, past her ankle. Up, past her knee. Up, until—

"John," Florence breathed.

It was encouragement, he could tell. There was a need in that voice he had heard before. He was starting to know it well.

Swallowing hard at the outrageous thing he was about to do, John's fingers skimmed the silk of Florence's stocking. Higher, higher, until he reached flesh. Warm, quivering flesh. Her thigh was even warmer now there wasn't two layers of fabric between them. And if he just trailed his fingers here, curving down her thigh toward—

Florence moaned, shifting her hips, pushing her buttocks down the seat so her secret place reached his fingers sooner.

For an instant, John closed his eyes, unable to take in the sight of her panting eagerness. Then his eyes snapped open again. He didn't want to miss a moment of this.

Biting his lip from stopping himself from muttering her name, John slowly trailed a finger along her slit. She was wet. Though he had promised himself he would go slowly, it was impossible to restrain his eagerness. He slipped a finger inside her.

"J-John."

"You said," he pointed out in a dark voice. "You said to show you.

This is how I can show you."

His pulse was throbbing in his ears and it wasn't the only part of him that was throbbing, but John forced himself to remain controlled.

So, he couldn't tell Florence that he loved her.

But he could damn well show her.

Slowly, he curled the finger inside her, luxuriating in her wetness, the welcome her body gave him. He stroked, moaning at the whimper Florence gave as her body twitched.

She deserved more. He needed to give it to her.

Not ceasing the gentle stroke he had already begun with one finger, John gradually slipped in another. And then a third. Florence's softness welcomed in, swelling against him as her ardor increased.

Soon her breathing was ragged, her hips twisting against him, and still John did not turn to look at her. There was something intoxicating about touching her like this, pleasuring her like this as they both watched the opera continuing before them on the stage—as though they were just here to experience a little light culture.

While instead, Florence was experiencing the twisting, flickering worship of his fingers inside her.

The mere thought almost made John come, but he forced himself to concentrate on her delight. It was Florence who needed to know how much she was adored, how precious she was.

How she was everything.

"Florence," John murmured as he slowly increased his rhythm. There was no answer. "Florence."

"Y-Y-Yes," Florence gasped. "Yes, yes, yes—"

"I have something to tell you, and you can't stop me now," he said with a teasing grin. "You're in my power."

"N-No I'm—"

"And I'm in yours," admitted John, just loudly enough for her to hear. "I'm going to make you come, Florence, and there's nothing you can do about it."

She whimpered again, her hands gripping the arms of the chair, and though she could pull away from him, force him to stop, ask him to stop and he would—she remained there, at the mercy of his lovemaking.

And just as she was about to reach her peak, when he could feel the thrumming pace of her nub, John closed the gap between his lips and Florence's ear, and whispered three short words.

"I love you."

Florence spasmed, her cry swallowed up by the bellowing duet on the stage. Her body quivered, her quim tightening around his fingers as her core exploded, and John could have wept to feel and see the pleasure that he gave her.

This was it. This was everything.

He could spend the rest of his life pleasing this woman and receiving nothing in return, and it would be enough.

Florence was more than enough.

Eventually she stilled. A few moments after that, she blinked a few times before meeting his eyes.

"That . . . that was . . ."

"I know," John said with a wicked smile, his pulse thundering as though it had been he himself who had been brought to a peak. His fingers shifted within Florence's folds and she gasped, a gasp that became a moan as he started to gently stroke. "Ready for a second?"

Chapter Fifteen

August 9, 1812

"AND NO MORE arguments," said Mrs. Bailey firmly. "I've had enough of these blessed arguments, and I simply won't have any more of them!"

Florence stood silent, red faced, and hating every moment she was forced to be here. Beside her mother. While she berated their housekeeper.

"But Mrs. Bailey," said Mrs. Harris quietly, "it is simply not possible. Without a gardener—"

"I will not have men peering at me through my own windows!" retorted Florence's mother, her voice rising in volume to a fever pitch, so loud it could almost certainly be heard from the street. Even with the front door closed. "The very idea! Why, my mother would have had a fit. No peeping Toms in this household—"

"B-But M-Mama," interjected Florence as calmly as she could. It did not matter. Her mother glared at her fiercely, increasing the discomfort in Florence painfully. "The g-gardener was not p-peeping at you, he was m-merely tying b-back the wisteria ag-gainst the—"

"I could have been . . ." Mrs. Bailey took a deep breath, then murmured *sotto voce*, "without certain clothes."

"Th-Then why d-didn't you c-close the curtains?" Florence could not help but ask.

It was a reasonable question. At least, it was a reasonable question when asked to anyone in the world except her mother.

Despite Florence's great desire for the conversation to be closed, the poor unfortunate gardener to have his job back, and the whole matter to be forgotten, it did not seem she was to receive her wish. Not if her mother had anything to do with it.

"Outrageous behavior, behavior I will not permit to continue," Mrs. Bailey was muttering as she pulled on her gloves. "And that's an end to it. Carriage!"

If Florence could have her own way—something she had not yet been permitted within the bounds of her home—she would not have taken her mother with her. She would have gone alone, or perhaps invited Miss Quintrell, if she was feeling very brave.

After all, one did not just take anyone to the modiste with you for . . . for this sort of appointment.

As it was, her mother had not insisted. She had assumed. And Florence did not have sufficient energy within her to argue.

Which had been her first mistake.

Her second mistake was, when they arrived at Madame Jacques's, to not immediately answer the question that was put to her by the proprietress. "You will wish to view your choices alone, Mademoiselle Bailey?"

But Florence would have had to have been very quick to reply before her mother cut in.

"Of course not," Mrs. Bailey said curtly. "Alone? How on earth will my daughter be able to make any decisions if she is attempting to do so alone? What poppycock! Move aside, good woman."

Barging past Madame Jacques to enter the private fitting rooms of the modiste, Mrs. Bailey's voice could be heard berating the assistant she had discovered there. "Who are you? What are you doing here? Do you know who I am?"

Florence inhaled deeply, closing her eyes for a moment to collect herself before shooting an apologetic look at the modiste.

Thankfully Madame Jacques understood the situation at once. "All mothers are highly excited about their daughter's trousseau," she said softly. "It is important not to be concerned, ma petite. It will all be over soon."

It could not be over soon enough. For a heartbeat, as Florence followed her mother's footsteps into the private area of the modiste, she wondered if it would have been preferable to bring her brother rather than her mother. As though that would have been an option. There would have been a small riot in the modiste's if a man had come in.

Or if she could not have her brother, a small voice whispered in the back of her mind, *perhaps John could have—*

No. They had already done so many outrageous things, Florence thought with flushed cheeks as she watched her mother argue with Madame Jacques about what true blue thread really was. She and John had pushed the boundaries of Society far more than she had even thought possible. Could she really even consider bringing him to a modiste's final fitting for . . . for this?

Florence swallowed. *Absolutely not.*

"Where's this wedding gown?" Mrs. Bailey was saying petulantly, after being thoroughly schooled on the difference between blue and aqua thread. "I don't see it. I was told—"

"Mrs. Bailey," said Madame Jacques smoothly, stepping forward to rescue her poor assistant from the onslaught. "How pleasant to see you again. If you will come this way—"

"I want to see the trousseau," interrupted Mrs. Bailey with seemingly little concern for her daughter. "Where is it? I demand to see—"

"It is over there, look through it at your leisure," Madame Jacques said, in perhaps a slightly sharper tone.

Florence tried to hide a smile. There were few people who could stomach her mother's tone for long when she was being this abrasive.

Mrs. Bailey glanced over at the expanse of clothes elegantly folded on a table, and sniffed. "Excellent. I will ensure they are of the quality we—"

"Miss Bailey," said Madame Jacques. "This way."

It was a small relief to step into a part of the modiste's which her mother could not—or at least, should not—enter. Standing on a small step and allowing Madame Jacques and another assistant to carefully place the wedding gown upon her, Florence attempted not to think about what would be coming in the next few days.

The wedding.

Not that she did not wish to be married. Quite the opposite. It felt as though the day itself was a long time coming. After all, John may love her now . . .

"I love you."

. . . but she had been in love with him for over two years. It was about time, Florence thought with flushing cheeks, that he noticed her for what and who she was.

No, being married to John was precisely what she wished for.

But the wedding itself, that was the trouble. Hundreds of people, for a marquess could not get wed without being forced to invite half the *ton*. All of them staring, watching her as she walked up the aisle.

A lump caught in Florence's throat as her lungs contracted. That was what she dreaded.

At least, she thought as her fingertips smoothed the fine silk of the gown which was having its final buttons done up, she would be wearing a most beautiful gown. Hopefully they could merely look at the gown, and not her.

"Voila," said Madame Jacques. "Here, ma petite, turn. The looking glass."

Taking a deep breath, and telling herself that no matter the reflection, she was not going to endure another fitting, Florence turned around.

And her lips parted.

There in the looking glass was a woman who looked a little like her. She had the same flaming red hair, the same hazel eyes, though they were wider than normal. Her lips and nose were precisely the same as hers, and they were even a similar height, if one took into account the box.

But the gown . . .

It was a masterpiece. Flowing just where it should flow and tucking in at just the right places, the fabric seemed to be more water than silk. The color was a delicate green, pale and shimmering in the sunlight streaming through the windows. The delicate embroidery at the cuffs, hem, and bodice in a rich gold seemed to heighten her coloring, not overwhelm it.

And that was it. It was simple, elegant, more refined than Florence had imagined when Madame Jacques had attempted to explain it to her.

Shaking, Florence lifted a hand. The woman in the looking glass did the same thing.

It was her. This was to be her wedding gown.

Tears threatened to tingle at the corners of her eyes. Florence brushed them away.

"A gown deserving of you, I think," said Madame Jacques quietly.

Florence gave a laugh which choked in her throat. "I am not sure—I don't think—"

"What in God's name is this?" screeched a familiar voice.

Florence allowed her hand to fall to her side as she sighed heavily. Naturally she could not have a moment of perfect happiness in public when her mother was accompanying her. That would be too much to hope for.

She swallowed the words, just in case she was tempted to say them. That was always the trouble, wasn't it? That she wished to speak such cruel things. Thankfully she always managed to hold her tongue.

She had to hold her tongue.

"I will deal with this," Madame Jacques said magnificently, casting a look at her assistant before sweeping out.

Florence turned, heart thumping. It was too much to hope, as raised voices became indistinguishable as they mingled over each other, that Madame Jacques could manage her mother alone.

No, she would have to follow. Another moment of her life she would never get back.

Steeling herself for a rather unpleasant conversation, Florence stepped down from the box despite the assistant's murmurs and followed the noise.

"—certainly not what my daughter ordered, and I think it shameful you are trying to pass off your second rates goods on—ah, there you are, Florence," said her mother forcefully, cheeks scarlet. "You will not believe the outrage you have been subjected to!"

Far be it from me to point out that you are always the one subjecting me to outrage, Florence thought darkly.

Aloud, she said, "Wh-What appears t-to b-be the—"

"This, this is the problem," Mrs. Bailey said darkly, pointing at a few garments on the table of the trousseau. "Your Madame Jacques is attempting to palm off goods on you which you most certainly did not order!"

It was unlikely. Florence had never met a more gentle saleswoman. When she had come to choose her trousseau from the elegant patterns, the little booklet, and a few samples which Madame Jacques had offered her, she had not forced Florence to buy anything.

Which was why she stepped over to the offending part of the trousseau in question. If there had been a misunderstanding, all Florence had to do was—

The instant she reached the table and saw what her mother was pointing at, Florence's cheeks burned.

Oh, dear Lord. No.

"—will not have it," her mother was saying in a stream of outrage.

"No self-respecting woman would ever dream of ordering such a thing, it is an insult to think—"

Florence attempted to swallow past the knot in her throat as she picked up the more delicate items she had ordered.

Silk, and lace, and clever designs which hid as much as they revealed. Which was a great deal. The undergarments she had, blushingly, asked Madame Jacques to include in her trousseau. For . . . for sleeping in.

Or not sleeping in, as the case may be.

"—woolen flannel is more than sufficient for one's sleeping attire," her mother was saying loudly for the whole world to hear. "I cannot imagine why any woman would wish—"

"M-Mother," Florence said hastily, turning around and wishing to goodness she could get her mother to stop talking. "Please. I-I ordered these, th-th-there is no m-mistake, and M-Madame Jacques—"

"She is attempting to take advantage of you, Florence, and you are such an innocent you don't even know it," said her mother dismissively as she waved a hand. "The last thing you need is—"

Oh, hell.

Florence had never thought her mother would ever discover the two or three elegant silk things she had chosen for her nightclothes. She had been shy about them, to be sure, when Madame Jacques had shown her the last few pages of the pamphlet.

"For the new bride," the modiste had said in a low tone without judgment. "Something a little different. All the rage in Paris, I assure you, and very . . . popular. With the gentlemen."

Florence's eyes had widened when she had seen the designs, but immediately understood what the woman had meant. And she wanted to look nice for John. Wanted to do something different. Show him just how adventurous she could be.

She had not expected her mother to discover that same adventurous spirit.

"—never been so insulted in all my—"

"Mother," Florence said firmly.

Mrs. Bailey blinked. "What?"

"I ordered these," said Florence, attempting to keep her voice as steady as possible. "It . . . it is n-no mistake. Please, you d-do not have to—"

"But these aren't going to keep you warm, are they?" Mrs. Bailey said with a confused expression. "No self-respecting mother would allow her daughter to do such a thing. Mine certainly would not have, and she'd have been quite right. Honestly, I don't know what you were thinking. You may as well not even be wearing—"

"That is the idea, Mother," Florence said wretchedly. *Oh, Lord, it was excruciating to discuss this in public, but apparently she had little choice.* "It is not for warmth, but . . . b-but for . . . well. You know."

There was silence in the modiste's. The women all stood, like a tableau, as the information the bride was attempting to tell her mother started to sink in.

Mrs. Bailey's nostrils flared. "I certainly do know—the question is, how do you?"

Oh, this was a disaster. How on earth was Florence ever going to look her mother in eye again?

"No, we'll be sending those back," Mrs. Bailey was saying to the modiste. "Burn them, for all I care, they're fit for nothing. We need five woolen flannel, full length, long sleeved—"

"Mother," said Florence, stomach churning as she attempted to find the strength to say what must be said. "Mother, I—"

"Miss Bailey made her order," Madame Jacques was saying calmly to her mother. "And it is Miss Bailey who is my client, Miss Bailey who is getting married—"

"I am her mother!"

"Mother, if you w-will j-just listen—"

"And I will not permit her to offer herself out to anyone, not even her husb—"

"Will you be quiet!" Florence thundered.

The modiste's fell silent. Her mother turned, mouth agape, to stare with abject shock.

Florence was panting so heavily, her shoulders were rising and falling at a great pace. But every other inch of her body seemed to have been turned to stone, muscles grinding against each other as she forced herself to take each breath.

This was it. No going back. The words had spilled from her mouth and now she had to continue.

"I am paying for these clothes with my own money," said Florence levelly, not taking her eyes from her mother. "My pin money, Mama. And that means that I get to make the decisions."

"But—"

"No buts," said Florence, far more confidently than she felt. *Was she truly doing this?* Finally standing up to her mother, and about frilly undergarments? In public? "It is my decision, I say, and I have made it. I wish to have them. I wish to wear them."

Her mother's eyes widened. "No daughter of mine—"

"Then I am not a daughter of yours!" snapped Florence, unable to help herself.

The words hung about the air like an echo of a minor chord with the notes all wrong, discordant.

Mrs. Bailey closed her mouth, her expression astonished but her demeanor—finally—silent.

Florence tried to force her lungs to calm, but it was impossible. This had been in the making for years, she knew. Building up, layer upon layer. Frustrations, irritations, anger.

And now it was pouring out. All she had to do was stem the tide.

"I . . . I appreciate your concern, but that sort of matter is no longer a concern of yours," Florence said quietly, her fingers brushing the silk of her wedding gown as though she could draw some sort of power from it. "And I—"

"But it's scandalous," whimpered her mother, seemingly unable to help herself. "Those clothes, they are—"

"What you decide to wear in bed is your own business," interrupted Florence, her cheeks flushing with heat. "As what I wear is mine."

She held her mother's look for what felt like a thousand years. The moment certainly stretched out far longer than she would have thought possible.

And then her mother blinked.

"Fine. Fine!" she said, pulling herself upright and glaring, cheeks pink and eyes inexplicably filled with what looked like pain. "If you wish to be wanton, to disgrace yourself before your husband, so be it! I wash my hands of you!"

Before Florence could even consider a response, Mrs. Bailey sniffed in the general direction of Madame Jacques, then marched out of the place. The door slamming behind her echoed around the modiste's.

Florence stared. She . . . she'd done it. She had finally spoken up for herself, spoken against her mother.

And the world had not ended. She was not crippled with doubt, with anxiety about what she had said. No regret accosted her.

She was . . . free.

"Well said, mon amie," said Madame Jacques with a smile across her lips. "Now, let's get you out of that gown, shall we? The whole trousseau can be delivered today if—"

"To Aylesbury House," said Florence with a dry smile. "I-I have a f-feeling it may not be safe if delivered to me."

The modiste gave her a gracious look. "As you wish."

Her heart was aflame and her spirits high as she stepped out of Madame Jacques's half an hour later. To think she had come so far, done so much in such a short amount of time. Finally spoken up to her mother! It was surely the most adventurous thing she would do tod—

"Florence!" said a voice she knew well as she walked along the pavement.

Then he was kissing her—John, his lips pressed against hers in a hurried anguish of desire, his hands around her waist.

It was over before Florence could truly appreciate it. John had pulled back, an expression of regret on his face.

What on earth—

Then she registered the gasps of outrage and shock that were surrounding them.

Florence looked about her. There was Mrs. Marnion, looking astonished. Lady Jenkins, a hand over her mouth. There were a gaggle of gentlemen over there, including Viscount Braedon, who were muttering together with wide eyes.

In fact, everyone on the street looked flabbergasted to see two people kissing—*kissing!*—in public.

"I am sorry," John murmured in an undertone, stepping close enough for her to hear but not so close that they would attract even more attention. "I thought—well, to be honest, I didn't think. I just—"

"Kissed me," said Florence happily, smiling up into the eyes of the man she loved.

John's smile was faint, but nevertheless discernable. "Yes, but that was selfish. I . . . well, I know how much you hate attention."

He was right. She did hate attention. But this was different—this was proof, public proof, that he adored her. How could she dislike that?

"Any attention b-because of you I will take," said Florence impulsively, slipping her hand into his arm. "But in recomp-pense, you must w-walk me home."

John's eyes glittered. "You drive a hard bargain."

After a few minutes of walking arm in arm, Florence's shoulders melted their tension and they left behind the gawpers who were surely sending gossip around the whole *ton* as they went.

And a question Florence had never asked crept into her mind. "Are you nervous?"

"Right now?"

She tapped at his arm as her pulse beat faster. "No, I m-mean . . . about the wedding."

John did not reply immediately, and when he did, his voice was low. "This all started as a marriage of convenience. Something that would take you out of the public eye, give me respectability. That was all we wanted."

Florence's stomach lurched. Not entirely all she wanted, but she would let him believe that. For now.

"And I could never have predicted this—all of this," said John, squeezing her hand. "I'm so happy, Florence—damn, sorry. Miss Bailey. God, I much prefer being in private with you."

She saw the gleam in his eye and knew precisely what he was thinking. "I always h-hoped it would be l-like this. I . . . well, I rather th-thought you might f-fall in love with me the f-first time round."

They had stepped across a street as she spoke, and so she did not concern herself that John did not reply as they navigated a cart speeding up and a carriage which rumbled past them.

When they reached the other side of the road, however, John was still silent. A pensive look had fallen across his face, and the longer he remained quiet, the greater Florence's nerves grew.

Had she transgressed, somehow? Should she not have mentioned—

"I was an idiot not to fall in love with you all those years ago," said John. "I hate that I needed a second chance with you—and I am going to do my utmost to ensure that I do not need a third."

Chapter Sixteen

August 11, 1812

JOHN SWORE AT his reflection.

"If your lordship would like a little help with—"

"I can do it," he said gruffly, turning back to the damned mirror with his damned cravat and his damned thumbs. "It's not like it is difficult, after all."

His valet, wisely, remained silent.

It was ridiculous. John had told himself he could get himself ready to see Florence without the help of another, and in many cases, that was true. He was mentally prepared. Their wedding was only a few days away, and this would be the last time they would see each other until then.

Florence had been most clear. She was a traditionalist, she had said with a smile, in most cases.

A smile crept across John's lips as he remembered the cases in which they had been most untraditional.

And as he was about to see Florence for the last time for two days, a length of time which felt impossible to go without her, that meant he wanted to look good.

"Ouch!"

John wrung his hand, his thumb throbbing after being trapped so perfectly within the fabric of his cravat. *Who knew these things could be so complicated?*

"I really do think—"

"I don't need your help, go on with you," said John—not unkindly. "If I need you, I'll ring the bell."

His valet gave him a look. It was a look that said, without any words needing to be spoken, that John was out of his depth, that cravats were some of the most complicated machinery in the world, and that he was being an idiot attempting to tie it himself.

However, the words out of the man's mouth were, "Very good, my lord."

The door closed behind him. John turned with a heavy sigh back to his looking glass.

It was probably ridiculous of him to attempt this, but there was something so delightful about preparing to see Florence on his own. Even if his thumbs were suffering for it.

His patience was also suffering. After another ten minutes had gone by and John had still managed to do nothing but get one end of the fabric tied in a knot he could not undo, he was starting to wonder whether calling his valet back would be the worst idea. After all, at any moment—

A heavy jangling echoed around the house.

John cursed under his breath.

Less than a minute later, the door to his dressing room opened and a footman dressed in livery stepped in, bowing low. "My lord, Miss Bailey is—"

"Yes, yes, and right on time, too," said John with a grin, unable to help himself.

He wasn't completely dressed. His cravat was still misbehaving, he had not permitted his valet to attire him with his waistcoat, and he had no idea where his jacket was. He wasn't, however, completely undressed, either.

Pushing past the footman, John stepped onto the landing and clasped the bannisters with both hands. "Florence?"

A face came into view, looking up the staircase with a frown. "John?"

"I'm almost ready for you, but not quite," he called, feeling foolish for his delay.

What, was he a popinjay now who spent more time in front of the looking glass than actually with his guests?

It appeared the same line of thinking was moving through Florence's mind. As she called up to him, there was a teasing lilt in her voice that he had only recently started hearing. "H-Have you b-beautified yourself for m-me?"

John considered swearing again, but there was a chance she could hear him, and that would never do.

Besides, his stomach was too busy lurching as he recalled Florence's own beauty. The luscious hair which had only yesterday been spread across his pillow. The soft skin which had been under his fingertips. The liquid desire in her eyes as she had—

"In y-your own t-time, I'm sure!"

John grinned. "I won't be long!"

That, of course, was a matter of opinion. He strode back into his dressing room but left the door open so he could still call out to Florence down the staircase, and frowned decidedly at the cravat in the reflection of his looking glass.

He was not going to be outdone by a scrap of fabric. He was a Chance! He was the Marquess of Aylesbury!

After another minute, John was almost ready to admit he was going to be outdone by a scrap of fabric.

"D-Do you plan to be late to our w-wedding, too?" called out a teasing voice.

John's stomach slipped sideways, as though the whole earth had decided to take a sudden lurch to the left.

Their wedding.

Two days away. Two days! That was almost nothing. The day

after tomorrow. Just two more sleeps, and he would be standing at the top of an aisle waiting for his bride.

His Florence.

It seemed almost ridiculous that just a few months ago, he could barely recall her name. She had been a mere passing flirtation, someone to entertain him while he had been bored. True, the kiss they had shared had been one of the best of his life, but it had been something he had been able to forget.

The idea of forgetting her now . . .

"There are t-two letters here!"

John nodded, forgetting for a moment that Florence was still downstairs in the hall waiting for him. She must have noticed the silver tray Humphreys was in the habit of placing on the dresser in the hall. John's habits were so varied, it was apparently impossible to find him when the post arrived. Easier to just place it there, by the front door, so the master could collect his letters when he came in.

"I bet one of them is from Cothrom," John called, frowning as he attempted to pull his cravat through the small hole he had managed to make.

There we go—a small twist there, a tug there—

"Your brother?"

John swore under his breath. Somehow the damned thing had fallen apart in his fingers. How on earth had that happened?

"J-John?"

"Wh—oh, yes, my brother," said John with a lazy grin, thinking of the oldest Chance. "He promised to send me some marital advice, God help us."

"N-Not sure if we need that," came the coquettish reply.

John's manhood twitched in his breeches. Dear Lord, she was a minx. Shouting that in their own house—as though no servant could possibly hear!

Oh, their marriage was going to be something special. Something different from all the staid, dull marriages made in Society every year.

Not for them the tired, polite mutterings of a couple who were forced together.

No, their lives were going to be full of passion, and—

Laughter echoed up the staircase and into his dressing room. "It has your brother's seal! What do you th-think it says?"

John groaned. "Heaven knows."

As long as the man did not attempt to give him advice for the bedchamber, he supposed he could take it with relative equanimity. The man did mean well. Cutting him from the family fortune was perhaps one of the best things Cothrom had ever done for him, after all.

Though he would of course never admit to such a thing.

"Open it up," John called, hoping the letter would suitably distract Florence from how long he was taking to come down. "You'll see how he berates me all the time!"

There was silence below as Florence undoubtedly took up his suggestion and read through the damned letter.

Perhaps Alice, Cothrom's wife, had advised him on the guidance, John thought wryly as he attempted, for what felt like the hundredth time, to tie the damned cravat. Now that would be interesting. Alice had certainly brought a calm to his brother's life that had never been there before. Perhaps her advice would be worth listening to.

So focused on his fingers and thumbs was John as he finally—finally—managed a serviceable knot that for a few minutes, he did not think about the letter from his brother which was undoubtedly being read downstairs. He did not think about it as he searched for his waistcoat, which had slipped to the carpet, or his jacket, which had been carefully folded then hidden by his nightshirt.

It was only as he buttoned up his waistcoat that John called out, "So, what is the old man complaining about this time?"

And Florence did not answer.

John frowned as he picked a little fluff from his jacket. It could not be that bad, could it? He had been honest . . . well, mostly honest with Florence about his own faults. She certainly already knew a great deal more about him than most people. Even his brothers. Especially his brothers.

And he knew her. Yes, he knew her, John thought with a grin as he slipped on his jacket. "You're not offended, are you?"

And still there was no answer.

A thrum of foreboding shivered through John's chest. It was most unusual for Florence not to answer him, even if she was having difficulty with her words.

Perhaps she was overcome by the well wishes, John thought as he found his top hat and glanced at his reflection to check he was suitably attired. Yes, that had to be it. Perhaps Cothrom had overdone the thing, his relief at having his younger brother married dripping out onto the page in an excess of enthusiasm.

As he left his dressing room and descended the stairs, it was to see Florence standing in the hallway, wearing an elegant gown covered with a spencer jacket and a reticule hanging from her arm. She was holding a letter. Her eyes did not depart from it as he approached her.

"What is Cothrom complaining about?" asked John jovially, repeating his question.

And Florence did not look up. Neither did she reply. She merely stood there, her face pale—far paler than normal, now he came to think about it.

John's pulse skipped a beat. "What is it?"

Only then did Florence look up. As she did so, the piece of paper in her hands moved. Became two.

There were two pieces of paper. Most strange. Had she opened two letters—or had Cothrom really had that much to say?

"I think," said Florence tranquilly, "this is yours."

John stood at the bottom of the stairs, mystified, as the woman he loved held out one of the pieces of paper to him. She did not meet his eye.

What could Cothrom have written to upset her so? Perhaps his brother, John thought darkly, had attempted to be funny and failed. Well, the man had many fine qualities, he would be the first to say that, but his humor—

"Take it," she said, still not meeting his eyes.

His curiosity overwhelming him, John obeyed. He reached out and took the paper, noticing curiously how Florence managed to pass it to him while not once touching his fingers. The lack of contact burned like ice.

He looked at the paper.

I promise that I am only marrying Florence Bailey for her money. For her stupendous dowry, and nothing else.

John Chance, Aylesbury

John's stomach lurched painfully and a roaring echoed through his ears, making it impossible to think.

No. No, this was not happening—this was a disaster. How could this have happened?

He looked up and saw Florence's face. Saw the hurt, the pain, the distrust. Saw the confidence they had built in one another, the connection which had grown since that fateful day when she had suggested a marriage of convenience, all fade away.

He had to fix this.

"Florence, I can explain—"

"I don't want to hear it," Florence said quietly. There was no cordiality in her voice, but also no censure. Just dull acceptance of an ending.

His heart rebelled at that, refusing to accept this was over.

Over? It could not be over. He loved Florence Bailey, and this was all one tremendous mistake. One of his own making, to be sure, but that meant he could unmake it.

He had to unmake it.

John took a step forward and hated that Florence immediately took a step back. "I know how it looks. It looks bad."

"You know what I said, how I felt about—ab-bout men wanting me only for my dowry," she said dully.

The flaring panic was making it impossible to think. "And that's not me, I would never—"

"You wrote it," Florence said faintly. "It is in your hand. Your signature at the—"

"I never thought you would see it," John said desperately.

It was the wrong thing to say. Something like fire flickered, just for a moment, in the eyes of the woman he loved. "I s-see. Well, that is—"

"No, you don't see—damn, I'm doing this all wrong!"

"I q-q-quite agree," Florence said in a monotone. "I s-suppose I sh-should have seen th-this after the w-wedding, when it was t-too—"

"No! Look, I can explain," John said fiercely, his pulse racing.

He had to explain. Had to, because Florence was looking at him as though he were a stranger. As though the idea of marrying him would be a torment, a punishment.

"I don't w-want to hear any explan—"

"You have to hear, because I love you, Florence," John said urgently, reaching out to take her hand.

Florence moved away. "S-Someone who l-loved me wouldn't—"

"Florence, please!"

He had never had anything to lose, not like this. Oh, his reputation, his name, but what did they matter? Only someone like Cothrom cared about such inconsequential things.

They were nothing to this. Florence clearly wished she were anywhere else. The pain in her expression could not have been plainer if he had hurt her, physically hurt her. It was as though he had bruised her soul, brought up welts across her heart as she saw him now for who he truly was.

A man always in need of a second chance.

"When I wrote that, I was being teased by my brother—I would never normally do such a thing, I was showing off," John said, waving his hands as though that could explain it, his words tumbling over each other in his haste to speak.

Florence's gaze was brutal in its clarity. "You s-still wrote it. It's your words—"

"I don't think that way anymore!"

"But you did," she said, her voice quavering in the force of her words. "You did, John. You looked at me and you thought, there's a pile of money just waiting to be—"

John swore under his breath. Yes, it had been about the money. At the beginning. But that had been so long ago—so long ago that he could barely recall feeling that way.

Not loving Florence? It was a different man, a different John. Not the one that stood before her, panicking that he had lost everything. How could he prove it to her?

"You have to believe me," he said forcefully.

Florence did not blink. "I do not."

"Everything we have shared together, since I wrote that stupid note, it has meant so much to me!"

"How can I possibly believe—"

"Choose to believe!" begged John.

Florence's eyes burned into him. "Choose to be lied to, choose t-to—"

"That is not what I said, and you know it," John said hotly, trying to keep his temper at bay. "Fine, I need money!"

The words echoed in the hall.

It was too late to save his dignity, but John didn't care about that. He barreled forward. "I ran out of money, gambled it away—didn't you notice that no matter where we went, I didn't play any game for money? And Cothrom, he cut me off, said he'd send me to the countryside in disgrace, and I thought—"

"You thought you could just marry a fortune."

John hesitated. Truth. That was what he had to tell, no matter the pain. "Yes—no . . . not exactly. And when I saw you, at the Knights'—"

"I see." Florence swallowed, hard, then said, "I should have known I was not the prize, but only my dowry. I just . . . I never thought you, of all—"

"I love you, Florence!"

"Will you let me finish?"

Such desperation was flowing through him, it was becoming difficult to prevent the words from spilling out. A voice at the back of his mind cried out that Florence hated being interrupted, but he did not seem to have the power to call back his sentences.

"It changed, don't you see, our marriage of convenience, it changed," he said, speaking over Florence once again. "And I had completely forgotten I'd written that stupid thing, it meant nothing, nothing compared to you, and I—"

"John Chance, you are being an idiot!"

John halted his words, his mouth open.

Florence had her fists clenched at each side, and her eyes sparkled with tears, but there was a determined look on her face he had never seen before.

"You once told me I should tell you if you were being an idiot," she said levelly, cool anger in every syllable. "And I am. You are being an idiot, and a rogue, and—and heartless!"

John swallowed. *This was a nightmare. This could not be happening.* "I . . . I never meant to . . . I didn't think—"

"That much is obvious," said Florence with a small sob breaking through her voice. "Do you have any idea how what this—what you've . . . You wanted to marry me for my money?"

He closed his eyes, just for a moment, as he heard the pain in her voice.

What had he done? Proven himself to be the worst kind of man, one who used a woman merely for what she had, rather than seeing her for who she was. And he had been foolish enough to write it down!

John glanced at the crumpled paper in his hand.

I promise that I am only marrying Florence Bailey for her money. For her stupendous dowry, and nothing else.

John Chance, Aylesbury

"Your brother wanted to send you this because he thought you would want to burn it," said Florence in a broken voice.

John's hopes leapt. "I will! It doesn't matter anymore, Florence, please, you've got to—"

"I d-don't have to do anything," she said in a muted tone. "I . . . to be used like th-this, treated like a f-fool because I cared for you. Because I knew m-myself to be in love with you, and th-that b-blinded me, completely, to who you are. To w-what you are."

Every word was sharp nails dragging across his chest. John was almost surprised not to see blood seeping through his shirt, dripping past his waistcoat and onto the floor. Actual daggers could not hurt more than this.

"Everyone thought I w-would end up alone," said Florence, a sad smile spreading across her face. "And in the end, you've p-proven them right."

"No," John said, panic rising in his lungs. "No, Florence, you can't leave—"

"I can," she said firmly. "I . . . I m-may stammer. I m-may be shy, and I am m-most definitely a wallflower. But I can s-still m-make up my own m-mind."

And Florence affixed him with a look, one that John would never forget. One that would remain burned into him, into his very skin, for the rest of his life. It was the look of a woman who had been hurt, yes . . . but who would rise above it. A woman who would shake the dust from her heels and walk away. Out of his life, into the world, never to speak to him again.

And he had to stop it, he had to, but he didn't know how. It didn't seem possible. What variety of words could he say to show Florence just how much he cared for her?

John dropped to his knees. "Florence, I love you. Let me show you, let me—"

"I am a w-wallflower, but that does not m-mean I deserve to be walked over," Florence said simply.

She allowed the other piece of paper to fall to the floor as she turned on her heel.

John lunged for her—just to touch her, to know the touch of Florence on his skin one more time.

He missed. She was too quick for him, her gown swishing before him and out of the door into the brilliant sunshine of the street.

The door closed. Silence fell in the hall. He was alone.

No, there was a sound. A strange dripping—gentle, and quite close.

John blinked. He was weeping.

Tears splattered down onto his waistcoat and shirt, onto the marble floor. And when he reached out to pick up the paper that Florence had dropped, just to touch something that she had so recently touched, his tears dripped down onto the letter Cothrom had written him, not knowing it would reveal him to be the world's greatest fool.

Aylesbury,

Well, you've done it! Just a few days to go until the wedding, and I'll be honest, I didn't think you had it in you to go through with a marriage of convenience. I hope that you'll find a partnership in your marriage without the bonds of affection.

I thought it was worth me sending this back to you. I don't need it, and Alice says it's foolish to have such a thing lying about our home where anyone could find it.

I recommend you burn it. Wouldn't want the wife to see it! So strange, I really thought for a moment you were falling in love with her.

Meet you at the altar. Who is your best man, by the way?

Cothrom

Chapter Seventeen

August 12, 1812

FLORENCE HAD INSISTED on a lock on her bedchamber a long time ago, and this was perhaps the first time she truly felt she had benefited from it.

The solid sound of the bolt shooting across gave a momentary release to her soul.

And then she was standing in silence again, with only the words which been shouted at her ringing in her ears.

"It changed, don't you see, our marriage of convenience, it changed! And I had completely forgotten I'd written that stupid thing, it meant nothing, nothing compared to you, and I—"

The memories were interrupted by a sudden thumping on the door before her. Florence jumped, the noise startlingly close, and took a step back from the door.

"G-Go aw—"

"Florence Bailey, you come straight back downstairs and finish your breakfast like a rational person!" snapped her mother through the door. "You're getting married tomorrow! You really think you can behave like a petulant child when I ask a simple question?"

Florence closed her eyes, leaning against the wall beside the door as her legs shook.

A simple question? Even for her mother, it had not been merely a simple question.

"What was it this Marquess of Aylesbury saw in you, anyway?"

A question which would have cut at the core of anyone who heard it. No one liked to be questioned on such a thing, to have it suggested that the man who was going to marry her the next day had to be a fool to do so.

But after what she had discovered . . .

"You know what I said, how I felt about—ab-bout men wanting me only for my dowry."

Another thump at the door. The hinges rattled but the bolt held. Florence made a private note to herself to thank Mrs. Harris for doing such an excellent job in selecting someone to fit it.

Her mother had not approved at the time.

"Florence Bailey, come down right now!"

Her mother's berating, which usually would have worked almost instantly, merely washed over Florence like a rising tide. What did it matter what her mother said? Or thought? Or did?

There would be no wedding tomorrow. No opportunity to wear that beautiful gown. No need to go to the church, no man waiting for her at the end of the aisle, no vows made to love and honor.

It was all over.

"I demand that you open this door at once! I will not have a daughter of mine hiding from direct questions, it's ridiculous! You come out here right now and we'll say no more about it."

Florence turned slowly so her back was against the wall, then slowly slid. Her ankles buckled right at the end but she was close enough to the floor by that time. Her buttocks hit the carpet and she sat there, drawing her knees up to her face as she buried her head in her hands.

"Florence Bailey, I have never known such disobedience! I will send for your brother, and he will force this door down. Do you hear me? Florence? I cannot believe such . . ."

The words faded, eventually. Florence knew there was nothing her mother could say that would make her open the door. She was of a mind never to leave her bedchamber again. What cared she for food? What did she need from the outside world—what had it ever offered her?

Naught but pain, suffering, and loneliness. If she had to be alone, she may as well be alone in peace.

Her exhaustion threatened to overwhelm her as she sat there. She had barely slept the night before, the argument with John roaring through her mind, making it impossible to close her eyes and lose herself to slumber.

"I ran out of money, gambled it away—you never noticed, did you, that no matter where we went, I didn't play any game for money? And Cothrom, he cut me off, said he'd send me to the countryside in disgrace, and I thought—"

"You thought you could just marry a fortune."

"Yes—no . . . not exactly.

Eventually Florence fell asleep. She must have done. When she opened her eyes again, she was still sitting on the floor, still leaning against the wall. Her shoulders and neck were stiff, as were her knees, but when she stretched them out Florence could feel herself unfurling, like a flower in the sun.

Just for a moment, she thought about John and smiled.

Then the memories flooded back. That letter, that note John had plainly written, declaring he thought of her as nothing more than a bank account. He was marrying a fortune, that was all. She was immaterial.

As she always was.

Florence glanced about her bedchamber. The curtains were still open, but the sunlight coming through the windows was different, paler than it ought to be.

From her position on the floor, she could see the carriage clock she kept beside her bed. Seven o'clock.

No wonder. She had slept the day away.

Despite her firm conviction, all those hours ago, that she would not require food for the rest of her life, her stomach had other ideas. It was growling most irritatingly, and though she attempted to ignore it for a few minutes, there was nothing she could do.

Groaning as she rose, Florence smoothed her rumpled gown as best she could, then placed an ear on her door. No movement on the landing. No sound could be heard, at least.

Slowly, her fingers stiff with exhaustion, she pulled back the bolt and opened the door.

There was no one there.

She did not encounter anyone as she crept along the servants' staircase either, which was odd. Just past seven o'clock meant it was coming up to dinner. Florence had expected a flurry of maids and footmen running about the place, preparing to serve her mother in the dining room.

And, usually, herself.

But Florence had discounted that idea before she'd even drawn back the bolt. The thought of sitting opposite her mother at the dinner table, being subjected to a plethora of questions—none of which Florence wished to answer—was anathema to her.

No, better to go down to the kitchens themselves. That way she could remain out of the way. Cook would give her a little something. Then she could creep upstairs again, and completely avoid—

"Mother," Florence said in shock as she entered the kitchen.

A most strange sight met her eyes. In fact, in all their years living here, Florence could not recall her mother ever stepping into the kitchen. That was the servants' domain, she had once heard Mrs. Bailey say. It was not for the likes of *them*.

Yet here she was. Her mother was seated at the worn kitchen table, smoothed with age and many hands, with a bowl of stew before her.

Mrs. Bailey dropped her spoon, splashing stew across her pristine white gown. "Florence."

Florence stiffened. "I-I don't w-want another argum-ment—"

"Neither do I," said her mother curtly.

Standing awkwardly, feet from the table, Florence was not sure what to do next. Her instincts told her to leave, that any encounter with her mother would lead to tears. Probably her own.

The trouble was, the stew smelled absolutely divine. A rich, gamey scent filled the kitchen, along with rosemary and what could be basil. Florence's stomach growled.

She glanced at the bowl of stew again, trying to weigh up whether she could carry such a thing up two flights of stairs without dropping it—and then something her mind had evidently noticed but not yet been able to inform her of managed to get her attention.

Her mother. She had been crying.

Florence's lungs constricted, making every movement painful. She had never seen her mother cry before. Mrs. Bailey did not cry. She was famous for it. Hadn't she once said that tears were a sign of weakness, and Baileys were not weak?

"I . . ." Florence swallowed. She could hardly leave without mentioning it, now she had noticed. *What had occurred?* Was it Philip—was he perhaps hurt? "You have had word?"

Mrs. Bailey swallowed hard, hands clasping and unclasping before her on the table. Then she nodded.

Florence's pulse skipped a beat. *If something had happened to her brother . . .* "Where is he? Philip?"

And much to her surprise, her mother shook her head. "It . . . it isn't Philip."

Heart sinking, Florence realized what must have happened.

Of course, she had been a fool not to think of it before. The wedding was tomorrow, was meant to be, wasn't it? Of course, there was no possibility going forward now, and John . . . and the Marquess of Aylesbury would not wish to go ahead with the thing, just in the hope she would turn up.

He had to know she was serious about her refusal.

And that meant, Florence thought with pain radiating through her, that John—the Marquess of Aylesbury, she corrected silently, had contacted her mother. There was no other way round it. The trousseau would be sent over, the flowers sent back . . . everything.

A broken engagement. A broken engagement the day before the wedding. A broken engagement the day before a wedding to a marquess.

No wonder her mother had been crying.

Florence tried to take in a fortifying breath, and managed to say without too many hesitations, "S-So. You have h-heard about my b-broken engagement with . . . with the m-marquess. You should know th-there will be no dis-dishonor. It is—"

"You think I care about that?" her mother interrupted as she looked up. "You think I care about dishonor, or reputation, or anything of that nature?"

Almost taking a step back in her surprise, Florence blinked, attempting to discern what on earth her mother could mean.

Because her instinct was to say . . . *yes. Yes, that is what has upset you. That is always what upsets you. When I am not clever enough or witty enough in company to impress. When the* ton *does not invite me to a ball, you feel slighted. When I announced my engagement, you planned which house my betrothed would give you.*

But something had changed since then. Florence was not sure what on earth it could be, but something had. Something intangible, yet which had a tangible effect on her mother.

Her mother was crying. Tears were trickling silently down her cheeks. "I am upset because . . . because my daughter had her heart broken. By a rogue, no less, by a—and she did not feel she could come to me. My . . . my own daughter."

Florence would have bet good money, and she had a lot of it, that her mother had been about to say something about the expense. The shame. The difficulty informing everyone that the wedding was off.

That it would now be quite impossible to marry off her daughter.

To hear her mother say such words—and to clearly mean them, to hear the break in her voice. . .

Her footsteps making almost no sound on the flagged stone floor, Florence caught the eye of the cook and a maid who were working in silence behind her mother.

Just one silent look was enough. Bobbing curtsies, the two of them quickly left the kitchen, leaving Florence and her mother alone.

Right. Well. Where did one start?

"It w-wasn't like th-that," Florence said awkwardly as she pulled out a chair.

Mrs. Bailey sniffed. "Oh, really? How is it different?"

Florence squirmed awkwardly in her seat. She had never had to comfort her mother in her life. True, her mother had never comforted her, either. But still. This was uncharted territory for the both of them, and she wasn't sure she liked it.

Her prickly, irritable, argumentative, corrosive mother was at least a constant. She always knew how Mrs. Bailey would respond to anything. She was one of the few parts of life depended upon to be the same in all situations.

Until, it appeared, now.

"Because from what I can see," her mother continued, tears spilling from her eyes, "my daughter had her heart broken, came home, slept, had some breakfast, then stormed away from me, all while keeping from me that her heart . . . that the wedding . . . that she was miserable, and I . . ."

Florence stared in amazement as her mother threw back her head and wailed.

"And I had to find out from Lady Romeril in the street!" bawled Mrs. Bailey.

Shoulders slumping, Florence congratulated herself silently in finally reaching the root cause of this sadness. *Of course.* It wasn't

Florence's actual heart that was the problem. It was being caught out by someone in public, and by Lady Romeril, of all people.

But just as she was about to leave and return to her room, stew or no stew, her mother reached out and took her hand. "And I hadn't been there to comfort you," she said in a thick voice, "when you most needed comforting."

Florence stared at her mother's hand on hers in amazement. This wasn't like her mother at all. She was at a complete loss to explain it, bewildered in the extreme with no idea what to say.

And so she said that. "I-I . . . I d-don't know what t-to say."

Her mother sniffed, but said nothing more in reply. The moment between them elongated, becoming more and more difficult to ignore.

Though she considered attempting to pull her hand away, Florence decided against it. She still wasn't completely convinced they had got to the bottom of this, but it would be callous in the extreme to immediately discount her mother's words.

"You . . . Mother, you are always so exacting. So vocal in public—"

"Oh, that's always because I'm so nervous," her mother said, wringing her hands.

It was all Florence could do not to stare. "Nervous?"

Nervous? Her mother—Mrs. Bailey, nervous?

Her mother was still wringing her hands. "I've always been nervous in company, ever since I was a girl, and so my mother told me always to have something to say, and say it loud, and as though you are confident. And she herself was always so certain, so forceful. So of course that's what I do, always have something to say, always have a remark, a comment—"

Of course.

Now that her mother had said it, Florence could not believe how she had missed it. Her mother always sought to fill the silence, make any remark, keep the conversation going even if it had reached a natural conclusion. Her words ran together, she spoke boldly but without thought. From . . . from nerves?

"We're so alike," gulped her mother, tears still pouring down her face. "I thought you knew!"

"How could I know?" Florence could not help but say. "You n-never told me."

"I thought it obvious—I thought the whole *ton* knew just how much I hated speaking out in public, how uncomfortable I am! Oh, Florence, the things that come out of my mouth in those moments . . . and then it's too late!" Mrs. Bailey sniffed. "I can never take anything back! But to hear of such a calamity that has befallen you, from another . . ."

Florence swallowed. "We . . . M-Mother, we have n-never been close. In that w-way."

There was no response to her words. At least, her mother silently wept, but as she had been doing so before, Florence was not sure that counted as a response.

She tried again. "We're n-not open. I s-suppose."

Mrs. Bailey sniffed. She released her daughter and started patting her sleeves, hunting for a handkerchief. "I suppose not. I . . . I . . . Neither was my mother."

Florence stared. Her mother may invoke her grandmother's standards and preferences often enough, but Florence had never heard her mother speak so openly about her own upbringing.

Her father had been an orphan at a young age, so she'd never had the opportunity to meet her grandparents on her father's side of the family, but she did have a vague memory of her mother's parents. An elderly gentleman who had been deaf, bellowing his good wishes at his tiny granddaughter with beaming eyes. And a woman . . .

Now she came to think of it, Florence could barely recall the woman who had been her grandmother. Her mother's mother.

She had been stern. At least, she had a stern expression. Florence could just about remember her features if she concentrated, but it was a challenge. They had lived in the countryside and had disapproved, from the few hints her mother had dropped, that the Baileys had decided to live in the capital.

And that was all she could recall. Her grandparents had both died before Florence had reached the age of five, so there wasn't a huge amount to remember.

Was her mother suggesting . . . well, was it possible that her mother had grown up in a home just as cold, just as lonely as she had?

"I always thought," her mother said with a watery smile, "hoped, that is . . . hoped I would break the cycle."

Florence breathed out the tension that had been building in her. "I b-beg your p-pardon?"

"Break the cycle," repeated Mrs. Bailey. Her eyes were red, but tears had ceased to fall. "Be different, I suppose. Be a different kind of parent, a different kind of mother to you than I had. But I fell into her habits, her phrases, her judgment. I couldn't stop myself, sometimes I didn't even notice I had done so until . . . until it was too late."

Her words echoed around the kitchen and in Florence's mind.

It was a revelation. She had never inquired of herself—or her mother, for that matter—why she was the way she was. It was not the sort of question one asked anyone, let alone a parent.

Florence's father had died years ago. Philip had left as soon as he was able, taking up rooms with a university chum who had inherited a house with plenty of space, and that was it. The two Bailey women had been left together.

Yet all this time, her mother had resented the way she had been spoken to by her own mother—and at the same time, not even noticed she was falling into patterns she herself had suffered from. That she was subjecting her own daughter to a treatment she herself must hate. All this time, her mother had panicked in company and just said the first words that came into her head. All this time, the pair of them had been equally plagued by nerves in company, but she had never known.

Florence did not need to think. The pity she felt for her mother was enough to drive her forward.

Rising from her seat, she did not say a word as she stepped around the broad kitchen table and pulled her mother into a tight embrace.

It felt . . . wrong. No, not wrong, exactly. But Florence could not recall the last time she had even touched or been touched by her mother, let alone embraced her. It was an alien thing, a discomfiting closeness that nonetheless she persevered through.

Because someone, to use her mother's words, had to break the cycle.

Her mother's sobbing returned and increased in volume for a while, her shoulders shaking, before the cries subsided. Only then did Florence carefully release her.

"It wasn't—I n-never th-thought that . . ." Florence swallowed hard as she slipped into the chair beside her mother. *Goodness, this was difficult.* "I did n-not wish to talk ab-bout . . . about it with anyone. It was n-not just you."

Mrs. Bailey swallowed, her face blotchy. "T-Truly?"

Florence tried to smile. "N-Now you sound like me."

Their awkward laughter echoed around the otherwise empty kitchen.

It was hard to take in. The idea her mother did not wish to be the way she was, that she had hoped to be different—it was startling. A revelation. One which Florence wished she had known years before.

How different things could have been. Perhaps they would have been able to enjoy each other's company. Perhaps their visits, attendance to balls, that sort of thing, would have been a burden they could have shared. Perhaps Florence would have turned to her mother the moment she realized her engagement to John—to the Marquess of Aylesbury was over.

Well, you could not go back. Florence could not turn back the hands of time and live those months, those years again. But she could choose how to live, going forward.

"I . . . I suppose it truly is over?" her mother asked in a small voice.

Florence's veins turned to ice. It was too difficult to speak. She nodded.

Mrs. Bailey sighed. "You . . . well. You seemed to really like him."

Only after she had taken a steadying breath was Florence able to speak. "I did."

The two words were said with such finality, she almost surprised herself. Was she starting to believe it? To accept that the marriage she had hoped for these long months, even years, which had seemed so close, was finally out of reach?

"And it can't be . . . repaired?"

Florence shook her head weakly at the hope on her mother's face. It was natural, she was sure, for mothers to wish for the best for their children. It was just so bizarre, seeing it in her own mother. "So that I c-can be a m-marchioness?"

It was, perhaps, the wrong thing to say. Her mother drew herself up proudly, and spoke with such strength of feeling, Florence was rather astonished she was still seated, and not parading up and down outside Westminster with the women making demands of Parliament.

"You could be a cottager's wife, if it made you happy," she said firmly, eyes still red. "Happiness is what matters, Florence, and finding that with a husband . . . I sometimes think I would have been a very different mother if your father had not . . . If you have found someone, someone you truly love, why let them go?"

Tears crept into the corners of Florence's eyes.

She was mostly bluster then, this mother of hers. Oh, the words would hurt, and she was thoughtless, and at times uncaring. But they were faults. Not failures of character.

And faults could be repaired. Together they could begin to undo the damage.

"Mama," Florence said, her voice cracking as tears finally fell. Her mother swept her into a comforting embrace before she could even get the next stammering words out. "M-M-Mama, he n-never l-loved m-me a-after . . . a-after all."

Chapter Eighteen

August 13, 1812

JOHN BLINKED BLEARILY at the two glasses of brandy before him. Each was held by one of his three hands.

Wait a minute. Three hands. Three hands?

Blinking rapidly as though that would clarify matters, John attempted to put the glasses down—a challenge, with the table always moving about the place—then tried to clasp his three hands together.

Only two touched.

Well, that was a relief, he thought vaguely as he tried, and tried, and tried to pick up his glass again. A man with three hands? That would be ridiculous.

More ridiculous than a man who lost his bride the day before his wedding?

The cruel voice at the back of his mind was back. John supposed he deserved it. There couldn't be many idiots of his particular caliber about, and it was only right he was criticized by all and sundry around him.

Including himself.

John sighed as he leaned back in his armchair. The study had been the only place he could think of to hide, though now he was three brandies in, he couldn't quite remember who he was hiding from.

No matter. They would certainly not find him here. Whoever they were.

"When I wrote that, I was being teased by my brother—I would never normally do such a thing, I was showing off."

"You s-still wrote it. It's your words—"

"I don't think that way anymore!"

"But you did."

Tears sparkled in his eyes as he recalled the complete nincompoop he'd made of himself. Had that honestly been his defense? That he had written those cruel words, and only recently stopped believing them?

Was he truly that dense?

Florence had certainly thought so, walking out of his life as though it were the easiest thing in the world. Refusing to heed him, no interest in reconciling. Disbelieving him. As she had a right to do.

Oh hell, it was all so tangled. John could hardly believe Cothrom had been so stupid as to put something like that in the post—but of course, it was a rare gentleman who allowed his wife to open his post, let alone a woman he was not yet married to.

When he'd gone over to Cothrom House, ostensibly to give the news that the wedding was off, Cothrom had been mortified. He'd talked about going over to the Baileys to explain things. Talking to the mother. Talking to the brother, if necessary. Sorting it out.

John had stopped him.

"What's the point?" he'd said lazily, as though it didn't matter. As though his heart weren't breaking. "She won't listen to reason."

"She's one of the most reasonable women you've ever met," shot back his brother. "The question is, will she listen to you?"

Apparently not. John had turned up outside the Bailey house and requested entry, but a stern looking housekeeper and an even sterner looking butler had forbidden him entry. When John had attempted to push past the latter, he'd discovered to his shock that the man was stronger than he looked. Strong as an ox. Certainly stronger than John.

And so he sat here. Drinking, thought John dully as he finally managed to catch a hold of his brandy glass and bring it to his lips. Why not? What else was there for him to do?

The door opened and two of his brothers stepped in.

No. Wait. One of his brothers?

"You look terrible," said a low, gentle voice.

John tried to smile, but his mouth was not behaving. It certainly wasn't obeying him. "Shhhut . . . shut up. Y'donn't look too preshious y'sel."

The face of Pernrith came closer, and then there was only one of him. Where did the other Pernrith go? "Oh dear."

"You oh dear," John shot back in what he thought was a clever and elegant manner.

"Aylesbury, how many fingers am I holding up?"

John focused. At least, as best he could. It would be a whole lot easier to answer this question if the blackguard didn't keep moving his hands about. "S . . . Six. Sleven. Eleven?"

Pernrith's brow furrowed. "Right. In that case—"

"Hey!" His last exclamation was in response to a very dirty and clever trick.

His half-brother removed the glass from his hands. "I think you need a drink."

John beamed. "Exshellent."

"A drink of coffee," the fourth Chance brother stated quietly. "I've asked your butler to send up—ah, there we go."

The door opened and a footman brought in a silver tray covered with a pot of coffee, two cups, a jug which could be cream, and a whole heap of sugar cubes in a saucer.

John turned away, face reddening. It was bad enough to be found in this sort of state, his mind managed to think, by a brother—by an illegitimate brother, not truly part of the family. How much worse to be viewed in such a manner by a servant?

His footman was undoubtedly just as embarrassed at having to see his master in such a state, for the man's ears were red and he disappeared from the study far more quickly than John would have thought possible.

At least, for a man carrying three trays.

"Here," said Pernrith with a bracing look. "We'll get some of this down you, and you'll feel as right as rain in no time."

A lump rose in John's throat. "No. No, nothing will—she'sh gone. Left me. She's left me, Pen."

There was a flash of something dark across the man's face, his hair swept back in a movement that momentarily covered his eyes, then the Viscount Pernrith was smiling blandly again as he so often was.

"That's it," he said gently, pressing a cup into John's hands. "Drink this."

It was scalding hot, burning his throat with a heat and sweetness that tasted as though the man had poured half the sugar cubes into it.

John choked, then forced another mouthful down. "'t's hot."

"Warming," said his half-brother. "Another gulp, please."

About ten minutes later, Pernrith refreshed his cup. Around half an hour after that, John was blinking blearily around the room with a greater sharpness than he had managed in quite some time.

More's the pity.

"You," he said bitterly to the man seated opposite him by the study fire.

Pernrith's gaze did not falter. "Me."

"I would have thought—Lindow—"

"Yes, well, I am sorry to disappoint," said the illegitimate Chance with a wry look. "But I am afraid the Earl of Lindow was otherwise engaged."

John rolled his eyes, attempting to push past his embarrassment at being so rude. Well, it wasn't the blackguard—the man's fault for being the product of his father's affair. He supposed.

Lindow had a different view of it, but there you go.

"Yes, he had a rather pressing and urgent matter," Pernrith said quietly. "Apparently."

John snorted. "Gambling, I suppose—or the horses. Good to know where I stand in my brother's priorities."

"And Cothrom wanted to come," continued his brother. "But he and the Duchess of Cothrom had . . . they are somewhat distracted at present."

"Oh, hell—"

"Not that," said Pernrith with a grin. "Or at least, not directly."

John stared, wondering whether the brandy was still having an effect on him. The man certainly was not making any sort of sense.

Pernrith's smile was gentle. "Just promise me you will not tell them that I told you about the arrival we shall be welcoming in the spring."

It took John a few moments to truly take in what the man was saying. Arrival? Had they ordered something from China, perhaps, on one of the large ships that arrived on the Thames?

Then he managed to put it together. "Dear God."

"Precisely."

"A little Chance?"

"It appears that way. At least, when I arrived at Cothrom House, the duchess was indisposed, and the duke was unwilling to leave her."

Duchess, John noticed. *Duke*. He was family, of a sort, yet still he resorted to such formalities.

Well, he could hardly blame him. Pernrith had never truly been made to feel at home in the Chance family. One of these days, this family was going to have to talk about—

"And speaking of people who are indisposed, though I grant you for very different reasons," said Pernrith, placing his own cup of coffee back on a saucer, "you are looking a little better."

John immediately scowled. "I was doing perfectly—"

"However you are intending to end that sentence, no, you weren't."

It was most infuriating to be spoken to in such a way. Particularly when you deserved it.

"Look, if I want to drink myself stupid of an evening, then I shall," he said threateningly. "I have the right."

Pernrith raised an eyebrow. "You do?"

"You must have seen it in the—Cothrom would have told you, at any rate," John said bitterly, wondering precisely how his older brother would have put it. "Florence . . . Miss Bailey. She has called off the wedding."

"Yes, I suppose so."

"And my life is over," continued John, unable to prevent the vulnerable words from spilling over. "The world, it's . . . it's lost all its color. I don't feel able to . . . all I want is . . ."

Her, he wanted to say. Florence. The woman who couldn't speak to me without flushing scarlet when we first met, and who kissed me like I was the center of the world. Touched me like all she wanted was me. Cried out my name like—

And laughed. And rode like the devil. And smiled.

"It doesn't make sense," John said, subdued.

Pernrith sipped at his coffee. "And why is that?"

Shooting him a glare which would have felled a lesser man—*he should have known it wouldn't work, the brute was a Chance*—John sighed heavily. "Well. She was just one woman, you know. Florence."

"Well at least you're not seeing double anymore," came the wry reply.

John's glare became a scowl. "Don't talk about her like—"

"Just one woman, you were saying," Pernrith pointed out, gesturing with a hand. "Your words. Not mine."

It was galling, to have his own words thrown back at him like that. John had known what he'd meant, even if he couldn't precisely spell it out now.

He shifted in his seat, wishing the damned thing was more comfortable. It had certainly felt more comfortable when he'd been drinking brandy.

She was just one woman. Florence. Just one.

But she had been *the* woman.

John knew that, knew it deep within his bones. It wasn't something you could explain to someone else. How could you describe the warmth of the sun to someone who had never felt it, or the soaring waves of the ocean to someone who had never seen the sea?

Words were there. They existed. But they couldn't translate the feelings, the sense of swooping in one's stomach, the delight and happiness that such things brought.

And Florence had been far more than that. So much more.

The only woman who had made John want to . . . made the world worth living within. How could he go on now, day by day, in a world in which Florence wished to have nothing to do with him?

"I feel wretched," he said quietly.

"You don't look too great, to be honest."

John glared at his half-brother, who had the decency to grin.

"Well," said Pernrith, spreading his hands with a shrug. "This Florence of yours—"

"Miss Bailey to you," snarled John, hardly knowing why it mattered.

The viscount nodded. "Fine, fine, Miss Bailey. From everything you've told me in the past, and everything I know about her from the gossip—" John groaned "—she was a wallflower. Just a wallflower."

"A wallflower who shouted down those who were rude to her," John pointed out, remembering the story Florence had told him about her mother in the modiste's.

Now that would have been a conversation he would have paid money to see. The idea of Mrs. Bailey holding one of the lace things Florence had described, and the way his love had stood up to her!

His stomach lurched painfully. *Not his anymore.*

"She is wealthy, isn't she?"

Agony twisted around John's torso. He barely had enough air to speak. He nodded.

"I-I d-don't want vultures circling me for my m-money. Ignoring me, happy to m-marry anyone attached to the numbers. I d-don't want to be w-wed for my b-bank balance. You need respectability. You aren't c-cruel. I chose you."

"Well, there are plenty of other wealthy women in London," said Pernrith with a shrug. "Quite a few, actually. There's talk of a pair of sisters who will be coming out into Society into the autumn, thousands each. It's a shame you can't wed both of them."

John glared. "You think this was all about money?"

"Isn't it?"

Trying to put aside the memory of the note he had written for Cothrom was difficult. John had been left with it, the only evidence he had left that he and Florence had been engaged, if only for a time.

I promise that I am only marrying Florence Bailey for her money. For her stupendous dowry, and nothing else.

John Chance, Aylesbury

"Florence is wealthy," he admitted, shoulders taut with tension. "But she enriched my life in . . . spending time with her. I felt wealthier because of it. Oh, hell, that sounds ridiculous. Do you know what I mean?"

John's gaze searched out Pernrith's, but there was nothing but the typical calm and blankness that the young Chance brother always had. It was infuriating.

"She was shy, though. Painfully shy, as I recall from the one time I met her," said Pernrith delicately. "That would have been grating. Tiring, over time."

Strange. John had hardly thought about it. Florence had spoken more clearly when they were alone together, but even when they were in public and she struggled through her words, John was so interested in what she had to say, he did not mind waiting a little longer to hear it.

"At least she had something worth saying," he said gruffly. "Not like half of these women in the *ton*, they just open their mouths and nonsense falls—you're *smiling*."

It wasn't an accusation, as such. But it was hardly a benign comment.

Pernrith was smiling. It was a self-satisfied smile, one John had never seen on the man's face before. Why, when he looked like that, it was most clear he was definitely a Chance. There was something about Lindow in the eyebrows, though John would be the last person to point that out.

And the idiot was still smiling.

"What?" barked John. "Spit it out, why don't you!"

He didn't. Not immediately. Pernrith shifted in his seat, leaning an elbow against the armrest and fixing him with a serious expression.

"Look," said the viscount finally. "I am illegitimate. A bastard, as I think Lindow refers to me."

John opened his mouth, hesitated, then closed it again. Well. There wasn't much to be argued about there, even if it felt strange having that spoken aloud. It was hardly done, to point such things out in polite Society.

"In many ways, I don't belong in your world. In your family," said Pernrith, his voice still low. "But your—our father took me in. The three of you—Cothrom, yourself, Lindow—you have been good to me. In your way."

A prickle of discomfort crawled across John's chest. It was not pleasant having such a thing pointed out to you. Particularly when one was heartbroken.

"But despite all that," continued Pernrith, "I feel honor bound to point out that you are being a complete idiot."

John's head jerked up. "What the devil are you—"

"I have just given you three excellent reasons to forget about Florence—about Miss Bailey, excuse me," Pernrith said. "Three reasons many gentlemen would easily grasp at to tell themselves they no longer had to care about a woman."

Heat was coursing through John's veins. "What are you—"

"She's a wallflower, she's wealthy but there are other wealthy women, and she's so shy, it's almost impossible for some people to hold a conversation with her." His brother—his half-brother ticked off his fingers. "All good reasons to move on. You've contradicted each one. You love her."

John scowled.

Love. What did that matter, when it came to it? Love had not prevented him from being a complete fool. Love had not made Florence understand why or how he had done that foolish thing. Love had not helped them understand each other, or given them the chance to patch things up and go ahead with the wedding.

The very expensive wedding.

Oh, damn. He was going to have a very uncomfortable conversation with Cothrom at some point this week.

But love—love wasn't the answer. How could it be? It hadn't solved anything, prevented any disaster. It hadn't brought them closer together. Somehow it had forced them apart.

Still. He could hardly deny it.

"My caring about Miss Bailey . . . about Florence, that was never the problem," John said heavily. "It was my idiotic past that destroyed our chance."

He should never have written that note. What had he been thinking?

He hadn't really been thinking, John thought darkly. He'd been showing off. Trying to prove to Cothrom that his heart wasn't going to be affected by a woman who had accepted his kisses then proposed a marriage of convenience.

"So." Pernrith's voice was low. "So you need a second chance."

John snorted, rising from his seat and giving a sigh of relief as his legs managed to hold him. The brandy was wearing off, then. "A second chance?"

"Fine, a third."

"Try a fourth, or a fifth," muttered John, pacing over to the window and jerking back the curtain to glance outside into the night. The stars twinkled.

"So you ask for them."

"You think I haven't already been over there?" John shot back. "You think I haven't written? You think I don't want Florence to accept my apologies—to love me?"

His voice broke on the final words.

If it even had been love, a cruel voice muttered in the depths of his soul. If affection could be broken so quickly, had it truly been affection in the first place?

He glanced over his shoulder and glared at Pernrith, who looked steadily back. "And even if she were ever good enough to take me back, I'd probably still need another chance every week we spent together."

"And do you want that?" Pernrith's voice had a steadiness and a certainty in it John had never heard before. At least, he had never noticed it before. How had he never noticed that it was Pernrith, of all the Chance brothers, who always had the calm response?

"Of course I want Florence—"

"I don't mean that, I mean something more," continued his half-brother doggedly. "To always be working to better yourself, always be looking for ways to improve, always hoping not to disappoint?"

John turned slowly and met his half-brother's eyes. They were unrelenting, and clearly determined to force him to reply.

He swore. "For you? No. For Cothrom? Definitely not. For her?"

Images rushed through his mind. Florence's pink cheeks upon

seeing him at the Knights'. Florence riding in Hyde Park, hair flowing out behind her, laughter in the air. Florence, slipping her hand in his as though it were the most natural thing in the world. And the world had felt right.

"For her?" John said hoarsely. "Yes."

Chapter Nineteen

August 21, 1812

IF SHE COULD be anywhere right now, it would not be here.

Florence's pulse was thundering in her ears, her fingers tingled most unpleasantly, and the worst of it was . . . it had been her decision to come here.

Her mother had been most astonished, sure enough. "You want to *what?*"

"I have t-to accept one of them at s-some point," Florence had said, spreading the several invitations she had received that morning alone across the breakfast table. "Eventually. I m-mean, I can't s-stay away forever."

Can I?

The last two words were unspoken, but Florence knew her mother heard them, nonetheless.

It was a pleasant idea, hiding away from the world and never having to trouble herself with it again. Remaining here, at home, where she was safe. Where the only people she would be forced to interact with were servants, those who had served the Bailey family loyally for years, her mother—rapidly becoming bearable—and her brother.

Though tempting, Florence was not quite a fool enough to believe that would be sufficient for the world.

She was a young lady, of good family, and of even better dowry. She had entered Society, and though she was perhaps older than some of the brides walking down the aisle, she was hardly a spinster.

Not yet, Florence thought darkly.

And that meant she had a duty, somehow, to Society itself. She could not simply ignore it, pretending it did not exist. She had to accept, even if she did not like it, that there were certain things a lady of the *ton* had to do.

And leaving the house more than once a year was one of them.

"You have certainly received a great many invitations," her mother had said with a frown. "More than you usually receive. Even after the engagement . . . after it was announced."

Florence's stomach had only tightened for a moment. And that was progress, wasn't it? Soon she would be able to hear John—the Marquess of Aylesbury's name without feeling as though her heart had just been ripped from her chest.

Soon everything would go back to how it was.

Boring. Dull. Lonely.

She pushed the thought from her mind. "They obviously wish to see me, now I am no longer engaged to . . . to the Marquess of Aylesbury."

Her mother's fierce eye was directed at her across the crumpets and butter, but it was not ire directed toward her, rather in her defense. "Vultures. They just want a glimpse of—"

"I know," Florence said quietly. "But eventually I w-*will* have to go. Accept an invitation. B-Be in Society, after it . . . it h-has all happened. I s-suppose there's n-no time like the present."

They had argued, needless to say, about which invitation to accept. Mrs. Bailey was determined it should be the one with the greatest prestige, whereas Florence had wished for the smallest gathering, the smallest crowd.

In the end, they compromised, leaving neither of them happy and each of them discomforted as they arrived at Lord Galcrest's dinner party.

"A mere viscount," her mother muttered as they entered the hallway, allowing their shawls to be taken by the footmen. "A scandalous step down after—"

"Th-Thank you, Mama," Florence had said, cutting across her with pink cheeks.

She could already hear the crowd through the doorway. There were hundreds of them.

Fine, perhaps not hundreds of them. In fact, as the two Bailey ladies stepped into the drawing room at Galcrest's footmen's behest, Florence saw there were in fact only about twenty people there.

At least ten too many.

Mrs. Bailey sighed. "A poor crowd."

"A c-crowd, nonetheless," Florence pointed out. "N-Neither of us is happy."

Her mother glanced her way, she could feel her stare. "And you do not wish to stay at home—to remain there, safe?"

Florence swallowed.

Yes, she wanted to say. *Yes, I just want to stay in my bedchamber and never leave. Nurse my broken heart, tell myself it would never have worked. That I should never have offered matrimony to a rake such as John Chance, Marquess of Aylesbury. That I should have listened to the surprise of the world and wondered why on earth a man like that would wish to marry someone like . . .*

Like her.

Pain and sorrow rose in her like twin flames, and there was nothing Florence could do to quench them. She would just have to learn to live with them, she supposed. The agonies of regret. The concerns about the future. The—

"Yes, that's her!"

The whisper was quiet, but not enough to be entirely lost in the cacophony of sound in the drawing room.

Florence did not need to turn around. She knew, without a shadow of a doubt, that she was the object of the gossip.

"—broken engagement—"

"—the Marquess of Aylesbury—"

"—what happened? No one seems to know . . ."

Gritting her teeth and trying to maintain a vague smile, Florence knew she should be grateful, in a way. It had been perfectly possible that John—that the Marquess of Aylesbury, she really should get better accustomed to thinking of him formally—that the Marquess of Aylesbury could have been open about the breach.

That she had been the one to make it.

That knowledge would have been scandalous in Society. If he had left her, she would be pitied. If the truth got out, that it had been Miss Florence Bailey who had walked away from a marriage with a marquess . . .

Well. Florence knew she certainly would not have received an invitation from Lord Galcrest, for a start.

Turning to her mother, she was immediately distracted by a pair of gentlemen who were pointing at her. Actually pointing!

Florence instinctively reached for her mother's arm, gripping it tightly. She needed the support, to know there was at least one person here at this dinner who was not gleefully wondering how she had managed to ruin her life.

Then she realized how tightly she was clutching at her mother. "I-I am—s-sorry, Mama, I—"

"No apology needed," said Mrs. Bailey, perhaps for the first time in her life not complaining when she had the chance. "I am here for you. Finally."

A wan expression crept across Florence's face as they strode purposefully, as though they had no concerns in the world, across the drawing room. There was a sofa currently unoccupied, and the two Bailey women sat down on it, still arm in arm.

It was a respite Florence sorely needed. Her legs were not going to hold her forever, and the last thing she wanted was to collapse. In public. At a Society event.

Oh, the gossip would be all over London by the morning.

Mrs. Bailey squeezed her hand. "Let them look. Hold your head up high, girl. There's nothing to be ashamed of."

The words were spoken gruffly, but each was spoken with support, love, and comfort.

Strange. In all this, a situation Florence would never have wished for and would never wish upon another living soul, there had been one silver lining.

She and her mother had never been in such good understanding. It may not last, she was aware of that, and there were still a great number of differences between them. But their mutual respect had grown, and the bickering had almost ceased. As had the near constant criticism. It was a marvel.

"It cannot be long before the dinner gong is rung," Mrs. Bailey said out of the corner of her mouth, as though afraid someone might accuse them of talking. "Then it'll be an hour or two of food and banal conversation, and then—"

"H-Home," finished Florence with a sigh. "I c-cannot wait."

Other ladies of the *ton* surely waited eagerly for invitations from Lord Galcrest. He was, apparently, a pleasant man, not that she had much memory of conversing with him. In fact, now Florence came to think about it, she could not recall ever meeting the man.

"M-Mama."

"Hmmm?"

Florence tried to hold her head high. People were still staring, she could feel the pressure of their gazes upon her skin. "When was it you made Lord Galcrest's acquaintance?"

"Lord Galcrest?" Mrs. Bailey blinked. "Who is he?"

Hoping to goodness no one else had heard her mother's words, Florence's expression faltered. "Why, he is the h-host tonight. I p-presumed the invitation w-was a courtesy to you."

"To me? I am hardly in the stage of life to be receiving compliments in such a manner," her mother muttered as she pulled out her fan and started fluttering it nervously. "The invitation was addressed to you, was it not?"

Florence attempted to remember. There had been so many invitations these last few days, and she had considered only the likelihood of crowds at each one, not the person who had sent it.

Lord Galcrest. Perhaps she had met him. Was he the viscount at the Knights' house party? Or was he—

Though momentarily lost in her own thoughts, she could not remain there for long. The gasps and murmurs spreading around the large drawing room were growing in volume. Florence turned her head to see what everyone was making such a fuss about.

"Perhaps there is a jester, or a musician," murmured Mrs. Bailey. "Some sort of entertainment, you know."

"It does not appear to be an entertainment," said Florence softly, craning her neck. It was not possible to see precisely what everyone was gawping at, but it was evidently something of great interest. Her pulse fluttered painfully. "Ah. Musicians."

A trio of strings had appeared, to the general polite applause of the guests. They began tuning their instruments, light delicate sounds that wafted through the drawing room.

Florence swallowed. This was all becoming too much. "You know, Mama, perhaps we should go home. There are far too many people here and . . . and . . . and . . ."

Her mother nudged her. "And?"

But Florence could not speak. How could she, when the one man in the world that she had no interest in seeing was walking toward her?

It was John.

No. It couldn't be. Surely she was dreaming—though this was more akin to a nightmare. Seated in public, with people around her already gossiping about her, and now John was here?

Florence shot up to her feet, dragging her unsuspecting mother with her as their arms were still linked.

"Florence!"

"It's . . . it's . . ." Florence could not hear to say his name.

He was looking at her. Still tall, still handsome, still with that intoxicating presence which made it difficult to think of anything else. Striding forward through the crowd of guests that clustered around him, probably attempting to ask him all the details of his failed engagement.

Florence's head spun.

She had to get away. She had to leave—there was no possibility of attempting to speak with him. The damned man would just try to reason with her again, try to convince her to accept him again.

And the very real danger was, she might. He was such a heady man, and she loved him so—

No. Florence tried to be firm with herself as her legs quivered and her lungs tightened, every breath an effort. No, she did not love him. Not anymore. How could she love such a man?

"What Lord Galcrest was thinking, inviting both you and—"

"I think that was precisely the point," murmured Florence, her attention transfixed just to the left of the man who was, slowly but surely, making his way to her.

Of course. Why hadn't she thought of that? If neither she nor her mother had any association with Lord Galcrest, someone must have requested that they be invited.

And who was the only person in the *ton* at this moment who wished to see her?

"He wouldn't dare approach you," whispered her mother at her side.

Florence swallowed hard, but it did nothing to dislodge the lump in her throat. "I wouldn't put it past him."

And she couldn't permit that. Just seeing John was painful in the extreme, her very being aching for him and yet rejecting all potential contact. Most unfortunately, seeing him like this, dressed to the nines in a perfectly fitted suit and looking her way with those dazzling eyes, made Florence realize that she was still very much in love with the brute.

Which could not be borne. She had no wish to be overcome by her emotions, and she certainly couldn't risk accidentally revealing that she was still in love with him.

She couldn't. She wouldn't.

I promise that I am only marrying Florence Bailey for her money. For her stupendous dowry, and nothing else.

John Chance, Aylesbury

The words she had read had been burned into Florence's eyes. She could never unsee them, never look at John without seeing them.

"I need to go," Florence murmured.

"Florence—Florence, where are you—"

But she did not remain to heed her mother's warning, or answer her question, or whatever it was that Mrs. Bailey was going to say.

Slipping her hand from her mother's arm, Florence started for a door. Any door. Anywhere had to be better than here, where onlookers were pointing, gossiping, laughing—where music was playing, clogging up her ears and making it impossible think, where John was—

Anywhere John was had to be a place she must leave.

The trouble was, he was faster than she was. Florence may have been able to outride him, escaping him on a horse without trouble, but there was no steed beneath her. John's strides were a great deal longer than hers, and just as she reached the door—

"Florence."

A whisper in her ear, a hand on her arm—a hand that Florence pulled away from immediately, cheeks blazing with fire as she turned to him.

"I don't want to hear another word from you," Florence hissed. John may not be aware of the staring gazes of everyone present, as he stood there with his back to the room—but she was. Painfully. Her back was pinned against a door that opened toward her, and now . . . now she was trapped here. Trapped before John.

Oh, this was intolerable.

"You may not want to hear a word from me, but you need to hear some," John said calmly, his voice low.

Florence swallowed as the murmurs around the room increased to a fever pitch. Perhaps they would lose interest, perhaps they would return their attention to the music.

No, that was impossible. This was too much of a scandal for anyone to look away, she thought dully. This was going to be in the scandal sheets tomorrow. And then everyone would know.

"You deserve to hear this," John said. "I—"

"What I deserve is to be left alone," Florence said, hating her voice was quavering with emotion but knowing there was nothing she could do about it. Knowing that she had to speak to make the damned man go away.

The damned man she loved.

John shifted on his feet, making it absolutely clear that she could not escape, blocking her route out of the room. So close that she would press herself into his chest if she attempted to pull the door open.

Florence swallowed hard, her throat dry. "Leave me alone."

Pain flickered across his eyes—or was that just her wishful thinking? It was hard to know. She had imagined this, this first meeting between them in public, so many times the last few days—but at no point had Florence thought it would come this quickly.

The pain of their last conversation was still weighing heavily. How could he—how could they . . .

"I know I don't deserve a second chance," John murmured.

Florence swallowed. There was nothing she wished to do less than admit to him, even with her body, that she had been utterly undone by their separation. Everything she was, everything she had wanted to be . . . it had melted away when she had discovered his betrayal.

"Look, here's the truth," said John hurriedly, as though aware she could attempt to leave at any moment. "I was an idiot, a fool, a complete rake to write that note—but more than you think. I was a coward."

Florence blinked. "A . . . a c-coward?"

Now that was an admission she had not foreseen.

The man she loved was nodding slowly as a pair of ladies stood on tiptoe in their attempts to see what was happening. "I didn't . . . hell, it's hard to admit this. I didn't want to look like a sap in front of my brother. A lovelorn idiot. I . . . I did not wish to reveal how deeply I already cared for you."

Florence's eyes widened.

It was precisely the sort of thing that she would wish to hear from him. Though that did not mean that it was true—in fact, it was exactly the sort of thing a gentleman would concoct to sound impressive, she was certain.

The question was, had John?

"I wrote the damned thing the day after I returned from the house party, when our agreement had been truly nothing more than convenience," John said, his words getting faster and faster, starting to tumble over each other. "I stopped meaning it within days. Hours. It was so far from my mind that I'd even forgotten I'd written it."

Florence twisted her fingers together before her, trying to remind herself that she was furious with the man.

Because it did make sense. She had seen the horror, the realization, in his eyes when John had seen the note. It was easy to believe that he'd forgotten the note had ever been written.

But it had been written. That thought brought Florence back to her senses. As much as she wanted to believe him, she couldn't.

All she had to do was tell him off, severely, then escape this hell of a drawing room.

Instead, her lips made the words, "I can't risk my heart getting broken again. That's not a chance I'll take."

And before John could reply, before he could even respond, Florence pushed past him along the wall and made for another door.

The people standing in her way scattered, squeals of shock and murmurs of curiosity following Florence with every step. And she was almost there, almost at the door to the hall—at least, she thought it was the door to the hall. And she'd be free, free of—

"Oh, I say!"

"Dear God, he's not—"

"What is the Marquess of Aylesbury doing?"

Despite all her instincts, Florence slowed. She could not ignore those words, the cries of shock, the gasps that filled the drawing room.

Much against her better judgment, and half certain that she would regret this the moment she had done it, Florence halted. She turned on the spot to see what everyone was making such a fuss about.

And she gasped.

"No."

"Florence," John said with a nervous grin from bended knee on the Axminster rug of Lord Galcrest's drawing room. "I—"

"What are you doing?" Florence hissed, heat burning up and across her face.

What did she hate most in the world? Attention? And what was John doing right now? Attracting all the attention of a room toward her!

Well. Toward him. But still!

"I am giving you the proposal you have always deserved," said the Marquess of Aylesbury with a serious expression. "Both the first time I met you, and the second time two years later."

The heat on her face felt like to burst into flames as Florence heard his words. How dare he embarrass her like this? How dare he—

The music the string trio was playing crept into her notice. She knew that tune. There was something about it . . . something delightfully—

Florence's stomach lurched. It was the aria, from the opera that John had taken her to. The aria which had been sung while he touched her with his fingers, brought her to pleasure—and told her that he loved her.

"Florence Bailey," John said softly from the floor, though he did not need to raise his voice. The whole room was listening now. "I am someone who has always needed second chances, and you know, I think I always will."

"So do I," muttered Florence, unable to help herself.

She also tried not to look at the expression on his face—one her lips wished to mirror.

What was wrong with her? Did she not loathe him for how he had treated her? Like she was nothing more than a pile of coins he was desperate to get his hands on?

"And that is why I am going to dedicate the rest of my life to improving myself and deserving you," John said steadily, his expression unwavering. "Even if it takes years for you to say yes."

Florence swallowed. "Say yes?"

"I was an idiot, and all I want now is to make you happy," John said, ignoring her question as a lady fluttered her fan and muttered something about this being the perfect proposal.

It was all Florence could do not to roll her eyes. Perfect proposal? He hadn't actually asked her to marry him! But as she looked into his eyes, she could see the truth. He loved her. John Chance may not be the most thoughtful of men, but when he did think, he thought of her.

It was enough to make her swoon, but Florence forced herself to remain both upright and aloof. He was the one who had broken her heart. If he needed to do a little more groveling, that was all to the good.

"You want to make me happy?" Florence said, as haughtily as she could manage.

John nodded.

"And what if you never speaking to me again would make me happy?"

It was a challenge for Florence to hold his gaze. She was painfully conscious of all those around them, staring at them as though they were just another part of the entertainment.

And that was what she wanted, Florence told herself firmly. For John never to speak to her again.

John's eyes twinkled. "Well, I admit it would be a very quiet marriage—but if those are your terms, I accept."

An exasperated laugh escaped Florence's lips. "You are completely impossible!"

"Does that mean yes?"

His words were spoken with an eagerness, a desire that Florence had only ever heard when the two of them had been alone. And they were most definitely not alone at the moment. Far from it.

He had chosen the most excruciating way to do this. In public, where she could not escape, without giving her any recourse to think. She should be furious at him.

But she wasn't. Florence hardly knew why she wasn't, but she did know one thing: if she could survive something like this, it was only because she loved him. And being happy without him was an impossibility. And that left . . . being with him.

She glared at John, then took a step forward. Mutters erupted around the room as she halted just inches before him, where he still knelt on the rug.

Florence frowned. "A second chance once a month?"

"Once a week I think is probably more useful, the rate I'm going," said John cheerfully, a wicked gleam in his eyes. "Can I get off my knees now?"

Taking a deep breath, and knowing that she was stepping into a happiness that was simultaneously complete and completely unknown, Florence nodded. "Y-Yes."

How John managed to immediately rise and sweep her into his arms, kissing her so passionately that one woman screamed—a woman who sounded suspiciously like her mother—Florence did not know.

It didn't matter how. The important thing was that she was right where she belonged. In John Chance's arms.

Chapter Twenty

August 28, 1812

JOHN SHIFTED AWKWARDLY on his feet and was tapped on the shoulder by an irritated Chance.

"Keep a hold of yourself!"

"I can't," muttered John, hating how his brother's voice echoed so loudly around the church. *Damn it, everyone would have heard that.* "I can't stay still."

Lindow snorted as he stood beside him, dressed rather uncomfortably from what John could see. "You should never have agreed to this. What were you thinking?"

"Thinking?" John repeated.

He had been thinking things that were simply not to be repeated in a church. Particularly not with the vicar glaring at him for his earlier outburst.

Besides, it wasn't about thoughts. It was about feelings—feelings he had been surprised to discover he had, then realized he could not do without. Feelings for her.

Miss Florence Bailey.

Panic sparked. He had run a risk, asking her to marry him again so soon after their first wedding date had passed by without a wedding.

Try as they might, they had not been able to keep the wedding of Miss Bailey and the Marquess of Aylesbury a secret. Despite only having sent out about ten invitations—mostly to family—John had been most astonished to arrive at the church nearly half an hour ago to find most of the *ton* already waiting inside.

Damned vultures. They wanted to see if Florence would actually go through with it and marry him.

The trouble was, John was just as curious.

"What if she doesn't come?" he muttered.

Lindow snorted. "Her loss."

"Lindow!"

"Well, what do you want me to say?" shrugged the Earl of Lindow with a grin. "That she'll have had a lucky escape?"

John knew he shouldn't punch his brother in the face. Not just because they were in a church, but because that sort of thing was frowned upon in polite Society.

He would have to wait until they were in impolite Society.

A man cleared his throat behind them, and both Chance brothers turned to see who was behind them.

John immediately glanced at Lindow, whose expression was wooden, but addressed the newcomer. "Pernrith."

"Aylesbury," nodded the illegitimate Chance who had, nonetheless, been one of the few recipients of an actual invitation. "Ready?"

"Of course he's ready," snarled Lindow, as if the man had just offered a terrible insult. "What are you—"

"Ah, there you all are," said another voice coming up the aisle as the congregation milled about before the bride arrived. "Damn it, Aylesbury, now I owe Alice a pound."

John nodded weakly as the oldest Chance brother and his wife strode up to them, arm in arm. "You didn't think I would show?"

"Just based on all I know you and all past behavior," the Duke of Cothrom said with a tight smile. "Nothing personal."

It almost made John laugh. Yes, he supposed it was not personal. That was just the way William Chance was. Always expecting the worst, and usually proven right. But this time, he, John, was going to do what was right.

He would just have to hope Florence would believe that.

"No bride yet, then?" Alice said with a teasing look as she and her husband slipped into the pew behind them.

John's stomach lurched. "Not . . . not yet."

"I suppose you're wondering what you'll do if she doesn't come," Alice said conversationally, seating herself and placing a hand over her belly protectively.

Not that she needed to, John could not help but think. She was not showing, at least as far as he could tell. He did not even officially know yet, though Pernrith had told him and he had told Florence. In fact, now he came to think about it, everyone relevant knew, except maybe Lindow. Except that Cothrom and Alice did not know they knew.

It was going to get a bit tangled.

"What if she doesn't come?" John said weakly, hoping desperately no one save his family could catch his words.

"Then she'll have more sense than I give her credit for," said Cothrom stiffly.

Alice tapped him on the shoulder at the same time as Pernrith shook his head and Lindow snorted. "William! How can you say such a—"

"You all saw the note he wrote!" protested Cothrom, raising his hands in surrender. "You know he's an idiot!"

"I most certainly do," said Alice levelly. "And—"

"I'm still here, you know," pointed out John, trying not to laugh.

"And if Miss Bailey is happy to accept an idiot, then why not let her?" continued Alice as though he had not spoken. "After all, I did."

John joined in with Lindow's laughter this time as they watched a pink tinge color their older brother's cheeks. "She's got you there, Cothrom."

"I suppose she has," admitted his brother with a sigh. "But you can't expect all women in Society to be willing to marry us idiotic

Chances."

"Never fear, I will be staying far away from the marriage bed," said Lindow with a shake of his head. "Now any old bed, on the other hand—"

"You are in a church," hissed Cothrom with blazing eyes.

"Not for much longer," Lindow said happily, as though he were not attracting scowls of outrage from half the people in the church. "I don't think she's coming."

John swallowed.

The thought had crossed his mind earlier that morning, and since it had, it was all he could think about. What if she did not come? What if Florence decided against it—decided he was far too much trouble? More trouble than he was worth?

Oh, he could hardly blame her. But he would live the rest of his life regretting her.

"Can't you just be happy for me?" he found himself saying to his brothers at large.

Cothrom placed an arm around Alice, pulling her into him with a wide grin. "Look, Aylesbury, if you end up half as happy as I am, then you will be doing remarkably well."

John tried not to look at the expressions of devotion the Duke and Duchess of Cothrom exchanged. It was so intimate, so sickly sweet, he felt as though he had interrupted them in the privacy of their breakfast room.

Or worse.

Lindow was pretending to retch.

"What a pleasant sentiment, Your Grace," said Pernrith politely.

"Yes, yes, very nice," said John with a sigh, nudging the brother beside him. "Leave off, Lindow."

"Fine," Lindow said smartly. "But as I'd like double the happiness, I won't be getting married at all."

John gave out a laugh, shaking his head. "I suppose that—"

His next words were drowned out by the organ, and a loud creaking of a door. Not just any door. *The* door. The door to the church.

She was here.

Voices fell silent throughout the church. The organ music stretched to the rafters as people took their seats, leaving only Lindow beside him remaining upright. John stared at the altar before him, knowing he should not turn before Florence had approached him.

But he couldn't help it.

Not because he wished to see what she was wearing. In truth, not that he would ever admit it openly, he didn't care what she was wearing. She wouldn't be wearing it for long.

No, it was because he knew precisely how Florence would be feeling in this moment.

Terrified. Shy. Hating the attention. Wishing he had capitulated and agreed to elope—something John had thought she had suggested in jest, but as it turned out, had been in earnest. Anything to escape the curious, watchful stares of the *ton*.

But while John Chance would have been more than happy to elope with the woman he loved, the Marquess of Aylesbury had to wed in the family church, witnessed by—at the very least—the extended Chance family. The entirety of the *ton* catching wind of their wedding date had not exactly been part of the plan.

And so John turned, hoping his devotion would be visible down the aisle so Florence would know how he felt.

She was so beautiful. So kind. The shyness that was a core part of her was making her cheeks pink, her red, flaming hair piled up under a white veil that gave her a mystical quality John had always known was there, but had only ever seen when the two of them were alone.

Here she was. Marrying him. Walking down the aisle, before hundreds, just to become his wife.

John's chest swelled. This was a difficult day for Florence—being gawped at was her absolute nightmare. Even with her brother, Philip, holding her arm, it was clear she was not enjoying the spectacle she was creating.

Just for a moment, he wished they had eloped.

But this was right, he knew. The whole world had to know he was marrying Florence because he wanted to, not because he had to. Not because of any agreement, or marriage of convenience. An elopement may have made it look as though they . . . well, needed to get married in a hurry.

As Florence drew level with him, John could see her fingers shaking as they held her bouquet of roses, and his affection for her grew even more.

Philip carefully placed Florence's hand on John's and nodded. John nodded in return, his attention following his future brother-in-law as he stepped to the other side of the aisle. He joined Mrs. Bailey, who caught John's eye and mouthed word "finally."

Stifling a smile, John heard Lindow beside him snort. Without letting go of Florence, or even turning away, he carefully lifted his right foot and stepped on his brother's left.

"What the devil—"

"We are gathered here today," said the vicar smoothly, shooting a glare at the Earl of Lindow, "to celebrate the union . . ."

"You look very beautiful," John breathed to his bride, unable to help himself.

Though it was scandalous of him to speak underneath the vicar's intonations, he could not help it. She was radiant. He had never seen a woman glow like that before. Did Florence even know she was doing it?

Her cheeks reddened. "Y-You have to s-say that. It's m-my wedding d-day."

Florence's voice was low, hardly more than a flutter, but it was a calming balm to John's soul. She was here. She was actually going to marry him.

"I have to correct you there," he said softly. "I have to say it because you are. And I'll keep saying it every day of our lives."

"Ahem."

Startled, John looked up to see the vicar examining him with a wry look. "A new vow. I like it."

John smiled weakly. "Ah. Hello."

"Hello, my lord," said the vicar, shaking his head as he beheld the two of them. "I hope I am not interrupting? May I go on with the service?"

Florence's hand gripped John's arm, and he knew she would be flushing most furiously. This was the life they had chosen. Florence would have to put up with his nonsense, and he would have to put up with . . .

Now he came to think about it, he couldn't think of anything in Florence he would have to put up with. Her mother?

"Yes, p-please," Florence said in answer to the vicar's question. "B-Before I ch-change my mind again."

There was a ripple of laughter behind them and this time it was John's turn to flush. "She doesn't mean it."

"Well, just in case she does," said the vicar, a twinkle in his eye, "let's get on with it."

And they must have done. John could hardly remember what happened next, the whole service a whirlwind of vows and promises and the knowledge, the wonderful knowledge, that he was going to have Florence with him for the rest of his life.

Forever.

Before John knew it, they had returned to the Baileys' home for the wedding reception.

Which was all very well and good, he could not help but think dryly, *when you had only invited ten people. But when another hundred or so decided to invite themselves* . . .

"More canapés, and open every bottle of wine in the cellar!" cried Mrs. Bailey smartly as she marched across the lawn issuing orders to the housekeeper who was bustling along beside her. "Send out for pies, we need pies—anything to feed the hordes!"

John chuckled as a hand tightened in his own. He turned to the woman he loved.

"Remind m-me," Florence said, her voice tight. "How m-many people did w-we invite to this thing?"

"Twelve, if you include us."

"And h-how many p-people have I been forced to greet?"

John looked about him.

They were standing in the French doors of the drawing room which opened out onto a small terrace and the lawn of the Bailey garden. The room behind them was packed to the rafters, and it was getting difficult to see the green of the lawn, there were so many people milling upon it.

"Oh, I would say around two hundred," John said. "Maybe more."

"And h-how m-many more do I need to meet?" Florence asked, her voice low.

John bit his lip.

This wasn't what he had wanted for her. This was supposed to be a calm, simple wedding. A small one. One that could be enjoyed, instead of endured.

"Perhaps another five couples."

It would have taken anyone by surprise. Even the most outgoing and adventurous woman would have been caught off guard by such Societal attention. Yet he could see the resolve sharpening in Florence's gaze as she beheld her many guests. But still she was a wallflower. She was shy. She did not appreciate crowds, and was far happier in the company of a very few. Perhaps even just one.

And John did not wish her to change, though he was proud to see such determination wash through her. To see Florence rise to the task, to see her put others first and push herself beyond what she was comfortable with.

A powerful, brave, and intelligent woman. And with the sort of packaging that would make a man pant.

How had he been so fortunate?

"Come with me," John whispered.

They managed to skirt around Lady Romeril who was seemingly giving a lecture on how a wallflower should attempt to find a husband, past Lord Galcrest who was telling anyone who would listen how he was instrumental in today's celebration, past Mrs. Bailey who was hastily pouring champagne for Lady Stratton and Mr. Hargreaves, past footmen running in and out of the house with platters of food . . .

Until they stepped back into the house by the side door and into the breakfast room.

John poked his head in and saw with relief that it was empty. "In here."

Florence stared in confusion as he shut the door behind them. The din of the wedding reception immediately died away. "Wh-Why are we here?"

"Because I know you," he said. "You need five minutes with no one talking to you or looking at you. It's quite all right. You can . . . well, you can recover."

Florence looked at him and his stomach lurched. *Dear God, he would do almost anything for this woman.*

"Thank you," she said.

"I'll leave you be," said John gently, stepping toward the door.

At least, he attempted to. Florence had reached out before he could leave, grabbing at his arm with a confused look on her face. "What do you think you're going?"

He frowned. "I . . . well, I knew you would need time to yourself. I thought you'd want to be alone."

"I do want to be alone," said Florence, a twinkle in her eye pinking her cheeks. "But I can b-be alone with you."

John swallowed, then pulled her into his arms, embracing tightly the woman he knew he could not do without. It was such a heartfelt thing for her to say, such an intimacy—he hardly knew how to thank her.

"I don't deserve this second chance," he said in a muffled voice to her shoulder.

"Probably not," said Florence. She pulled back and kissed him on the corner of his mouth. "But in a way, maybe I don't either. I've . . . well, I should have known my fortune would have something to do with it, and I didn't ask because . . . because I didn't want the answer. I was a coward, too, in my own way."

"Perhaps this is why this means so much," said John with a sigh.

"Means what?"

His grip tightened around her, the feeling of Florence, the weight of her against his chest, the knowledge that now they had forever. "Everything."

Epilogue

September 1, 1812

THERE WAS SOMETHING about the thrill of the movement beneath you. The knowledge that the two of you were moving as one. The sense that the rest of the world could fade away, and as long as the two of you were still there, everything would be fine.

Florence smiled. Nothing compared to what she felt when she was with John, but horse riding came perhaps a close second.

There was a chill in the air as the hooves beneath her pounded along the path, and it carried the scent of autumn. The seasons were changing, just as she was embarking on this new season of her own life.

As a wife.

Florence lifted up a hand and whooped in the cold, crisp early air. "Yes!"

It had been a wrench to tear herself away from the warm arms and even more warming fingers of John that morning, but Florence had been unable to stay away. The Aylesbury estate had been far more than she could ever have imagined.

The one in Scotland, that was. Who knew?

Mountains loomed on the horizon before her, with acres and acres of pines sweeping down the sides of the hills toward the Aylesbury estate. The beauty of the place had dazzled her when the carriage had brought them here only days ago, and she wasn't sure whether she would ever grow entirely used to it.

Forest became parkland, where red deer roamed. Parkland became the arboretum, with several kinds of trees Florence had never seen before. And the arboretum swept gracefully into the gardens that encircled the house. Herb and rose and kitchen, all in their own red brick rooms. Despite the days they had spent there, Florence had not yet discovered everything there was to find.

And she had not seen a single soul. Other than the servants, of course. And they kept out of their master and mistress's way.

The isolation was perfect. As was its owner.

"Slow down there!" called John from behind her, panting as his horse struggled to keep up with hers. "You're riding like the very devil is behind you!"

"Isn't he?" Florence called back over her shoulder with a grin, spurring her horse onward.

There was something truly magical about this. Being here, with John. Knowing she could speak clearly and would always be heard, always attended to. Knowing the words she spoke were considered weighty and important by the man she loved.

The man who loved her.

Though perhaps "loved" wasn't a strong enough word. Adored? Worshipped?

Florence smiled as she gently eased her mare from a gallop into a mere canter. After a few moments, John drew up beside her on his own steed.

"You really can ride faster than I can," he said, more than a little ruefully, wind tugging at his hair.

Florence laughed, and her happiness increased as she felt no tension in her lungs, nothing stopping her from allowing the laugh out.

Being with him, with John . . . it was like nothing else she had ever experienced.

Trusting him, finally, had perhaps been an act of faith. He had certainly needed more than one second chance. But taking this chance on him, giving him the opportunity to woo her—even though she had been, for the greater part of it, his wife . . .

It was not something Florence was going to regret in a hurry.

"Of course I can ride faster than you," she said aloud, her laughter continuing as their horses slowed to a trot. "You thought I was t-teasing?"

"It doesn't matter what I thought," John said with a chuckle, reaching out for her. "It's what you think that counts. It will always be your opinion that counts."

A splash of heat covered Florence's cheeks, but she did not look away. She did not need to. This man, this wonderful man—he understood her shyness. Finally.

And most importantly, he did not see it as something to change, to alter, to fix.

He did not think like her mother and cringe every time Florence opened her mouth and stuttered her way through a sentence. Even though she tried not to.

"I could ride out here all day with you," John said, as they trotted over the lawn toward the large manor house which was their current home. "But I promised my steward I would look over the tenant accounts."

Florence rolled her eyes expressively. "Are you certain you're not going inside to read up on the racing that's taking place in York next week?"

It was perhaps a jest too soon. That was one of the things she was still learning about this mercurial husband of hers. Just when she thought she had entirely understood him, there was something else that confused her to no end.

It was riveting. No man had ever caught her attention quite like John Chance, Marquess of Aylesbury.

"Most definitely not," said John firmly, looking a little hurt.

Florence giggled. "Because your favorites aren't riding, are they?"

Her husband lifted a wounded hand to his chest. "I can't believe you would say—"

"I'm right, though, aren't I?"

"Well they aren't riding, as it happens," said John with a grin as they trotted into the stable yard. "Mere coincidence, I assure you. No, it's Lindow. He's bought a share in a horse, believe it or not, the fool."

And Florence was assured.

Oh, she wasn't so foolish as to think a man could kick a habit like gambling in a matter of minutes. She knew there would be times when her husband would make mistakes. Knowing John, they would probably be rather large ones.

But she was certain of one thing, Florence thought as they guided their horses around the gardens and into the stable yard. No matter what happened, no matter what opportunities would come his way, John would never betray her. Their marriage bed, sweet and delectable as it was, was somehow above and beyond all the mistakes that John could make.

Anything else . . . well, he would tell her, and they would work through it. That was the true meaning of love, wasn't it? Making mistakes, and being honest, and being forgiven.

Florence laughed as she glanced over at the man who had taken her heart, and given her . . . *Did he know? Had he guessed?*

"Now then," said John, dismounting smoothly from his steed and walking over to her mare, hand outstretched. "By my reckoning, I would say I have about twenty minutes before my steward will be expecting me."

Florence could have dismounted on her own, but she didn't. Instead, she took John's hand in her own, heat pouring through it thanks to their utter disdain for wearing gloves, and ensured she slid down his chest in a most sensuous manner as she dismounted.

"Really? Twenty whole minutes?" she breathed, looking up at him with wide, almost innocent eyes. "Goodness, I can't think of anything I'd like to do for twenty whole minutes."

She almost wasn't permitted to finish her sentence. John covered her lips with his own with a moan, and Florence responded immediately, pulling him close, tugging on the lapels of his riding jacket.

There was something so very heady about kissing one's husband in public.

Well. Not entirely public. The stable yard here wasn't exactly in public, but anyone could come across them.

Not that Florence particularly cared about that. She could only think of the aching heat dripping down her breasts and across her stomach until it settled between her legs—legs that were swiftly no longer on the ground. John had lifted up first one, then the second leg to curl around him, his hands now on her buttocks.

And Florence kissed him. Teased open his mouth with a whimper, lavished her tongue upon his own, trembled as he—

"We shouldn't be doing this here," John said in a ragged voice, pulling away only so he could start to trail kisses along her neck.

Florence tipped her head back and gloried in the connection. *It was just her and John, alone in the world.* "No one will interrupt us, who would be—"

"Ahem," said a strained voice. "Ah. Oh dear."

Florence froze. So did John, but he swiftly unfroze to place her back on the cobbles of the stable yard.

They both turned.

George Chance, Earl of Lindow and third Chance brother, was standing there with an awkward grin on his face and a hand raised in greeting.

John swore.

"Lindow!" said Florence hurriedly, pulse frantically beating now for an entirely different reason. *Oh, Lord, to be caught so by her brother-in-law!* "I d-did n-not know—you did not s-send word that—"

"I thought I'd surprise you," said the Earl of Lindow with a grin. "And I suppose I did."

"The house is that way, Lindow," snapped John with a wry shake of his head. "You never heard of knocking on the front door?"

"I thought I'd be useful and stable my own horse," replied his brother as Florence wished the earth would kindly swallow her up, and John too while it was at it. Lindow jerked his head behind him. "But now I see I should have—"

"Yes, you should," said John. There was no unkindness in his words, but Florence tried not to smile as she saw—and felt—the rather hard evidence of his desire for her against his breeches. "Why don't you go up to the house, tell Humphreys you're here, and that my wife and I will be over shortly for breakfast."

Florence glanced up at her husband. "F-For—"

"In twenty minutes or so," said John, glaring at his brother. "Understand?"

When she finally snuck a sidelong glance back at the Earl of Lindow, Florence saw that her brother-in-law most certainly understood.

"Ah," said the third Chance brother weakly. "Yes. Right. You know what, I'll just go up to the house and—"

"Thank you, Lindow," said John resolutely.

Only when the younger of the two brothers had turned the corner and disappeared from sight did Florence allow herself to lean her head on her husband's shoulder. "Oh dear."

"Oh dear is only the half of it," growled John, his hands swiftly returning to her buttocks. "Now, where were we?"

"John!"

"What? I want to kiss my wife," said John, nuzzling her neck in a way designed to produce the most confusion.

And it was working. Heady desire was flooding Florence's mind, quickly dulling all concern that they had been caught most scandalously in their own stable yard. And that they had a guest waiting. And the steward too, now, probably. And breakfast.

And yet . . .

"John—"

"I never should have invited him," said John heavily, hanging his head and looking morosely into her eyes. "All I wanted was to have a few quiet weeks with my wife—"

"Quiet?" Florence raised an eyebrow.

Her husband flashed a wicked grin. "Well. I didn't intend to keep you quiet that much, truth be told. When I told Lindow he should come up for a week's shooting, I meant late October, not now! I'll have to pack him off to Bath to be with his precious racehorse, or something. Try to keep him distracted."

"Well, he's here n-now," Florence said with a sigh. "It would be cruel to send him back. It's such a long way to Bath, and . . . well, he m-might be lonely."

As expected, John snorted. "Lonely? Lindow? He has a different woman in his bed every week, and—"

"Sounds like a lonely man to me," Florence said serenely.

That was one of the things she adored about John. He would look at her sometimes, usually after she said something calm, benign, and utterly dull, and would find treasure in it as though she were some sort of saint.

It was most endearing. Utterly mad, yes. But endearing.

"You are a very good person, you know that?" John said.

"I don't feel like a good person when your fingers are squeezing my buttocks like that," Florence pointed out with faintly burning cheeks. "Still, it's not easy for him—"

"Not easy for him?" Her husband rolled his eyes. "What about me?"

Florence blinked. She had been unaware John was having any difficulties—he certainly hadn't mentioned any to her. "What do you mean, what about you—what's wrong?"

"It isn't easy, you know," John said, a teasing grin flickering across his face. "Trying to keep my hands off my wife."

And all the tension that had suddenly bunched in her stomach disappeared. Most of it, anyway.

Florence glanced about them for a moment. It was a very public place to be kissing. Stable hands and groomsmen and gardeners usually roamed about this place from morning until night.

But for now, it was empty.

Perhaps now was the right time then. It probably wasn't the best place, but that was by the by.

"Well, I am afraid, John, you w-will have to keep your hands off m-me in a few months' time," Florence said, some of the shyness that was always rippling under the surface appearing again.

John's fingers halted their delightful teasing of her buttocks. "Dear God, why?"

Florence swallowed.

She was sure. As sure as she could be. Even the doctor was sure, and that meant that it was time for John to know, too. Though as much as she had rehearsed this moment, words had escaped her and all she could do is look up into his blue eyes and say . . .

"J-John," Florence stammered, hardly knowing why her voice had failed her now. "I . . . I am with child. I mean, I think. Probably. Almost definitely."

John stared.

And it was like that meeting, in the Knights' drawing room, all over again. A moment of connection across a crowded room, her gaze meeting his own, and knowing, even if she didn't understand it, that the rest of her life was going to be changed. That nothing she had yet known was going to be like what was still before her.

And that she would be sharing it with the very best man. Oh, the best man she had ever met.

Then John was hugging her, pulling her into a tight embrace that knocked the very air from Florence's lungs.

"Oh, Florence—really? T-Truly?" His breath fluttered in her ear, a shake to it she had never heard before. "A-A baby? You're a-absolutely certain?"

Florence pulled back with a laugh. "Goodness, you sound like me again!"

Only then did she see that her husband, the bold man with the bravado of a king, was dashing away tears.

"John!"

"I'm fine, it's just . . . oh, Florence," whispered John, his hands now tight on her waist, holding her up, as though she could fall at any moment. "A baby."

"I know, it is all very sudden," said Florence in a rush. "I know we have not been married long, and you probably wished to spend more time enjoying our—"

John kissed her hard on the mouth—but this was not merely a kiss of lust, of desire that could only be completed one way.

No, this was a kiss of adoration: of truest love, an affection deeper than a mere flight of fancy.

When he pulled away Florence was dizzy, and rather glad for the steadying hands at her waist.

"I love you, Florence Chance," John said seriously, though there was still a hint of mischief in his eyes. "And I promise you, I will not ruin this second chance you have given me."

"Good," said Florence firmly, heart singing, knowing she had found the happiness she had always thought would be denied her. "Because I won't let you."

A short letter from the author

Hello! Thank you so much for reading *A Second Chance*, the second novel in my Chances series. I truly hoped you enjoyed it and fell in love with John and Florence just as much as I did.

I've always wanted to write a series of brothers, but I could never "meet" the characters that were quite right. After waiting years to meet them myself, I have had a lot of fun writing the four Chance brothers—and I think Lindow and Pernrith's stories are going to be just as much fun as Cothrom and Aylesbury's.

Being an author can be a lonely business, but knowing that there are readers from all over the world who are going to adore my stories makes it all worthwhile. Thank you for your support, and I hope you love reading more of my books!

Happy reading,
Emily

About Emily E K Murdoch

If you love falling in love, then you've come to the right place.

I am a historian and writer and have a varied career to date: from examining medieval manuscripts to designing museum exhibitions, to working as a researcher for the BBC to working for the National Trust.

My books range from England 1050 to Texas 1848, and I can't wait for you to fall in love with my heroes and heroines!

Follow me on twitter and instagram @emilyekmurdoch, find me on facebook at facebook.com/theemilyekmurdoch, and read my blog at www.emilyekmurdoch.com.

Printed in Great Britain
by Amazon